The New York Saints novels are

"Strong . . . Scott does a fine job of balancing sports and passion." —*Publishers Weekly*

"Sexy, well-written, layered, and engaging . . . Emotional intensity and dynamic conflict combined with a lively setting make this baseball-themed romance [series] a hit." —*Kirkus Reviews*

"Awesome . . . Sports and romance. What more could you want?" —*Night Owl Reviews*

"Deliciously sexy." —*Ereadica*

"Amazing!" —Deirdre Martin, *New York Times* bestselling author of the New York Blades series

Also by
Melanie Scott

The Devil in Denim
Angel in Armani
Lawless in Leather

Playing Hard

Melanie Scott

St. Martin's Paperbacks

This is a work of fiction. All of the characters, organizations, and events portrayed in this novel are either products of the author's imagination or are used fictitiously.

PLAYING HARD

Copyright © 2016 by Melanie Scott.
Excerpt from *Playing Fast* copyright © 2016 by Melanie Scott.

For information address St. Martin's Press, 175 Fifth Avenue, New York, NY 10010.

ISBN: 978-1-250-07720-2

Printed in the United States of America

St. Martin's Paperbacks edition / February 2016

St. Martin's Paperbacks are published by St. Martin's Press, 175 Fifth Avenue, New York, NY 10010.

10 9 8 7 6 5 4 3 2 1

For the boys of summer.

Acknowledgments

Thank you to Eileen Rothschild for editing superpowers and all the team at St. Martin's Press. Thank you also to Miriam Kriss who continues to be a great agent to have on my side. For all my fabulous writer gal pals who are always there during the good bits and the bad bits with wise words and good booze and my friends and family who embrace the writer weirdness. And last, but certainly never least, to all the fabulous readers, reviewers, and bloggers out there who let me know you love my books and share the joy of all the good stories with the world, you're the best.

Prologue

Sunshine and baseball. Two of his favorite things. Oliver Shields shifted on the plastic seat and stared down at the field where the New York Saints were currently in the middle of a training session. All he really needed for perfection would be a cold beer in his hand.

Sadly, he was going to have to make do with Gatorade. He took a swig, then put the bottle down and adjusted the ice pack on his right hand. He'd been too slow, had lunged for a ball early, and it had clipped the tops of his fingers. Dan Ellis, their coach, taking no risks so early in spring training, had sent him off to ice the fingers for a few minutes.

So now he got to sit in the Florida sunshine, relax, and just enjoy watching the guys do their thing. Nice.

Things were coming together. They had a few new players as always, guys just picked up or being trialed—which sometimes made things interesting, but this year everything had gone relatively smoothly.

Down on the field the new guy who'd just subbed into Oliver's first-base spot while he was icing his hand completed a flawless double play. Finn Castro had good hands and a good arm.

Unfortunately, from what Oliver had seen of him so far, he also had a cocky mouth. Some new guys came in all bluster and arrogance, but usually they settled in quick enough.

Finn? Well, he hadn't settled down yet. Oliver and Hector Moreno, their catcher, had fifty bucks riding on how long it would be before Dan stepped in and tore a few strips off the kid, but so far it hadn't happened.

As if he could hear Oliver's thoughts, Dan Ellis turned and bellowed, "Shields, get your ass back down here."

Oliver grinned and put down his dripping ice pack. Time to get back in the game. As he walked onto the grass, Finn was coming off.

"Nice play," Oliver said.

Finn smirked and brushed past him, his shoulder meeting Oliver's just that little bit too forcefully.

"Hey," Oliver said, turning after him, but Dan bellowed his name again and he dismissed the kid from his mind as he slipped on his glove. No point letting a noob with a chip on his shoulder ruin his day.

An hour later, when Dan decided to stop being a sadist and called a halt to the session, Oliver was feeling good. His hand was fine, the day was still beautiful, and he might even get in a few laps in the hotel pool before dinner. He lingered for a couple of minutes to talk with Dan and Hector and Brett Tuckerson, the starting pitcher. The three of them were the senior players on the Saints and Dan liked to check in and see what they thought of the new guys. Opinions given, he headed for the locker room.

As he reached the door, he heard Castro's voice, laughing. Then, "Shields. Fucking wimp. Did you see him, icing his hand like a seventy-year-old? He better watch out. That first-base spot is going to be mine before the season is out. Dude should give it up and retire before he starts embarrassing himself."

Little shit. Oliver felt the burn in his gut. He was used to the odd rivalry on the team. Healthy competition. There was always someone younger coming along who thought he deserved a shot. But Oliver had fucking earned his first-base position through fourteen—soon to be fifteen—years of hard work. And good arm or not, no cocky bastard like Castro was going to take it from him.

He pushed the door all the way open, maybe a bit too hard. It crashed against the wall and Finn and the guys he was talking to—most of them rookies—turned as one.

"You know, Castro," Oliver said as he walked into the room and dropped his glove onto the nearest bench. "You'd think a guy who'd been traded dirt-cheap by his old team might have the sense to shut up and try to get along with his new teammates rather than mouthing off."

Finn's mouth went flat, green eyes cooling as he rose from the bench he was sitting on. "You got a problem, old man?"

"Yeah," Oliver said, meeting Finn's glare evenly. "You. Let me give you a tip. The guys who run the Saints don't like egotistical, wannabe little boys. They like guys who can fit into the team and do the damned job they're given. So why don't you focus on that instead of talking yourself up." He stepped forward. The two of them were close enough in height, but Oliver had a few pounds on Finn.

"Who says it's talk?" Finn said. His chin came up, shoulders squared.

Little fucker really didn't know when to give in. Stupid. Or stubborn. Which amounted to the same thing. Oliver grinned at him. If Finn wasn't going to back down, then Oliver would be happy to show him how things were done at the Saints. "Castro, better players than you have tried to take my spot. And I'm still here. Not going anywhere until I'm good and ready. So I suggest you shut up and get used to the outfield. Because that's where you'll be spending your time this year." He bit off the *if you stay* that belonged on the end of that sentence. Finn's expression was 100 percent pissed off. The kid really didn't know when to quit.

Finn took a step toward Oliver. "Why don't you go—"

"Castro," Brett said from the doorway. "Shut the hell up and sit the hell down."

To Oliver's surprise, Finn did. So maybe the kid wasn't completely stupid. At least he was smart enough not to get on the wrong side of the team captain. Oliver tipped his chin at Brett, who rolled his eyes in reply, and then walked past Finn to his locker. He didn't miss the glare and the muttered "douche" that Finn directed at him. But he ignored it. Hopefully the kid would get the message about his current position in the team hierarchy and lose the attitude. But if he didn't, it was going to be a very long season.

Chapter One

Wall-to-wall hot men and all Amelia Graham really wanted was more comfortable shoes. It was official. Her life was sad. If there was a list of people who had lost their mojo, it would clearly say "Amelia Graham" at the top. In bold. Underlined. She winced at the mental image and tried to find her party spirit. But her feet hurt—stupid new shoes—and the wall-to-wall hot men seemed far more interested in the hordes of superhumanly glamorous women filling the room than in her. She looked good but these women were New-York-model-level gorgeous. And if the sky-high stilettos most of them wore were hurting their feet, they were far better at ignoring that fact than Amelia was.

Which only proved that her name belonged on the sad list. If Em could see her now, she'd be rolling her eyes in disgust. Of course, it was Em's fault that Amelia was stuck at this party in the first place. Her best friend had steadfastly refused to move to New York, remaining at home in Chicago. Which meant that when Em's brother Finn—Amelia's de facto brother by way of lifelong best-friend-hood with Em—had been transferred from the

Chicago Cubs to the New York Saints, Amelia had rein-
herited first-line Finn Support status. All the other Castros were still back in Chicago, so it was Amelia who got
to play cheer squad and sounding board and whatever
else he needed. Back on Team Finn. Not that she'd ever
really been off it. And it was a role she was happy to play.
After all, she owed the Castros a lot, and Finn especially.
She could never repay that debt. Being there if he needed
her was the least she could do. Still, she'd been in New
York for seven years now and they hadn't been as close
as before she'd moved here. Until he'd moved here, too.
She'd helped him find his apartment and showed him
around when he'd first arrived in New York and somehow they'd fallen back into old patterns.

   Not quite as it used to be, though. Sometimes weeks
went by without him calling. After all, he traveled a lot
for games and he'd found a crowd to run with quickly
enough—Finn was blessed with the same dark good
looks as his sister and a bucketload of charm as well and
never had trouble making friends—but he still called her
when he was at loose ends and wanting to be entertained.
Or wanted a familiar face at his games. And Amelia
couldn't help being there to answer. Plus there was Em,
who wanted reports on how Finn was doing. Something
Amelia had been used to when Finn was in high school
and he'd told her things he wouldn't necessarily tell his
sister. Now, at twenty-nine, it was kind of weird to be
asked to keep an eye on a twenty-five-year-old guy who
was a professional baseball player.

   But she couldn't say no to Em any more than she could
to Finn.

   So she'd said yes when Finn had invited her out tonight, even though it was the first Sunday she hadn't
worked in a month and all she really wanted to do was
sleep. But the Saints were celebrating the fact that they'd

made it to the American League Division Series for the first time in a long time and she was feeling guilty that she hadn't actually made it to that many of their home games this season due to work craziness. Amelia liked baseball, having kind of absorbed her knowledge and affection for it through Finn, so a baseball party should have been fun. So she'd come. And now, somewhat predictably, she was bored, watching Finn dance with random women.

She sighed and rattled the two rapidly melting ice cubes that were all that was left of her drink. There really had to be something wrong with her. All these gorgeous men and no one had caught her eye. Which was troubling. She had something of a thing, to her chagrin, for guys who oozed confidence, and professional athletes oozed it more than anybody. But all too often it seemed that über-confidence had a downside. Too many of the guys who had it were a little too fond of themselves and a little too sure of their place in the universe. It had been that way with the jocks she'd steadfastly avoided dating in high school and college, and it was the same with the men she'd met on Wall Street since she'd graduated. Both groups leaned toward master-of-the-universe worldviews. The Wall Street guys just did it in expensive suits rather than baseball uniforms.

She'd resolved the last time, after another crash and burn with an investment banker who'd been exactly that type, to stick to nice guys in the future. Maybe the fact that she was bored tonight—surrounded as she was with men who should be Amelia catnip—meant she had a chance of succeeding in keeping that resolution.

Though, if she was going to stick to her guns, tonight was probably not the best night to put her plan into action. She was guessing that ordinary nice-guy types were an endangered species at this party. Finn had let slip enough team gossip about how the single guys tended to blow off steam that she could be fairly certain of that. So maybe she should just give it another hour and then make her excuses to Finn and leave. Go home to comfy slippers and watching whatever seemed good on Net-flix while she baked some late-night muffins. Maybe the pistachio chocolate ones she'd spotted on one of her fa-vorite food blogs the other day. Finn wouldn't care if she left now that he was surrounded by beautiful women, so she was off the hook there.

Time to be sensible.

Like the guy she wanted. She sighed and put the empty glass down on the small, high table near her elbow. If she was going to stay, she needed another drink. Though maybe a soda first. Whoever had made the cocktail she'd just finished definitely hadn't skimped on the alcohol. The buzz of it was warming her veins just a little too well. Not good if she wanted to be sensible, smart Amelia. One soda, one more cocktail, and then one swift getaway.

Maggie Jameson and Raina Easton definitely knew how to throw a party. Oliver Shields took his tequila from the bartender and turned to survey the room, taking in the heaving mass of partying New York Saints players, wives, girlfriends, and whoever else had been invited. The play-offs. The Saints had made the fucking American League Division Series for the first time in God only knew how many years. Of course, he should know, having spent the last fifteen years playing for the Saints, but after his first two tequilas had gone down fast, the statistic, one that most of the time he had to try hard to ignore, refused to come to mind easily.

He was finally going to the play-offs. Halle-fucking-lujah. He had to hand it to Alex Winters. He hadn't liked the man when Alex had first bought the club with his two best friends, Lucas Angelo and Malachi Coulter—not only because Alex had succeeded in getting Oliver's onetime girlfriend Maggie Jameson to become Maggie Winters—but the terrible trio knew what they were doing. This was the third season since they'd purchased the Saints from Maggie's dad, and the team had made the goddamned play-offs.

Which was why every man and woman even remotely connected to the Saints was currently blowing off steam for one night of insane partying before it was back to the grindstone. After tonight it would be tunnel-vision focus and a lot of sweat. Eyes on the prize twenty-four seven if they were going to achieve the next seemingly impossible goal—making it to the League Championship Series and then, if the stars aligned, to the World Series.

Ollie sipped his tequila—one of the other things Raina Easton knew how to do was stock a damned good tequila in her burlesque club—and watched the crowd. Across the room he saw Maggie's dark head next to Alex's blond one and found himself smiling. They were good together. They worked. In the way that he and Maggie, as much as he'd never wanted to admit it, never quite had.

Damn, that was way too serious a thought for tonight. Tonight, he'd decided, was for celebrating. He'd been pretty damned dedicated this season. Practically a monk. But even monks needed to give in to temptation occasionally, and this room was just chock-full of temptation, though no one had actually caught his eye yet. Which was why he was still drinking tequila alone at the bar instead of busting a move down on the tiny dance floor with some gorgeous woman. Like Raina was with her fiancé, soon-to-be-husband, Mal Coulter. Raina was a former Broadway dancer, among other things, so she was making Malachi work hard to keep up, but the two of them were grinning at each other like fools. Next to them, Finn

Castro was dancing with a short blonde Oliver didn't recognize.

The sight soured his mood slightly. Castro had been a pain in the butt all season. A smart-ass whenever he thought he could get away with it. Temperamental. Too fond of partying. And always pushing for a chance to step into Oliver's position. The only thing that had saved him from being traded again was the fact he'd been playing very well. Not good enough to take Oliver's slot, but Alex had gotten more than his money's worth. Pity Castro was such a dick. A dick who was just going to have to keep making his peace with life in the outfield. Oliver wasn't going anywhere.

He drained his tequila, savoring the smooth burn for a minute, then decided that maybe it was time to slow down. He'd driven tonight, not wanting to break training completely. Also, if he did find some temptation to yield to, he preferred to drive them back to his place himself rather than use a driver.

Turning back to the bar, he waved at the skinny bald guy tending it and said, "Club soda," at the exact same moment a woman slid through the crowd at the bar and ordered the same thing.

She turned to look at him and said, "Snap," with a smile in big blue eyes almost the exact deep shade of the Saints logo. He found himself smiling back automatically. She had a pretty face, curving lips, and dimples to go with the eyes. Her hair was pulled up into some sort of messy bun arrangement at the back of her head, wisps of it coming loose around her face. In the low lighting of the bar, he couldn't really tell what color it was . . . maybe blond, maybe red, maybe something in between.

The bartender slid two glasses across the bar toward them. Ollie nodded at her. "Lady's choice."

"Thanks," she said and leaned forward to take the nearest glass. Her dress was sleek and black and finished north of her knees, showing off a very nice pair of legs and equally sleek black high heels, but it wasn't the usual plunging, painted-on thing that girls who came to trawl Saints parties for talent wore. Who was she exactly?

He reached for the other glass, using the movement as an excuse to move slightly closer. "So, what has you hitting the hard stuff tonight?"

She stirred the soda with the straw. There were no rings on the slim fingers. "I could ask you the same question."

He started to say *I'm in training*, then stopped. For once he didn't feel like being Oliver Shields, first baseman. And his mystery companion hadn't shown any sign of recognizing who he was. "What if I said I'm on duty?"

Her eyebrows arched slightly. "On duty? Are you security? One of the guys' bodyguards?"

She didn't know who he was. This could be fun. "I could tell you but then I'd have to kill you. And that would just cause problems." He hit her with a smile. "Now I've told you, your turn."

"Me? I'm an economist at Pullman Waters," she said. "Wanna hear about the outlook for Southeast Asian currencies in the next few months?"

He nearly choked on his soda, and she burst into laughter. Deep throaty laughter that sank into his gut and spread outward and downward. Damn. His vague curiosity about her kicked itself up to *very interested*.

"Sounds fascinating." He didn't really know what an economist did but he was willing to find out.

"Really?" Amusement lurked in her eyes.

"'Round here the conversation revolves around baseball, so it's something new."

She laughed again, and his body reacted in the same way to the sound. He curled his fingers a little tighter around the glass.

"You get points for not falling asleep immediately," she said, smiling.

"I find it hard to believe that anyone could fall asleep on you."

She tilted her head but her smile didn't fade. And there was a glow of mischief in those big eyes he liked. "If you're going to flirt with me, you should tell me your name," she said.

Damn. He didn't feel like giving up his anonymity just yet. "Ladies first."

"Oh no, you started this, you go first."

There was a sudden loud cheer from the direction of the dance floor. He turned to see one of Raina's performers balancing on Sam Basara's shoulders. The kid—who was shaping up into a very nice pitcher—was grinning like all his Christmases had arrived at once as the girl on his shoulders did a pretty good bump and grind given her position.

"Interesting," said his mystery woman from beside him.

He turned back to her. "These guys get a little crazy when there's something to celebrate."

"Oh?" She closed her lips around the straw and sipped, and he suddenly found his attention riveted by the deep pink of her mouth. He leaned slightly forward, and a hint of her perfume—something heady and rich—reached him. His gut tightened again, and his attention zeroed in on her.

Who was this girl?

"Not too crazy," he said. Though right now he felt like getting a lot crazy. If crazy involved her.

"Everyone has to blow off steam sometime," she said.

"So what are you celebrating?" Her eyes were laughing again.

She had to be teasing him. "You don't know? Did you crash the party or something?"

"I'm here with a friend."

A friend. That could mean a lot of things. A flash of disappointment hit. Of course she was here with someone. But she definitely wasn't dating any of the guys on the team. He knew all their wives and girlfriends. There were a few guys who were single. Like him. But none of them had mentioned bringing a date. Maybe she was here with a girlfriend?

"A friend—" he started to say then stopped as Finn Castro muscled his way up next to them and grinned at the mystery woman. Oliver felt his jaw tighten, a sensation far less pleasant than his reaction to her.

"Milly. There you are. I was looking for you." Finn turned his focus to Oliver, and his smile died. "This guy bugging you?"

She shook her head. "No, we were just talking while I got my drink." She looked from Finn to Oliver and back again, the pleasure in her eyes fading a little.

Oliver smiled at her and then narrowed his eyes at Finn, trying not to let his annoyance show on his face. Castro. Of course, she had to be here with Castro. Because life apparently had it in for him. "Finn," he said, trying to sound polite.

"Shields," Finn replied, and beside him Milly's eyes widened slightly, her expression turning wary as she glanced at Oliver. Oliver felt his gut tighten, wondering just what shit Finn had been talking about him. Plenty, he was sure. Their relationship hadn't improved any since that first incident in the locker room, and Castro didn't bother to hide it. He was barely polite to Oliver at work, so Oliver couldn't imagine Finn had anything good to say about him away from it.

Finn jerked his head toward the dance floor. "Come on, Milly, let's dance."

Milly—what that was short for?—held up her glass. "I haven't finished my drink." Her expression was still wary as she looked between the two of them.

"You can finish it with me."

"Finn, you're being rude." Her expression turned exasperated. Her tone wasn't *annoyed girlfriend*, more *sisterly irritation*. Interesting. Oliver felt a flash of hope that she might actually stay and talk to him.

"I'm just looking out for you," Finn retorted. "Shields here likes to sleep around. He's not the kind of guy you want to get involved with."

Oliver stiffened. "Excuse me?"

Beside him, Milly said, "We were just talking. Besides, I'm a big girl, Finn. I've been choosing my own dates for a long time now."

Finn scowled. "Yeah, well, don't pick Shields. He has a different girl every week."

Oliver bit back the urge to tell Finn exactly where he could shove his bullshit. That wasn't going to help the situation or impress Milly if she was really a friend of Castro's. Besides which, Finn was clearly on his way to drunk. Glassy-eyed and looking for trouble. And he was full of just enough youthful arrogance and stupidity to pick a fight. Which was the last thing anybody needed.

"I believe that's a case of the pot calling the kettle black," Milly said. She glanced up at Ollie, her expression somewhat assessing, and she focused on Finn again. "What happened to the blonde?"

"I came to find you. You said you'd dance with me."

She studied him for a long moment. Sighed. "Okay,

I'll dance with you. But how about we get you a cup of coffee first?"

Damn it, she was going to go with Castro. Time to step back from the plate. "Good idea," Ollie said. He smiled at Milly. "It was nice to meet you, Milly the economist."

And then he turned and walked away.

Amelia watched Finn dancing with the same short blonde he'd been flirting with earlier and tried not to think about Oliver Shields. Or give in to the desire to smack Finn for ruining things. She'd managed to pour one cup of coffee into him and they'd danced for a song or two but then the blonde had returned bearing beer and Finn had abandoned Amelia in about five seconds flat.

Leaving her with nothing better to do except think about Oliver. She knew about Oliver Shields—damn it, she should have recognized him and refused the drink. Finn had told her plenty about the guy. How he did his best to keep Finn from getting any time at first base and how he was tight with the Saints' owners and was using his position to make sure Finn didn't get the credit he deserved. Amelia had taken most of this with a grain of salt—she'd known Finn long enough to know he liked getting his own way and tended to have zero tolerance for anyone who stood between him and a goal. Oliver wasn't the only Saints player whom Finn had talked about in a less-than-positive way, but he seemed to be the one Finn really had a beef with.

Which was a pity, because the one thing Finn never mentioned about Oliver was that the man was stupidly hot. Night-dark eyes, tanned skin, and a wicked smile in a tall, lean body. Broad-shouldered, dark-haired, and smoky-voiced. Damn. Pretty much all the things she liked in a guy.

The universe was taunting her. Because hot or not, the man was a baseball player. And apparently Finn's worst rival. Maybe it was just as well Finn had interrupted them. A few more minutes of Oliver Shields flirting at her and she was fairly sure she might have thrown common sense to the wind and thrown herself at him. Which would have been all kinds of awkward once she'd found out who he was.

But luckily Finn had come along and been Finn.

Which he was all too good at. She sighed. She loved Finn like the brother she didn't have, but being Team Finn was hard work sometimes. She could hardly re-sign from the job, but maybe she needed to ease back a little. Finn was an adult. He was going to have to figure out how to be one. Which included getting along with his teammates.

She glanced back across the bar but couldn't spot Oliver. And couldn't help the pang of regret that he hadn't been someone else.

Oliver Shields was mighty pretty. And mighty appealing. Even if he wasn't Mr. Right, it had been too long since the last Mr. Wrong. A man as gorgeous as Oliver would make a pretty good Mr. Wrong.

But now she'd never know. The last thing Amelia wanted to do was cause a problem between Finn and one of his teammates. If Finn couldn't make it work at the Saints then he could be in trouble. The kind of trouble that had led to the Cubs trading him at the end of his first season with them. The kind of trouble that Finn had gotten into on and off over the years. A little too much partying to blow off steam at times. Though to date he'd been lucky and managed to avoid any serious consequences. Up until he'd been traded, anyway.

Amelia had hoped that being ditched by the Cubs would lead to him turning over a new leaf, but if tonight was an example of what he'd been doing all year, then apparently not.

Crap. Easing off on Team Finn might have to wait until the end of the season. And she definitely didn't want to do anything that would set him off. Like having a fling with a guy he hated.

So she, Amelia Graham, would take one for the team and not break her rule and not try to seduce Oliver Shields. Though of course, there was always the possibility that he might have turned her down. She thought of that smile again. And the dark warmth in his eyes. Nope. She didn't think she'd been calling that play wrong.

Bloody Finn. He was a flaming hypocrite.

Sucking now-warm club soda through a straw, she watched Finn dancing with the blonde. Close dancing. In a way that made it clear that he was planning on introducing her to some extracurricular activities later that night. She suppressed an eye roll. Finn had always been surrounded by willing women. One day he was going to meet the woman who would tell him no and Amelia very much looked forward to standing on the sidelines when that happened and cheering her on. But it didn't seem like tonight was going to be that night.

So she might as well call it quits. She didn't really know anyone else at the party, and if Finn had abandoned her for the blonde then he wasn't there to introduce her to anyone new. It was getting late and her feet were hurting more than ever. It was time to just go home. Back to Manhattan. Where she would curl up in bed alone and try not to think of Oliver Shields and what might have been.

Somewhere around one a.m., Maggie Jameson ambushed Oliver as he made his way across the club looking for distraction. It was well over an hour since Finn had pulled his bullshit and Oliver had struggled to shake the nasty mood that had settled over him in the aftermath. Castro. Still, Maggie didn't deserve to get caught in the cross fire of his lingering irritation, so he forced a smile when she stepped in front of him.

"What's up, Mrs. Winters?" he asked. "Come to your senses and decided to leave Alex for me?"

She grinned at him, looking beautiful as always, her long frame wrapped in a very short, very red dress that matched the red gems gleaming in her ears. "In your dreams, Ollie."

He grinned back. Once upon a time, Maggie had been his dream. But that was a long time ago. "Are you out of official party-wrangling mode yet?"

Maggie and Raina and Sara—the third of the trio of women who ruled the owners of the Saints—usually worked like a well-oiled machine to ensure that Saints' functions ran like clockwork. Which Ollie thought was rather unfair. It meant they didn't always get to relax and enjoy the parties as much as they deserved to.

"Just about," Maggie said. "Things will wind down soon." She studied him for a moment. "Meet anyone nice tonight?" she asked.

That was Maggie speak for "Are you hooking up?" Or maybe "When are you going to settle down, Oliver?" Which was a subject that he considered to be none of her business since she'd long ago declined to be a candidate for said settling.

"Still looking," he said, trying not to think of Milly the economist and her perfume and her pretty eyes.

Maggie smiled. "Oh good, then you won't mind doing me a favor."

Crap. He'd walked into that one. "Define favor," he said cautiously.

"Helping out one of your teammates," she said. "With a ride. You drove, right?"

"Maybe."

"I saw your car parked outside the club."

Busted. "All right, yes, I drove. Who needs a lift?"

She hesitated. Just for a second. Then, "Finn."

"Castro?" Ollie said disbelievingly. He did his best to get along with Castro at the club, but he'd made his opinion of the guy clear to Maggie on several occasions. Finn's actions earlier hadn't improved that opinion one bit.

"Yes. He's had one or two too many. Alex and Mal and Lucas think it's time for him to go home."

Translation, the guy was wasted and Maggie was in damage control mode. "So put him in a cab."

"He's not that drunk. He'd probably just get the driver to take him to another club as soon as they got out of sight."

True. The last thing they needed was Finn doing some dumb-ass thing while under the influence and getting the Saints' name plastered in the papers or all over the morning news shows.

"He was here with someone earlier. Milly or something." His jaw tightened at the thought of her. And of Finn chasing her off. Though she'd let herself be chased off. Sort of. So maybe she hadn't been interested in the first place. Or maybe she was just being a good friend. Damn it. He needed to stop thinking about her.

"If I'm understanding Finn correctly, then she went home," Maggie said.

"So send him home with someone else." He understood Maggie's reasoning for not wanting to trust Castro with a cab or one of Alex or Mal or Lucas's drivers, but he really wasn't in any mood to help out.

"He lives about two blocks from you," Maggie said. "You're the best candidate."

He'd been vaguely aware that Castro lived somewhere near him. He should have paid more attention. Then Maggie would be trying this with some other sucker. "How do you know I won't succumb to the temptation to kick him out of the car halfway across the Brooklyn Bridge?"

"You won't do that," Maggie said.

"Why not?"

"Because you think I'm awesome," she said with another brilliant smile and he resigned himself to having a very unwelcome passenger for his trip home.

They drove in near silence. Castro hadn't said a word since Mal and Dan Ellis had practically escorted him from the building and into Oliver's car. He'd pulled out his phone and started texting someone as soon as Oliver had started the engine. Which suited Ollie just fine. He really wasn't interested in talking. He focused on the road, suddenly tired. The adrenaline of the win and the party was fading, and he felt every one of the twenty or so hours he'd been awake.

As they hit the end of the Brooklyn Bridge and eased into Manhattan traffic, he yawned.

Finn looked up. "Tired, old man?"

Jesus. The guy didn't let up. No wonder the Cubs had sold him cheap. He was a decent batter and a very good fielder, but he was trouble. He shook his head. "No, just bored by the company."

"Yeah, well, you can just let me out at SubZero and I'll be out of your hair and you can go home to bed."

Un-fucking-believable. "Not gonna happen. I'm stopping nowhere but your apartment building."

"Shit. You sucking up to the bigwigs or something? Just take me to the damned club."

"Look, Castro, I don't know who gave you the bug up your butt, but let me clear something up for you." Oliver let the car glide to halt as the lights ahead turned red. "When the owner of your club and your coach evict you from a party for being wasted, the smart thing to do for your career is to go home, sleep it off, and apologize in the morning."

"If I wanted advice, I'd ask for it," Finn snapped. "As if you've never partied."

Apparently the kid was determined to dig his own grave. The light flashed green and he stepped on the gas. "Fine. But I'm still taking you to your apartment. You can do what the hell you want after that. It's your damned funeral."

The SUV that hit them halfway across the intersection came out of nowhere.

Chapter Two

The bag of takeout was frying her arm through the too-thin layer of her coat. She would have moved it but the October day was unexpectedly cold and the takeout was keeping the worst of the chill out. She smiled gratefully at the doorman as she reached Finn's apartment building and practically jogged through the door into the warmth.

Juggling the take-out bag, her purse, her laptop bag, and the key to Finn's apartment proved impossible. She was tempted to give in and knock but that didn't seem fair when Finn was recovering from a concussion. His head had to be killing him.

Or maybe not. When she managed to open the door and get inside, Finn was sprawled on one of the giant red leather sofas in his living room, playing a video game on his massive TV. The sound was turned off, and there was no other light source in the room.

"Should you be doing that?" she asked from the doorway. "I thought you were told to avoid anything with a screen for a few days."

Finn didn't look up. "You sound like Emma."

Given it was Emma who'd reminded Amelia about the list of things Finn wasn't supposed to do when she'd called earlier to request a baby-brother lunchtime checkup, that was an accusation she couldn't deny. But that didn't mean she was going to let Finn know.

"I brought you pot stickers. And wonton soup." Finn's favorite foods. Well, they had been when they'd been growing up. "Have you eaten?"

He looked around at the question and she saw the wince that crossed his face with the movement. "No."

"How's your head?" She put the food down on the coffee table in front of the sofa and dug into the bag for the carton of pot stickers.

Finn put the video game controller down and rolled his eyes. "If I eat this, will you stop nagging?"

"I'm not nagging, I'm asking how you are," she said, trying to keep her voice level. Long lunches were hardly the norm at Pullman, and she was pushing her luck by taking this one. It had taken forever to get the food and then all the way to the Upper East Side, and she was starving. Arguing with Finn wasn't going to help her mood, or Finn's.

She fetched bowls from the kitchen and came back to the lounge. "Here." She held out the bowl to Finn and he obligingly tipped about two-thirds of the first carton of pot stickers into it.

"There," he said. "Let's eat."

"I think you need another lesson in fractions," Amelia said. "That one I gave you when you were in elementary school doesn't seem to have stuck."

"I'm bigger than you," Finn said.

"You've been doing nothing but lying around all day," Amelia countered. "You'll be busting out of those tight baseball pants if you're not careful."

He grinned at that. She tried not to grin back. Finn

and Em came from a background that included Polish, Irish, Spanish, and French ancestors. Whatever the precise mix was, it had produced good-looking specimens in this generation. Both Castros had skin that always looked slightly tanned, dark-green eyes, and dark-brown hair that was close enough to black. In Finn's case it also came with a face chiseled to perfection by helpful genes—strong cheekbones and a square jaw that was a reminder of just how stubborn he could be. On Em the cheekbones were high and the face more angular but just as attractive. Both of them could charm the birds from the trees. Which was why Amelia was sitting here when she should be at work, making sure Finn ate and trying not to smile when he smiled at her.

She ate her share of the pot stickers a little faster than could be termed polite and reached for the second carton—securing her share before Finn could devour them all. The perfectly cooked dumplings eased the hunger pangs, and her mood started to improve.

Leaning back in the chair—and wishing that she was wearing something more comfortable than a suit—she studied Finn.

He ate steadily but the fact that she had beaten him to the second batch of pot stickers told her he wasn't feeling 100 percent.

"Did the team doctor—what's his name again—come to see you?" she asked when Finn put his empty bowl down.

"Jones," he said. "I thought you weren't going to nag."

"Well, either you can tell me what happened and I can tell Em, or you can not tell me and deal with Em yourself when she gets sick of waiting for an update."

"You wouldn't sic Em on a recovering invalid, would you?" He gave her his best puppy-dog eyes.

Luckily she was largely immune to Castro puppy-dog

eyes. At least when they came from Finn. Em was harder to resist, but that was because her puppy-dog eyes came with nearly twenty years of best-friend you-got-my-back-and-I-got-yours instinct built in. "I won't need to sic her on you. She'll do it herself. So what did the doctor say? Are they going to let you play?"

"Doc Jones was here this morning. I have to get another checkup tomorrow but it looks like it," Finn said. "We don't have to fly to Boston, so that helps."

Flying with a concussion was a no-no, she knew that much. The Saints were playing the Red Sox for the division series. So that was lucky. Though part of her wondered if Finn should be playing so soon. Damned stubborn Castros.

Finn slurped soup, and she suddenly felt exhausted. She'd gone home from the Saints' party ready to call Em in the morning and announce that the Amelia-Graham-looks-out-for-Finn-Castro program was about to be canned. Instead she'd gotten a semi-hysterical phone call from Em telling her that Finn had been in an accident. The memory made her gut tighten. After all, it was only Tuesday, and the accident had been Sunday night. Or Monday morning, really.

"That seems fast," she said. "Only gives you one more day to rest."

He slanted her a look that suggested he wasn't that interested in her medical opinion. "If the doc says I'm okay, I'm okay."

She held up her hands. "Fine. I won't nag." If she did, he'd just turn stubborn and decide to play no matter how bad he felt. So she'd leave the nagging to Em and just try to be supportive. Team Finn, as always. He was hurt, so she couldn't bail on him. After the divisional series was over, maybe. It seemed unlikely that the Saints would make the championships. The Red Sox were far more experienced. Not that she was going to utter that traitorous thought to Finn.

He was thrilled to be playing in the division series. It was his first time.

"Are your parents and Em coming out for the game?" she asked.

"Mom and Dad are going to come to the first Staten Island game," Finn said.

"And Em?"

"She doesn't know if she can get away. She's got a case starting tomorrow. Some big fraud thing that's going to go on forever."

She knew that part. But she suspected Em might surprise Finn with an appearance. Though if it wasn't one of the two Boston home games or the first Saints game at Deacon Field, she might just miss out. The division series was best of five.

A yawn suddenly overtook her, a reminder that she hadn't had enough sleep in two nights. She fought it, shaking her head to wake herself up. She wasn't up to baseball math or trying to plan how to get Em out here—even though she'd love to see her. She had to get back to work before her boss noticed how long she'd been gone. If she powered through the afternoon, maybe she could leave at a reasonable hour for once. Get an early night.

"What are you doing this afternoon?" she said as Finn put his bowl down.

He waved a hand at the TV. "Pretty much this."

More TV. Not what the doctor ordered. But Finn wasn't good at doing what doctors ordered. Though she'd have thought, with his chance to play in the divisionals at stake, that he'd be toeing the line for once. Her stomach tightened again. He was getting his chance because Oliver Shields had been hurt worse than him in the accident. Oliver whose smile she hadn't been able to erase from her memory despite her best intentions. She hesitated a moment; mentioning Oliver might just send Finn into one of his moods. But then she decided she didn't care. She might not have completely given up on Team Finn just yet, but this seemed to be a moment when being Team Finn required calling him on his shit for once. If he hadn't been drinking so much at the party, the accident wouldn't have happened. "Have you thought about going to see Oliver in the hospital?"

Sure enough, Finn's expression turned cranky. "Shields? What the hell for? He—"

She held up a hand. "He got hurt driving you home, Finn. Seeing how he's doing seems the decent thing to do." She nailed him with the look she used on the interns at work when they were being annoying. "Have you even talked to him?"

Finn's face went from cranky to sulky. "No."

"Well, you should."

"Why?"

"Because you're not seven?" she said softly. "It doesn't matter if you don't like him or don't get along. He's your teammate and he was helping you out. And now he's missing the play-offs because of you."

"You're just saying that because you want to jump him."

"I've met the man exactly once," she said. "Nobody's jumping anybody." Unfortunately. She had to admit that Oliver was eminently jumpable. Though currently presumably out of action for a while . . . she dragged her thoughts back to the topic at hand. "I don't seem to remember anyone passing a Finn Castro Is Ruler of the Universe Bill, so even if I did want to jump him it would be none of your business."

"The guy's a jerk. And a player."

"Finn, I've been managing my love life on my own in

New York for seven years now. I work on Wall Street. Not to mention I grew up around you and your jock friends. I can look after myself." And everybody else.

"I'm just saying, he's not the sort of guy you want. You don't want to end up like your mom."

She sucked in a breath, stomach twisting. "That's not fair. Or the same situation by any stretch of the imagination." Her dad had been a football player in college on scholarship. Until he'd gotten her mom pregnant, decided to do the right thing, and married her. Then bailed six-ish years later. Her mom didn't like to talk about it. Amelia had always wondered if it was resentment over losing any chance to go pro that had killed their marriage and made him run. She knew her mom never liked it when she'd dated jocks in high school. And she'd made damned sure Amelia had had all the sex ed and birth control a girl could want.

"I'm just saying. Hell, Milly. I know these guys."

"Because they're like you?"

"Maybe." He winced as he shifted on the sofa, and her mood softened a little. But not completely.

"It doesn't matter what Oliver is like, I'm not trying to date him. So stop changing the subject. I know you don't like him, but he's on your team. And he's been there a lot longer than you have. He's a senior player and you're new. Don't screw things up. You told me he's tight with the owners, right?"

"Yeah, well, because Maggie Winters used to sleep with him, back when dinosaurs roamed the earth," Finn said.

Oliver had dated Maggie Winters? That information shouldn't give her a pang in the chest, but it did. "All the more reason not to piss him off. You don't want to get on the wrong side of your bosses," she said a little more sharply than she had intended. She took a breath, tried to soften her tone. "Look, Finn, the Saints are a good shot for you. Their fortunes seem to be on the rise. The smart thing to do would be to see if you can catch a ride along with them."

"You're an expert on baseball now?" he snapped.

No, but she was pretty good on the ways Finn liked to screw things up. "I just think—"

"Milly, you need to get this straight. The only thing that I'm interested in when it comes to Shields is the fact that he's out of action. Because that gives me an opportunity. And I'm going to take it. So don't expect me to be sitting in his hospital room being buddies. We're not friends. We never have been. He's been in my way all season— and rubbed my nose in it—and now he's out of it." He looked at her, scowling still. "Hell, don't look like that. I didn't want this to happen to him but it has. So I'm going to take my shot. You can bet your ass he would if our positions were reversed. He's had fifteen years in the spotlight. Now it's my turn."

She actually couldn't speak for a moment. Hell, she'd known Finn could be single-minded about baseball. It came with the talent, she supposed, that driven kind of focus to get where he wanted to go. But she'd never seen him be so cold-blooded about it. Even if Finn didn't get along with Oliver, being so ruthlessly determined to take his place was . . . well, pretty crappy, actually. Still, there was no point trying to talk sense to him when he was in this mood. Instead she stood and picked up her stuff. "Look, I have to get back to work, and your head must hurt. I'm going to go. I'll talk to you later, okay?" She waited. Hoping he'd say something even vaguely apologetic.

He didn't respond, just lay back on the sofa and

reached for the video game controller. And in that moment, she decided she wasn't going to be having such an
early night after all.

His hand hurt like a son of a bitch. Oliver shifted himself
back up the hospital bed, which only set off an answering throb in his bandaged ankle, and hid his wince. He'd
spent the last two days since his surgery half stoned on
morphine but was determined to make do without it
today.

Which wasn't improving his mood any.

But fuck, he had a right to be pissed. He was missing
the play-offs. Might miss the start of the next season.

All because Finn fucking Castro couldn't handle himself and some moron in a Hummer had decided that red
lights didn't mean "stop," they meant "gun through the
intersection and take out anything in your path." Both
Finn and the Hummer driver had walked away from the
accident with bruises, a few cuts, and concussions.

It was Oliver who'd woken up in a hospital bed after
surgery to be told that a piece of metal had sliced up his
right hand, and his chance to finally play in the divisional
series after fifteen fucking years of professional baseball
was over. The sprained ankle—Lucas had told him he
was lucky that he hadn't actually broken it—and various
other cuts and grazes were just the icing on the cake.

He played first base. He needed his damned hand to
work.

Lucas hadn't been able to tell him that it would recover
fully. The slice had been deep. Apparently the surgery—
Lucas had dragged the best microsurgeon in the city out
of bed—had taken hours. Nerves and tendons sewn back
together. But that didn't mean they were going to be as
good as new. And without full function, more than his
chance at playing in the divisional series would be gone.

Lucas had told him it was too early to panic; he had to wait and see.

Maggie, white-faced, had told him that the police were charging the Hummer driver with half a dozen offenses. Alex, who'd been there with her when Ollie woke up, told him that if he wanted to sue the driver, the Saints would pay.

Oliver didn't care about money. He cared about losing his career. And ever since that moment of waking up, even during the times he'd been delirious on morphine, he'd felt nothing but rage.

Rage and flashes of pain, and then the drugs would suck him back down into sleep full of dreams that he couldn't remember but made him wake up gasping each time.

Which was why he wanted to ditch the drugs. Or at least wean himself onto something less heavy-duty. It had been three hours now since they had taken out the morphine drip and his hand was starting to complain. Loudly.

But he wasn't going to ask. Not just yet.

Drugs weren't going to help him recover sooner. Not soon enough to make any difference anyway. He was missing the play-offs. Nothing to be done about it.

He felt his good hand curl at the thought, resisted the urge to smash it against the bed frame. Just. Instead he dropped his head back on the pillow, closed his eyes, and yelled "Fuck!" in as loud a voice as he dared, not wanting to have three nurses come barreling through the door to pester him.

"Sorry, is this a bad time?" a voice came from the doorway. Female. One he didn't immediately recognize.

"Go away," he growled.

He heard a sigh but no sound of the door closing again. Then another sigh and footsteps came closer to the bed.

"I said go away."

"I heard you," his unknown visitor said. "But I wanted to say something first."

"If you're a reporter, I'll have security here in about three seconds," he said, still keeping his eyes closed. He knew exactly where the call button was. He'd been bargaining with himself to delay picking it up and asking for a painkiller.

"I'm not a reporter," she said.

"Are you a doctor?"

"No. Economist."

His eyes flew open. Milly the economist? What the hell was she doing here?

He blinked as he turned his head, the lights in the room dazzling him for a second, but when his vision cleared, it was definitely her. Milly of the big blue eyes and wicked laugh. Here in his hospital room.

Wearing a very sleek suit in a greenish-brown shade that made her hair—pulled back in a bun that was far more orderly than the style she'd worn at the club—look more red than blond.

"Do you remember me? I'm Milly—Amelia—Graham. We met at the party."

"Yes. What are you doing here?" he said, confused. Maybe he should pinch himself. Maybe he'd fallen asleep and was having another very weird dream. But if he was dreaming, surely she would be wearing something far more seductive than a suit. And she wouldn't be carrying a brown paper bag with lollipops printed on it.

She moved closer to the bed, extended the bag. He sat up—carefully so as not to jostle his ankle too much—took the bag, and peered inside.

It was full of candy. Sour gummies. Cotton candy in a tin. Chocolate of several different varieties. Red Hots.

Tootsie Rolls. Jolly Ranchers. "Candy?" he said, still confused.

"I broke my arm a few years ago," she said. "When I was on painkillers, I didn't have much of an appetite because they made me nauseous, but candy was okay. And I didn't know if you liked flowers." She paused, surveyed the room, which was brimming with the flower arrangements that the Saints, his manager, his family, and apparently every other person he'd ever met in his life, had sent. As if flowers could help. "But apparently you do."

He frowned. "People keep sending them. I keep asking the nurses to take them to other wards. But then more arrive."

"Sucks to be popular," she said with a tentative smile.

He put the bag on the tray table thing beside his bed. Then changed his mind and grabbed for it again. She was right, he wasn't eating much. Even in the fancy part of the hospital that Lucas had gotten him into, the food had done nothing to lessen the queasiness from the drugs. Even ginger ale—which he loved—hadn't helped. Maybe gummy bears would work.

"So you're a gummy bear man?" Milly said.

"As long as they're the sour ones," he replied. He realized that opening the pack of candy was going to be difficult with one hand and used his teeth instead. Once he'd managed that—the whole process a lot more awkward than he would have liked—he put it down on his tray table. "Want one?"

"No, thanks," she said.

He ate a bear, studying her. She looked . . . nervous, he decided.

"You gonna tell me why you're here?" he asked.

Her shoulders slumped a little, then straightened again. "I came to say sorry," she said.

"Sorry?" He was confused again. "What do you have to be sorry about?"

"Finn," she said. "If I hadn't let him chase me off at the club, then you wouldn't have gotten into this accident."

Well, he couldn't argue with that. Fucking Castro. He started to scowl involuntarily.

"You came to see me to say sorry for Finn?" Finn who hadn't been to see him at all. Finn who was already home. Who still had two working hands. "Did he send you?" His frown deepened.

"No," she said, in a very definite tone. A frown appeared on her face. "No. In fact I didn't know you'd been hurt until yesterday when I finally got the full story about what happened."

That sounded about right. "And how is Finn?" He made himself eat another gummy bear.

"He has a mild concussion. He has to rest for another twenty-four hours, then they'll assess him again before the . . ."

Before the divisional series started. On Thursday. Two days from now. Which meant Finn would most likely play. Might even score some time in Oliver's now-vacant first-base spot. Suddenly the gummy bear wasn't the only sour taste in his mouth.

Amelia was looking at his leg. Or rather at the strange tented shape the metal thing they'd put over his ankle to keep the weight of the blankets off it made in the bedclothes. Then her gaze moved to the swath of bandages that had turned his hand into something out of a Mummy movie.

"That looks like more than bumps and bruises. Finn didn't tell me what happened to you."

"Finn doesn't know," Oliver said. The team hadn't released an official statement about him yet. "But yes, severed tendons in my hand is worse than bumps and bruises."

She turned pale. "S-severed?"

"Yes."

"Will you . . ." She hesitated again. Then took a breath. "Will you be able to play again?"

"The doctors are being noncommittal. The words *early days* keep getting used. Hard to tell." He'd torn his ACL and come back from that. But he'd been ten years younger then. And ACLs didn't take months of therapy. And now it was likely that his right ankle would be weakened from the sprain. It was, of course, the same leg as the knee he'd hurt earlier. Same hand, too. Apparently the right side of his body had done something to piss the universe off.

According to Lucas, it would be nearly the start of spring training before they had a good idea of his prognosis. Whether he'd be able to play major league again.

His good hand curled. He didn't want to think about that. He wasn't going to think about it.

Time for a distraction. Right now, Milly was his best shot at one. Looking at her was definitely distracting. In a good way. But if he was reading the situation right, she was only here to do what Finn clearly wasn't man enough to do and apologize. He studied her a moment, and their eyes met. She blushed, pink flooding her pale skin in a rush.

Interesting. Maybe Finn wasn't the only reason she was here. Before she'd found out who he was, before Finn had interrupted them back in the bar, Milly the economist had been into him. Team Oliver, not Team Finn. The question was how to find out whose side she was on now. He tilted the bag of candy toward her. "Sure I can't tempt you?"

Was he imagining things or did her cheeks go even pinker?

"No, thanks." She smiled as she shook her head. And for the first time all day, he felt vaguely good.

"Not a gummy girl?" He smiled back, hoping to keep her smile going.

"I am. But I already ate half a bag of Reese's Pieces on my way over here."

His attention strayed to the curve of her mouth. It was painted with soft pink. Freshly painted? Had she messed up her makeup eating chocolate? What would Milly the economist taste like if he kissed her now? Sweet like chocolate? Salty like peanut butter?

Well, no time like the present. If she turned out to be taken he could at least dull the pain with his next dose of whatever the heck it was they were going to give him instead of morphine.

"Do you mind if I ask what exactly your relationship with Castro is?"

She tipped her head to the side, one hand straying to the gold loop in her ear. "It's complicated."

"I'm not going anywhere. Complicated as in crazy-ex complicated or something else?"

Her laugh rang out across the room. Damn, he'd forgotten just how sexy that laugh was.

"Ex? You thought Finn and I were—"

"He seemed pretty possessive at the party."

"He's just overprotective. I'm kind of his de facto big sister."

His eyebrows rose even as a ridiculous sense of relief—she wasn't one of Finn's exes—flooded through him. "How does that work?"

"His actual big sister is my best friend. We grew up together. But I moved to New York after college and she's still in Chicago. So now that Finn's here, I'm kind of the big sister on-site."

"Isn't he old enough not to need a big sister keeping an eye on him?"

"Yes," she said. "But it's a hard habit to break. And Em—his sister—is a worrier."

He understood worrying female relatives. He'd only just managed to talk his mother out of camping in the hospital foyer instead of staying in a hotel. It had taken the combined charms of Lucas and Maggie and Alex to help him pull that off. Luckily Heather, his youngest sister, was about three weeks away from making him an uncle for the fifth time and not allowed to fly out from San Francisco to visit him. And Leah, his other sister, was out with Heather, being aunty. He was pretty sure they'd be bugging him via Skype as soon as he was set free from the hospital.

And if Castro's sister was a worrier, then she had reason to be. Castro had been traded by the Cubs to the Saints at a bargain rate. Cheaper than his talent warranted. Ollie hadn't quite gotten a direct confirmation out of Maggie that there were other issues at play, but the baseball world was small and it hadn't been hard to get the dirt that Finn had a taste for partying and a dislike for listening to the advice of his teammates that hadn't endeared him to his previous team. Habits he hadn't given up in the six months he'd been with the Saints. Ever since that first clash at spring training, he'd made no secret of the fact that he wanted Oliver's spot. Now he might just have gotten his wish. "So you were at the party as a babysitter?"

She pulled a face. "No, just came along because he asked me. I thought it would be fun. It's been busy at work—"

"At . . . where was it again?"

"Pullman Waters," she said.

The name was vaguely familiar. "Investment bank?"

She nodded. "Yes. Small. We specialize in Asian markets. And that's all I'm going to say or you'll fall asleep."

"Didn't we have this conversation once before?" he asked. "I remember telling you that a sensible man wouldn't fall asleep on you."

Right before Finn had barged in and ruined the moment.

Her cheeks went pink again, then her expression turned intriguingly regretful. But regretful moved to apologetic. "I'm sorry," she said again. She looked at his hand, a not-quite-well-enough-hidden wince crossing her face.

Pity. He didn't want pity from her.

What did he want, then? She'd just told him she was practically Finn's family. Which meant that as distracting as she was, she also came with complications. There was no love lost between him and Finn. A situation that wouldn't be improved if he made a move on the guy's de facto sister or whatever the hell she was.

He shook his head, wished he could clear his head. The morphine or whatever the hell it was they'd been given him might have stopped working on his hand and ankle, but it was still doing a number on his brain. Still, foggy or not, he wasn't much inclined toward sparing Finn's feelings. He liked this girl.

"What exactly are you sorry for, Amelia?"

"It's Milly."

"Nah. You look like an Amelia. Millys are fluffy. You're not." he said, then wondered where the hell that had come from. This was why he hated morphine. Loosened his tongue a little too much.

She grinned. "They have you on the good drugs, don't they?"

"Nope, haven't had anything for hours."

Concern chased the amusement off her face. "Why on earth not?"

"I don't like morphine."

"Oh good grief. What is it with athletes and the need to prove you're Superman?"

"Well, they tend to frown on most drugs in the MLB. Better not to get used to them."

"You just had surgery. I'm guessing that means no baseball for you for a while. You should take the drugs."

He desperately wanted to agree with her. But he wasn't going to give in. No drugs. Lucas had offered him a nerve block earlier, but he'd said no. "But I have you to distract me. And you haven't told me what you're sorry about."

"Right now, I'm sorry you're too stubborn to take drugs. I imagine that hand hurts quite a bit." She glanced at the watch on her wrist. Which was, unless he was mistaken, a Cartier Tank. Classy. Expensive classy. Amelia was doing all right on Wall Street, it seemed.

"I need to go," she said. "Visiting hours will be over soon."

"Soon, not yet."

She shook her head. "It's been kind of a long day. I still have some work to do when I get home."

"I'm sure I'm more fun than Asian economies," he said.

That earned him half a smile. "Maybe you are. But Asian economies pay the bills." She bent to pick up her purse, clearly intent on making a getaway now that she'd done her duty.

Chapter Three

"That's all I get? Gummy bears and an apology and a five-minute visit?"

Amelia froze half bent over. "Excuse me?" She fumbled her purse as she grabbed for it and it fell to the floor with a solid thunk. Heat flooded her cheeks as she grabbed for it a second time. What the hell did he mean by "that's all I get"?

"Well, your de facto brother is kind of responsible for my hand being screwed."

She straightened with a jerk. His eyes, still wild and dark, were studying her. It was unfair, she decided, that even in a pale-blue hospital gown, with stubble darkening his jaw and dark circles under his eyes, Oliver still looked all sorts of good.

But she couldn't think about that now. No, now she had to work out if he was teasing or if he was actually mad at Finn and thought she owed him something.

"There's chocolate-coated pretzels and salted caramel bark in there," she said, trying to sound unconcerned.

"I don't want candy, Amelia," he said.

"It's Milly," she corrected. For the second time.

He tilted his head. "Finn called you Milly."

"Lots of people do."

"Amelia suits you better," he said. "It's pretty. Like you."

Pretty? He thought she was pretty? For a moment everything went kind of foggy and swimmy. Then she remembered where she was. "Are you sure you're not on drugs?"

He shook his head. "Nope." And then he hit her with a version of his smile that wasn't quite as full wattage as it had been in the club but was still annoyingly charming.

Holy crap. He really thought she was pretty. The room suddenly felt uncomfortably warm.

"You're not a closet masochist, are you?" she said, desperate for something to fill the silence between them. Then she heard the words that had actually come out of her mouth and wished the boring gray linoleum tile floor would open up and swallow her.

Oliver laughed, and the sound was even better than his smile. "Are you asking if I'm kinky, Amelia? Isn't that a little forward for our second date?"

"This is hardly a date. Let alone a second one."

"I don't know. First you flirted with me in a bar, now you're hunting me down in my hospital room. Face it, you can't get enough of me."

Her eyes narrowed. "I'm not the one who's trying to talk me into staying. Maybe you're the one who can't get enough of me."

He laughed again. "Maybe so, Amelia. Which brings me back to our original topic. Or it will after I tell you that I'm definitely not a masochist. But I am a professional athlete. We already covered how the league feels about narcotics."

"And we already covered that you're probably not playing professional baseball for a while," she retorted.

The smile dropped from his face as quickly as a door slamming shut. Idiot. Why had she said that?

"No. Not this season."

Or maybe never again? She looked again at the bandaged hand resting on his lap. She had no idea how bad his injury was, but severed tendons sounded pretty damned serious. Oliver was a first baseman like Finn. He needed his hands. What if he never played again? God, what if driving Finn home had ended Oliver's career? What would that mean for Finn? For both of them?

Could Oliver sue Finn? Was he the type of guy who would sue? He didn't give off asshole vibes, but he was a professional athlete. He had to be earning serious cash. Finn might just have been part of the cause of that income stream vanishing completely. Though surely if anyone was to blame it was the asshole who'd been driving the Hummer.

Or her, for not making sure Finn had switched to coffee back at the party. She squelched the horrible surge of guilt back down. She'd been squelching it ever since Em had called her to tell her Finn was in the hospital. It had been an accident. No one was to blame. And Oliver wouldn't blame Finn.

"Which brings me, Amelia, to the question of your particular offering."

"Offering?" she said, having lost track of the conversation as her mind came up with worst-case scenarios.

"Gummy bears." He shook his head at her, smiling that damned smile again. "Like I said, gummy bears just aren't going to cut it."

"They're not?" Amused was good, wasn't it? Amused meant "Not about to announce that he's going to sue Finn for everything he owns." Which possibly would be a disappointing lawsuit. Finn wasn't exactly focused on providing for his financial future. She'd tried dropping him recommendations for financial advisers in the past. She'd given him names of people she knew and trusted. But he'd never, as far as she was aware, contacted even one of them. Finn so far seemed happy to spend his money on fancy gadgets, including a yellow Porsche that was a textbook hyped-up boy's toy, designer clothes, and over-priced booze in all the latest cool clubs.

"No."

He was looking at her again. Watching with those dark eyes. She felt exposed, naked. His expression seemed to tell her that was exactly how he wanted her.

"What d-do you want?" She heard her voice catch slightly, heard the weird breathy tone, and wanted to sink into the floor again. She needed to get ahold of herself. But all she could think of was what she might do if he answered, *I want you, Amelia.* Possibly something dumb like crawling up onto the bed and kissing him. Jock or not. There was no denying how sexy he was.

"I want . . ." He paused, watched her a moment longer before a smile flickered over his face. "A distraction."

She didn't know whether to be relieved or annoyed. Perhaps both.

"I'm sure this hospital is willing to provide endless hours of entertainment for its VIPs."

"You might be surprised," he muttered. "But that wasn't the kind of distraction I meant."

She folded her arms. "Oh? Perhaps you should spell this out for me, Mr. Shields. What exactly is it you're expecting me to do for you?"

"Give me a second chance."

She blinked. That wasn't the answer she'd been expecting. "A second chance to do what, exactly?"

"We were interrupted, back at the party."

Here came that swimmy feeling again. Like she needed to sit down and take a few deep breaths. Bad idea. She stayed where she was. He was just another guy. She could handle him. "Sort of," she agreed. She waved a hand at the room they were in. "But I get the feeling that you're not in any condition to be trying to sweep anyone off their feet right now."

His smile was lopsided. "Are you casting aspersions on my abilities, Amelia?"

"No. Just being practical."

"You like practical, do you?"

"I'm an economist," she reminded him.

"Facts and figures and statistics."

"And predictions."

"Predictions aren't truly practical, though, are they? Not when they can go wrong."

"Well, economics is complicated. It's like trying to put together a jigsaw puzzle that has a million pieces. And some of the pieces keep changing shape."

"So you like a challenge then?"

"I guess," she said warily.

"Good. So do I."

"Is that what I am? A challenge? The thrill of the chase? I'm not much interested in being the shiny thing that keeps you occupied until you can get back on your feet." That wasn't entirely true. The thought of being the object of this man's singular focus was oddly intriguing. But she knew athletes. Single-minded. Take away the usual obsession—aka the sport they played—and they often found another. And Finn had said that Oliver was a player off the field as well as on. Apply the theory of *It takes one to know one* and Finn should be a reliable judge of that sort of thing.

And she had enough experience with athletes who'd had their shiny thing taken away to know they weren't a good risk. Her dad had provided an object lesson in that fact. Besides, she had her own dreams to chase. She'd spent a long time playing cheerleader to Finn's and Em's dreams. She didn't begrudge them that, but that didn't mean she wanted to add someone else to the list.

"Despite what Finn might have told you, I don't treat women as disposable," Oliver said. She felt her brows lift, and he held up a hand. "I'm not saying I've lived like a monk or never hurt someone, but I'm not twenty-four years old anymore and I don't spend my nights screwing a new girl at every game."

"But you're single?" The question tumbled from her mouth before she could stop it.

"Yes. And that's for a number of reasons. But not because I want to . . ."

"Keep chasing?"

"Close enough. I'm not in it for the thrill of the hunt." He shifted suddenly on the bed and winced, pain clear on his face this time.

"How long did you say it was since you had some painkillers?" she asked.

He waved the unbandaged hand at her. "I'm fine."

"You don't have to be a big tough guy and impress me with your manly ability to withstand pain," she said. "Stoicism isn't an attractive trait. Call the nurse."

"I don't want the drugs," he said. "They make things foggy."

"There must be something they can give you that's a bit less potent."

"I'm not sure Advil is going to cut it," he said. Then grimaced, as though he realized what he'd just admitted.

"So it does hurt," she said softly. "Call the nurse, Oliver."

"And if I don't?"

"Then I'll be forced to conclude that you're really in no condition to make sensible decisions. Or go on second dates."

"Third dates."

"Don't quibble over numbers with an economist," she said mock-sternly. He was paler now, she thought, than he'd been when she arrived, his olive skin looking gray and washed out. "Call the nurse and I'll think about what you're . . . proposing."

"That hardly seems fair," he said. "I'm the wounded one here. You're meant to minister to me."

"Well, I might if this was the eighteenth century," she said, suppressing a smile. "And I did bring you gummy bears."

"If this was the eighteenth century, I'd be demanding that Finn hand you over to me in retribution for his wrongs," Oliver said. His eyes had gone intent again.

A chill stole over her. Retribution? Was he serious? Or was he flirting as a distraction from his pain again? "I'm pretty sure he would have to be an actual relative to hand me over," she said, trying to keep the conversation light. "And those stories never end well."

Oliver shrugged. "You're reading the wrong stories. The ones I read involved the maiden falling in love with the vengeful knight."

"I wouldn't have picked you for a romance novel fan."

"Maggie used to read them by the bucketload when she was younger. In between baseball statistics anyway. I wanted to see what the attraction was so I swiped one. Then I discovered they had sex in them. At seventeen, that was pretty compelling." He grinned then, and she felt her stomach curl.

"You've been with the Saints since you were seventeen?"

"Yes. But you're changing the subject, Amelia."

"You're the one who's changed the subject. We were talking about the fact that you need drugs."

"Who needs drugs?" asked a female voice from the

door. Amelia jumped, startled. She turned and saw Maggie Winters—Finn had introduced them very briefly at the party—standing in the doorway.

"Oliver's hand is hurting and he's being stubborn," Amelia said.

"He does that," Maggie said with a nod. She hovered in the doorway, looking over at Oliver with a questioning expression. "Am I interrupting something?"

"No," Amelia said. She bent down and retrieved her purse. "I was just leaving. It's late." Seize the opportunity for retreat while it presented itself. Before Oliver Shields and his pirate charm could talk her into something crazy. "Enjoy the gummy bears, Oliver," she said and headed for the door. Maggie stepped back to let her go, watching her with an oddly curious smile.

Oliver watched Amelia practically bolt out the door and bit back the desire to shout *fuck* again. He'd almost pinned her down. But now she was gone. And he was suddenly painfully aware that his hand hurt like hell. He set his teeth, looking at the clock on the wall. He'd told himself it would be at least four hours before he asked for something. He wasn't quite there yet.

"So, who was that?" Maggie asked, walking into the room.

"You don't know her?"

"Should I?"

"Her name's Amelia Graham. She's one of Castro's friends. His sister's best friend or something."

"Amelia?" Her brow crinkled for a moment. "Was she at the party? I think Finn introduced me to someone at some point."

"It's not like you to forget a name."

"There were over two hundred people at that party, Ollie."

"Finn calls her Milly."

"Oh? And what do you call her?" Maggie asked. Amusement danced in her eyes. It was the first time he'd seen her looking happy since he'd woken up in the hospital. But he wasn't about to try to explain his strange fascination with Amelia to Maggie.

"Nothing. I met her at the party. We talked for a couple of minutes but that was it."

"Yet she's bringing you gummy bears in the hospital?" Maggie asked skeptically.

"Finn told her about the accident. I think she was just being nice." That sounded unconvincing even to him.

Maggie shrugged out of her coat. "I see. And has her niceness rubbed off on Finn? Has he come to see you yet? Or even called?"

He shook his head.

Maggie sighed. "He should. I'm going to get Dan to talk to him."

"Don't push it, Maggie. The kid needs to figure out how to do the decent thing himself. Or decide if he's going to be an asshole his entire life."

"The kid is nearly twenty-six," she pointed out.

"He's still a kid, though." Amelia's kid brother, kind of. If he was going to try to get to know her, then he was going to have to find a way to get along with Finn.

"Yeah, well, if he doesn't want to find himself traded again, he better start growing up."

Her expression had turned fierce. Maggie had grown up with the Saints; her dad had owned the team before Alex, Mal, and Lucas. Now she worked as Alex's right-hand woman. She didn't like players who caused problems. Which Finn did. Ollie got the feeling that Finn might just have stepped over a line with Maggie. Not a good idea.

"You have the play-offs to focus on. Finn can wait."

Maggie looked suddenly stricken. "I hate that you don't get to play." Her hand curled around his left hand. His good hand.

"Yeah. Me too."

She looked away. Looked down. Swallowed. "I shouldn't have asked you to drive him home."

Her voice sounded one step away from tears. Christ. He didn't need Maggie crying over him.

"I didn't have to say yes," he said. "It was an accident, Mags. Nothing you or I can do about it." He squeezed her hand then let go. "Now, how about you see if you can find out when Lucas is going to let me out of this place?"

"Got a minute?"

Amelia looked up from the currency outlook report in her hand and manufactured a smile. Her boss, Daniel Carling, wasn't the type to come to his underlings' offices very often. "Of course," she said, rising a little in her chair. "Do you want me to come to your office?"

He waved a hand, the gesture a little too magnanimous to be casual. "No, we can do it here."

She sat back in her chair, stomach rolling. Do it? What on earth did he want? "If that suits you." She waited for him to settle himself in the chair opposite her. Her office was tiny but it was still an office. One she'd worked hard for since she'd joined Pullman five years ago.

"How was your meeting earlier?" Daniel asked.

She blinked. "The one for the Australasian currency model?"

He nodded, one hand straying to the immaculate French cuff of his shirt. "That's the one."

"It was good," she said briskly. "The IT guys are confident they've fixed the critical bugs so now they're just fine-tuning the logic and then we can start testing it with real data."

"Did they give you an ETA?"

"End of the month."

"You think they'll meet that target?"

"I'm cautiously optimistic." She ventured a smile. "They've been good at hitting milestones so far."

"Good." His impeccable British accent, as usual, gave no clue as to what he might be thinking or feeling. If he had feelings. Daniel Carling made blizzards seem warm. He was good at his job but not someone who believed in being friends with his coworkers. "How long have you worked here now, Amelia?"

"Five years," she said, knowing full well he knew the answer to the question. Daniel had joined the bank only a year ago, taking over from her old boss when he'd jumped ship to a rival firm. Iceman or not, he understood economics and so far hadn't tried to micromanage the team of economists she worked in. But he had put each of them through a series of seemingly casual lunches with him when he'd first arrived, grilling them not so subtly about their job histories and more.

"That's a long time," he said.

It was, in a way. But she liked working for Pullman. The money was good, and they'd made it through the global financial crisis less battered than many other banks, so she was happy to stay for now. She waited as Daniel studied her with ice-gray eyes that matched the silver starting to show in his hair and the polished cuff links at his wrist. He took cool, calm, and collected to an art form. But she had gotten somewhat used to his act over the last year. He didn't completely intimidate her anymore.

"Are you still interested in working in one of the overseas offices?" he said eventually.

Yes! She almost shouted the word but that was hardly the impression she was hoping to give. She took a breath, tried to sound calm. "If an opportunity came up that was suitable for me," she said, "then, yes, I'm interested." Pullman had offices in Hong Kong, Saigon, and Sydney. She'd wanted to travel for as long as she could remember, but apart from one distinctly shoestring-budget trip to Mexico one spring break, she'd never left the United States.

"Good to know," Daniel said.

Amelia studied him. He didn't know how she'd grown up. How tight things had been after her dad had left. Her mom couldn't afford fancy vacations when Amelia had been little, and then she'd gotten sick. Expensive sick. Breast cancer. Complications. Years and years of not enough money and too many bills. It had only been the kindness of the Castros—who'd insisted Amelia live with them when her mom had been in the hospital, who'd given them the garage apartment at their house when there'd been no rent money, and who'd given her mom work when she'd been well enough to work—that had kept them from complete disaster. Not to mention what Finn had—

No. She pushed the memories away. She had to focus on Daniel. On her goals. On what she'd been slaving for since she'd left college. She'd paid off the small student loans she'd incurred despite her scholarships and she'd saved enough for a deposit to help her mom buy a tiny apartment. Between all of that, the New York cost of living, and buying the kinds of clothes she was expected to wear for work, there'd been no money or time for travel.

One day. One day she'd visit all the places she'd read about and seen on TV. Until then, she would stick to her plan. She'd given herself six years on Wall Street to make sure she'd built a nest egg, taken care of her mom, and added some weight to her résumé. If she couldn't get a transfer with Pullman by then, she was going to woman up and apply for jobs in London or Hong Kong or Australia. Anywhere that wasn't the United States.

She'd been here just on five years but so far an opening hadn't come up. Not one that they seemed to think she was qualified for anyway. There had been a few in the first two years she'd worked there, but she'd been told she was too junior. Then there'd been belt-tightening post-GFC. Then Daniel had taken over the department. Daniel who was clearly in it to climb higher up the ladder in the finance world himself and didn't seem all that interested in what his team wanted.

"Has an opportunity come up?" she asked.

He toyed with his cuff, straightening the silver link a fraction of an inch before he unleashed his chilly smile. "Perhaps. I heard a rumor that Hong Kong may have something soon. So I was just checking in."

She didn't believe that for a minute. Daniel did nothing casually. Time to check the internal vacancy ads on the intranet. And put some feelers out to the Pullman grapevine. "Well, I'm definitely interested if there is something."

He nodded. "We'll see. I will add that getting this model live before the end of the month wouldn't hurt your chances should something become available. You most likely wouldn't be the only person under consideration."

So, screw up this project and she was out of luck? That she could believe. Daniel liked healthy competition among his staff. "I won't let you down. Was there anything else you needed from me?" Hopefully not. She had more than enough work to keep her busy late into the evening. Later than she'd been planning, probably. Because now she had to go over the project plan and see if there was any way she could compress the time frame. Hong Kong. It was what she'd always wanted. She couldn't mess this up.

"No, I'll leave you to it," Daniel said. He stood and smoothed down his jacket before leaving the office without another word. Which left Amelia none the wiser about what was going on. Was there really a new project somewhere that she hadn't yet heard about? Something hush-hush? She needed time to check in with the office grapevine.

But first the currency model. Daniel had been clear enough. She needed to deliver on this project or even if there was a new project, she wouldn't be considered. Time to knuckle down. If she worked all weekend—Crap. She'd forgotten the Saints game on Saturday. She couldn't not go, but the game would eat up an entire night. Even part of the afternoon if the Castros invited her to have dinner before the game. Which they usually did when they were in town.

She couldn't say no to them. Besides which, she wanted to see them and Em. Em had seemed calmer when Amelia had Skyped her last night to give her the latest update on Finn, but who knew how long that would last? Particularly if she was in the middle of a case. When Em was in court, she worked like a dog. Made Amelia's hours look positively part-time. Unfortunately it also turned her into Em-the-lawyer who could get very cranky. Amelia should send her another court-day care package. Cookies and chocolate and her favorite gin.

Gin. That sounded good. An icy gin and tonic and bad movies with her best friend. It had been far too long since they'd hung out. Someone really needed to invent a way to move Chicago closer to New York. Skype was a godsend but it wasn't the same as giggling together in person.

Maybe she should just try to convince Em that she really needed to come to one of Finn's games so they could do that.

She sighed. The reality was, she didn't have time for talking Em into anything just now. She needed to get her work done. If there was any possibility of an overseas assignment, then she was going to make sure Daniel Carling thought she was the best thing to happen to economics since the invention of international trade.

Which meant no more time trying to fix things she really couldn't fix. She needed to just put her head down and work.

The first half an hour was a struggle as her brain kept insisting on trying to decipher if there were any hidden meanings in what Daniel had said, but eventually she got back in the zone. Let herself get lost in the numbers for a while. Numbers were easy. They behaved, for the most part, logically.

They were soothing.

So soothing, in fact, that they sucked her in as usual to the point that she jumped when her office phone rang. She gave herself a mental eye roll and then hit the speakerphone button.

"Amelia Graham."

"Hello, Amelia."

If she'd been actually holding the phone she would have dropped it. The voice was instantly recognizable. Oliver Shields. What the hell was he doing calling her?

"Who is this?" she asked, trying to play it cool.

"Why, Amelia, have you forgotten me already? After you flirted shamelessly over gummy bears?" Oliver asked.

"I did not flirt shamelessly." She tried to sound indignant rather than embarrassed. Because there'd been at least a hint of flirting. The way Oliver's voice rumbled over the phone did distracting things to her nervous system, which made her want to flirt a little more. "How did you get this number?"

"You told me where you worked," Oliver said. "I used the magic of the phone directory and called the switchboard."

She couldn't help feeling pleased. He'd looked her up. She grinned to herself and then shook her head. She was getting carried away. "Is there something I can do for you, Oliver?"

He laughed. Was it wrong that she was already way too fond of the sound of his laugh?

"Now that, Ms. Graham, comes under the category of leading questions."

He sounded more himself than he had last night. Well, more like the guy that she'd met in the bar. She'd only talked to the man twice, for heaven's sake. She didn't have a large sample to go on. "No, it comes under the category of polite inquiry. Did you call for an update on how the yuan is performing against the yen?"

"Nope," he said cheerfully. "I'm calling to let you know I'm out of gummy bears."

Her smile widened. Now, there was a flimsy pretense for calling her if ever she'd heard one. Oliver Shields was making up excuses to talk to her. That information made her both happy and nervous. "You're in a hospital, Oliver, I'm sure they sell gummy bears in the gift shop. And you must have at least twenty-two nurses willing to do your bidding."

"Ah, but I'm not in the hospital anymore," he said.

"You're not?"

"Don't sound so surprised, Amelia."

"But you only had surgery a few days ago."

"Yes, and my doctor is happy with my progress, so he kicked me out."

She wondered if that was true. Or if Oliver had found a way to convince everyone to let him leave the hospital earlier than he should. But Lucas Angelo was a surgeon. He wouldn't let one of his star players leave before it was safe to do so.

"So where are you?"

"At my apartment. Gummy-bear-less." He put on such a sad voice for the last part of the sentence that she laughed despite herself.

"They just let you go home alone? No nurse or house-keeper to help you out?"

"The nurse left an hour ago with everyone else. He's supposed to come back later. My housekeeper doesn't come every day."

"I'm sure there are places that would deliver gummy bears to you," she said, trying not to feel sorry for him. She remembered the first few days home after she'd busted her arm. She'd been exhausted from not sleeping well, and every simple task seemed to take three times longer than it should. And hers had been her left arm. Not her dominant hand with a bonus injured ankle.

"They might get the wrong kind," Oliver said. "Plus they aren't you."

Her breath left in a rush. She'd been ready to find another excuse but it was hard to resist Oliver Shields saying "they aren't you" in that voice. Something about it curled around the logical parts of her brain and arrowed straight for the parts that *wanted*. Wanted him. Against all her better judgment and all the complications that would come with him.

"I can't come now," she said, feeling resolve float away like a balloon snared by an unexpected breeze. "I'm working."

"Can you come later?"

"I work long hours." Now she was stalling. She knew she was going to. It was simply a question of whether she could maintain a few shreds of dignity and hold off long enough that it wouldn't look like she'd come running just because he'd crooked his finger. She wasn't that girl. She wouldn't be that girl. She wanted, yes, but she wasn't ready to let him know that yet. Not before she'd decided if he was worth the complications.

"I'm not going anywhere. C'mon, Amelia. We didn't exactly finish our conversation about second chances yesterday. I'd like to see you. I'd come to you but I'm fairly sure Lucas will put me back in the hospital if I go out before he gives me the okay."

It sounded good. To finish her day with an hour or so of Oliver's company. But good, in this case, came with trouble. She'd told Finn that she knew how to handle herself and her love life and that was generally true. But Oliver wasn't the norm when it came to the guys she dated. He had all the things she liked—and that usually didn't work out—in a man. Plus he was an athlete. Her mom would have a heart attack. But she wasn't in high school anymore, or even college. She wasn't going to get knocked up. No one's life would be ruined.

Finn might take it badly, that much was true.

And she owed Finn. But she couldn't keep living her life bound by that loyalty. Or, for that matter, by her mother's fears.

She liked Oliver. Or what she had seen of him so far. Very much.

Surely a little flirtation couldn't hurt anyone?

She wanted to believe that was true. Normally she could spot the ones who were only temporary straight off and she'd learned how to keep her heart out of the equation in those situations. Learned how to have some fun without heartbreak. She wasn't so sure it would be so easy to keep Oliver at arm's length. But she was going to try despite all the reasons he might be a bad idea.

Because she wanted to see him again. Flat-out couldn't resist the opportunity.

"Okay," she said. "I'll come tonight. But it will be after nine."

"It's okay, Amelia, I have nothing pressing on my schedule in the morning," he said in a dry tone. "Just some more quality lying around."

"Tell me your address." She knew he lived somewhere on the Upper East Side near Finn. Finn had told her that much after the accident.

Oliver gave her the information and she wrote it down in a daze. Oliver Shields's address. His home. Where she would be in just a few more hours. With him.

She looked down at her clothes and sighed. Once again she was wearing a suit. Sure, it was a very nice suit, and she was also wearing very nice shoes, but it was hardly what she'd call sexy. Though it wasn't that different from what she'd worn yesterday and Oliver hadn't seemed to mind then. He'd flirted with her despite being in a hospital bed. Maybe he liked the pseudo-librarian look. She could take out her contacts and put on her glasses and see how that played.

"Amelia?" Oliver said and she realized there had been a gap in the conversation while her mind went off on tangents.

"Sorry," she said, hoping she sounded less flustered than she felt. Damn the man. Maybe she should rethink this. But she knew she wouldn't. "I need to get back to work. Is there anything else you need?"

"This day to go a lot faster than I think it's going to."

Heat flooded her cheeks. She pressed her hands to them, willing the feeling away. Damn. He was good. Which was a pity because it wasn't like they could exactly get up to much with his hand, surely? Even if she wanted to. Or rather decided to give in to the fact that she wanted to.

"I can dig you up some old economics research papers on the Web," she said. "That should put you right to sleep."

"Don't do that," he said.

"Do what?"

"You always joke about your job being boring."

"We've talked exactly twice," she pointed out. "That's not hardly always."

"This is the third time," he corrected. "And you've joked about your job all three times."

"Most people don't find economics all that interesting," she said. "It's not really glamorous." Most guys didn't seem to find economics a sexy occupation. Though at least the Wall Street guys had some idea what she actually did. Which simplified matters.

"Perhaps, but you think it's interesting. You're obviously pretty good at what you do or you wouldn't be working where you are. You should be proud of yourself. Screw anyone who isn't."

She didn't know what to say to that. "Thank you. Maybe I'll get you extra gummy bears."

"Just come by and see me. You and your big brain can beat me at Scrabble or something"

"Scrabble?"

"Well, I can't take you out just yet, Amelia. So I have to find other forms of entertainment. Board games, I can manage one-handed." His voice went low. "Unless you had something else in mind?"

"No." Her voice actually squeaked slightly as she spoke. "Scrabble is great."

"Good. We can play for gummy bears. I'll see you tonight. I'll tell the concierge to expect you."

Chapter Four

Oliver's apartment building wasn't exactly what she expected but true to his word, when she walked into the lobby, the short stocky guy with neatly trimmed graying hair and wire-rimmed glasses behind the desk took one look at her and asked, "Ms. Graham?"

"Yes," she said. "I'm here to see Oliver Shields."

He smiled at her approvingly. The discreet silver name badge on his lapel read ANTHONY.

"He told me to look out for you. Take the second elevator. He's on fifteen." No apartment number. Did that mean Oliver had a whole floor? She knew there was a lot of money in baseball, but the Saints were hardly the richest team in the league. Still, Oliver had been playing for a long time. Maybe he was good with his money. Or maybe he'd gotten some sort of deal. A sweet sublet like she'd scored when she'd moved to New York. Though her apartment was nowhere in the same league as this one.

"Fifteen, got it," she said. "Thank you, Anthony."

"It's Tony, ma'am," he said. "You go on up."

She followed instructions and soon enough was

standing outside the elevator on Oliver's floor. There was only one door in the hall, and she stared at it.

Oliver Shields was behind that door. Her palms felt clammy in the warm air. She peeled off her coat and scarf while she kept staring at the door as though it might explode. Was she really going to do this?

Apparently the answer was yes. Because she walked over to the door and knocked. The sound was surprisingly loud. Almost loud enough to drown out the pounding of her pulse in her ears.

"It's open." Oliver's voice came from inside. "Come on in."

She turned the handle and the door swung open. No sign of Oliver.

"Second room on your left."

She followed the sound of his voice. To find him lying on a sofa in a pose so similar to Finn's the previous night that she almost laughed. The only difference was that Oliver had a book in his lap instead of a video game controller in his hand. His right foot was encased in a black foam-and-plastic contraption, and his right hand was in a plaster cast, nothing visible but a thumb and his fingertips. When he saw her, he grinned with such delight that for a moment she froze, caught in the answering pulse of happiness that spiked through her like an electric shock.

Then she regained control of her senses. Hauled back the reckless emotions and shoved them down. Sensible. She was going to be sensible about this. No broken heart. No emotional wreckage. Stay in control. She held up the bag of candy she'd bought for him. "Gummy bears as requested."

"You are my new best friend," he said. He still looked so delighted she couldn't help smiling back.

"Not sure gummy bears are great recuperation food."

He shrugged and pointed to the chair nearest him. "Have a seat. I'd get up but I'm meant to be resting my ankle."

"I think that's called changing the subject. That looks worse than just a sprain." She nodded at the black boot thing on his foot.

"No, it's definitely just a sprain. I've been scanned and x-rayed six ways from Sunday to make sure. Lucas would've preferred me to be on two crutches to keep it immobile for a while but that's not going to work with this." He lifted his injured hand. "So it's a walking boot and a stick for me for a couple of weeks. Which means I deserve gummy bears."

She tore the bag open and handed it to him. "There. All the sugar a man could want. One hundred percent nutrition-free."

"I assure you my fridge is stashed full of nutritionally balanced food," he said. "Maggie and Sara—that's Lucas's wife, did you meet her at the party?—were here earlier and they stocked me up."

"Maggie Winters?" She couldn't quite keep the hesitation out of her voice.

"That's the one." He stopped, lifted his eyebrows. "Let me guess, your friend Finn told you that Maggie and I used to date."

"He may have mentioned something about it."

"Did he also mention that it was before she went to college? Or that she's very happily married to my boss?" He wagged a gummy bear at her. "She's a very good friend. She'll always be a good friend. But you have nothing to worry about. Maggie is not interested in me and I got over my yen for her a long time ago."

She wanted to believe him. She had no reason not to. Though if tall leggy brunettes were his thing, she wasn't sure why he was interested in her. She was none of those three. Well, her legs were okay, but she was firmly in the middle height range whereas Maggie had to be about five foot ten. And her hair couldn't decide what color it was, let alone shape itself into the sleek dark-chocolate waves that Maggie Winters's did. She'd only met the woman twice but there was no denying she was beautiful. Whereas Amelia was just . . .

"Amelia," Oliver said.

She blinked. He was watching her with a very smug expression.

"What?" she said, feeling flustered.

"You were checking up on my past. That means you like me."

"You're right, you need the gummy bears. You've obviously got low blood sugar and it's making you delusional."

He laughed. "I like you, Amelia. And you like me, too." He offered the gummy bears to her. "Want to share my sugar?"

"I bet you say that to all the girls," she said waving him away.

"Nope, I can honestly say that you're the first woman who's tried to seduce me with gummy bears." He laughed again, and bit the head off the bear he'd been waving around. It was unfair that he managed to look sexy eating a gummy bear.

"Who says I'm trying to seduce you at all?" The thought of just how many women might have tried to seduce him over the years—and how many he might have said yes to—was a little depressing. Most of them probably had far more lethal weapons in their arsenal than knowing his weakness for weird candy and Scrabble.

But his past was just that: the past. And given she didn't believe for a second that he was Mr. Right rather than Mr. Right Now, his past shouldn't bother her that much. *Shouldn't* being the operative word. One she wasn't ready to confront. Time for a change of subject.

"I don't see a Scrabble board," she said, surveying the gleaming wooden coffee table. Its surface was bare apart from a half-empty coffee mug, a copy of *USA Today* open to the sports pages, and an orange pill bottle.

Oliver looked slightly embarrassed. "I forgot to ask Maggie to grab it for me. It's somewhere in the closet in my spare bedroom. Do you want to look?"

Playing Scrabble was clearly a safer option than just sitting here talking to the man. That could lead to disaster in so many ways. "Do you really want to play?" she asked. He looked slightly better than he had the previous day—for a start he'd shaved—but he still looked exhausted.

"Scared I'll beat you?"

She stuck her nose in the air. "You're the one who should be scared. Point me at the closet, Shields."

He nodded toward the door. "Down the hall. Second door on the right. Games are on the shelves to the left, I think."

"I'll be right back."

Curiosity spiking, she followed his instructions. The hall was lit by a series of bright downlights that cast a line of shining circles on the polished concrete floor. They led all the way to the room at the very end of the hall. She wondered if that was his bedroom. Then she dragged her thoughts back to where they should be. The hall walls were dark gray and hung with vintage sports posters, not all of them for baseball. When she stepped into the second room on the right, she was expecting more dark and masculine decoration but the walls were white and the spread covering the bed had vivid abstract splashes of bright blue and leafy green.

On the far wall was a series of black-framed

photographs. Unable to help herself, she took a closer look. Family, she decided. A dark-haired man and a woman with equally dark wild curly hair grinned at the camera from half the photos, their arms wrapped around Oliver at various ages as well as two younger girls. Sisters. She hadn't thought about Oliver, the baseball bad boy, having sisters. Most of the other pictures showed Oliver in baseball gear. Starting from an age when the bat he held was almost taller than he was.

His face changed from chubby-cheeked and adorable to gangly and adorable to something that was like a less well-defined version of the man he was today. In the last one he wore a Saints uniform—not the current version, though. Seventeen, she remembered. Practically a baby. But he wasn't a baby any longer. Nope, he was 100 percent man. One that made her want to do things that involved words you couldn't play on a Scrabble board.

Scrabble. Right. She remembered what she was supposed to be doing. Finding a board game. If she took too long Oliver was going to think that she was snooping. Which she was, but she wasn't ready to let him know that.

Turning her back on the pictures, she moved to the closet. The door opened easily, revealing neatly stacked shelves that were way more organized than hers back in her apartment. Was he neat, or was his housekeeper?

Either way, it made her search easy. The top shelf on the left was full of small plastic storage boxes, the one below that had a good assortment of trophies that she would have liked to dig through, and the next one had just about every board game under the sun. Clue. Trivial Pursuit. Pictionary. Something called Settlers of Catan. Risk. Snakes 'n Ladders. Candy Land. Star Wars Monopoly, which made her laugh. The Scrabble box was easy enough to spot and she pulled it out after moving a little black box labeled CARDS AGAINST HUMANITY that rested on top of it.

"What's Cards Against Humanity?" she asked when she got back to the living room with her prize.

Oliver shook his head with a grin. "Something that requires more people and a lot of booze." He held out his left hand for the Scrabble set. "Speaking of booze, do you want something to drink? Or eat? I'm sorry, I can't be much of a host right now. But help yourself to whatever is in the fridge."

She'd eaten a salad earlier at her desk but she was still hungry. "Wait here. I'll go look. Do you want something to chase down the gummy bears?"

"I think there's some ginger ale in there," he said. "Maybe some of that?"

Ginger ale. That gave her pause. "Are you feeling okay?"

He nodded. "Yeah, just not very hungry. Don't fuss. I like ginger ale. I drink it a lot when I'm not in training."

His expression went dark for a second before his smile returned. But not quickly enough for her to miss it. Not in training. Which he wouldn't be for months, thanks to Finn. She felt her own smile start to slip and turned on her heel to go fetch him his drink.

Oliver watched Amelia head toward his kitchen and took advantage of the opportunity to admire the way her neat black skirt hugged her curves. She looked like a sexy librarian and brought him gummy bears just because he'd asked her to. He liked this girl. Maybe a little too much.

Which was a pity, because he definitely couldn't do much about it at the moment. He turned carefully and set the Scrabble set down on the coffee table, easing his leg—awkward in the walking boot Lucas had forced on him—into place in front of him. The position made it difficult to lean forward and try to put the board out onto the table. The movement jostled his ankle, sending a spike of pain up his calf.

He bit back the curse that sprang to his lips. Deep breaths. Breathe through the pain. He was used to dealing with the odd injury and sore muscles, and it wasn't the first time he'd sprained an ankle. He could handle it. And truthfully the throb in his ankle was less painful than his hand. Which ached like a son of a bitch despite the painkillers. But he could handle that, too.

He had to handle it. He had to get back in the game.

He would get back in the game. No room for doubt.

He wasn't done yet.

"One ginger ale."

Amelia's voice startled him and he knocked the tray of tiles off the table. Then realized he couldn't bend down to pick it up in his current position. He bit down the *fuck* that rose in his throat and tried to look as though the whole damned situation wasn't pissing him off. He didn't want to scare her off because he was being a miserable prick.

"That doesn't look comfortable," Amelia said. She had a plate of cheese and crackers balanced on top of a glass of water in one hand and his ginger ale in the other.

"Nothing is particularly comfortable at the moment." He managed not to snarl. Just. None of this was her fault.

"Well, lucky for you I can do more than just deliver gummy bears." Without any fuss she put the food and drinks down, slid the glass to where he could reach it, sank to her knees, and started picking up the tiles. When she'd gathered them all, and put them and the tray that held them on the table, she sat back on her heels and studied the board for a moment before she looked back up at him. "So, you like board games, huh?"

"My nephews and nieces like board games. I like my nephews and nieces," he said.

She peered at him over the top of the tortoiseshell-framed glasses she wore. "That doesn't explain the one that requires booze."

He liked her in glasses. Looking at him like that with amusement glinting from those blue eyes. Hot. "So I like them, too," he admitted.

That earned him a flash of her pretty smile. "Competitive streak?"

"Who, me? Nah, I leave that for the baseball field."

Her amused look deepened. "Now, why do I find that hard to believe?"

"Trust me, I've mellowed in my old age."

"You're hardly old."

"In baseball years, I'm close to geriatric," he said. And for the first time ever he was feeling like that might be true.

She snorted. "Now you're just angling for sympathy."

He put on his best pathetic face. "Is it working?"

"Nope," she said. "Though I think there's a better way to do this Scrabble thing."

"Is it wrong if I hope that means you want to play the dirty version?" he asked, more to see what her reaction might be than from any belief that that was what she wanted. Or that he was up to doing what dirty Scrabble might lead to.

She put on a stern expression but he was fairly sure from the laughter in her eyes that she wasn't upset. "Why, Mr. Shields," she said. "I'm not the kind of gal who dirty-Scrabbles on a first date."

Whether he was up to it or not, he couldn't help feeling disappointed. But cheerful that she wasn't offended. "This is our third date."

"You wish. And no, that wasn't what I had in mind."

"Pity. I'm sure that would cheer me up even more than gummy bears."

"Sorry, you're just going to have to stick to getting your thrills from sugar for now."

"For now?"

She pointed one of the tile holders at him, expression stern. "Stop changing the subject."

"To be perfectly honest, I can't even remember what we were talking about." Because his mind had wandered off down a very interesting tangent involving Amelia and getting some thrills. It was a good tangent. He wanted to stay there a little longer. Enjoy the scenery. But that didn't seem wise when he had the real live woman here in front of him. Wearing more clothes, perhaps, but no less enjoyable.

"We were discussing my brilliant plan to make this a bit more comfortable," she said. She picked up a cracker, popped it into her mouth, and chewed happily.

"Which is?"

She swallowed and then fished her phone out of her purse. "There's this app that's pretty much Scrabble. Words with Friends. Do you have your phone?"

He shook his head. "It's switched off for now."

"Why?" She looked confused.

"Because I don't feel like answering thousands of questions about my injuries and my future," he said. He needed to get someone to organize a new number for him. Plus his phone—which had been in his jacket pocket when he'd had the accident—had a crack across its screen. He had no idea why it hadn't fallen out when the car had rolled, but it hadn't. So a new number and a new phone. "The press sucks sometimes."

Amelia looked disappointed. "Oh. I didn't think about that. They should leave you alone. I know social media drives Finn a bit mad, and you're a lot better known than he is." She chewed her lip. "Do you have a tablet?"

"It was in my bag in the car. I haven't gotten my stuff back yet." His car had been towed after the accident, but he hadn't yet bothered to find out where it had been taken. It wasn't like he was going to be driving anytime soon. The car was a write-off anyway. He needed to add "new car" to the list of stuff to buy.

She winced. "Sorry." Then her face brightened. "I know, I have my iPad in my purse. I'll log out on that and we can make you an account and I'll play on my phone. It should be easy enough for you to use a tablet with your left hand." She made a little shooing motion at him. "Put your leg back up while I get this organized."

He was about to protest that there was no way it was going to take him that long to move, but then he realized it probably would. Stupid ankle. He grabbed a gummy bear and bit its head off savagely before he eased back onto the sofa. Which hurt both his ankle and his hand when he bumped the splint against a cushion. He checked his watch. Thirty more minutes before he could take the next dose of painkillers. And given he'd insisted on switching to Advil, even taking another dose wasn't going to help that much. He was just going to have to suck it up. So he pushed the pain away and smiled at her as she handed him the iPad.

Two hours later, he played the word *sexy* and smiled innocently at Amelia as she narrowed her eyes at him. His previous three words had been *flirt*, *date*, and *bed*.

"I thought we weren't playing dirty Scrabble," Amelia said.

His smile widened. "If you think *sexy* is dirty Scrabble, Amelia, then you've been playing it with the wrong guys."

"Oh, and you're the right one?" She tapped her screen a few times then looked at him with challenge in her eyes.

He refreshed his screen and laughed as he saw she'd played *optimist*.

He returned the favor with *hopeful* and was rewarded when she couldn't stop herself laughing when she read it. God, her laugh was sexy. Hell, all of her was sexy. Her laugh, her brain, the way she bit her lip when she studied the screen to decide her next move. Made him want to lean in and bite it for her. Though he was hardly in any shape to make a move and he didn't want to scare her off. But he couldn't resist just pushing it a little further.

"Tell me I have something to be hopeful about and I'll be good," he said.

"You can be hopeful that you might beat me eventually," she said, grinning. She'd so far won every game. Which should have spiked his competitive streak but he was enjoying her company too much to care.

"Winning is good but I had something else in mind." He held her gaze, watched her cheeks flush.

"Such as?"

Was it his imagination or did she sound just a little breathless?

"Will you come play with me again?" he said.

Her cheeks went an even deeper shade of pink. But she didn't look away. "Yes."

"Are you sure Finn's okay?" Em asked the next afternoon, screwing her face up. In the tiny screen of Amelia's phone, it looked kind of funny.

"Look, all I know is what he told me. He said the team doctor cleared him. So he's on his way to Boston. I guess we'll find out whether he plays tonight or not. So stop worrying." She studied Em's expression. She knew that look. Big sister in overdrive. All because Finn had been given the okay to play in the game tonight. "Aren't you meant to be in court?"

"We're having a recess."

"Then shouldn't you be studying case files or something?"

"I know what's in my files, Milly," Em said. "Stop trying to change the subject. Or at least, if you don't want to talk about Finn then tell me something else fun. I need some good gossip."

I played Words with Friends with a hot baseball player hovered on the tip of Amelia's tongue, but explaining that to Em would also mean explaining why she was breaking her no-jocks rule and who Oliver was, which would bring the topic of conversation back to Finn. She had no doubt Finn had complained about Oliver to his sister just as much as he had to her. Given Em's current level of stress about Finn, Amelia doubted Em would take her side. Besides, she wasn't sure she was ready to tell anyone about Oliver just yet. "I've got nothing," she said. "It's all work, work, work around here."

"You went to the party with Finn, didn't you? Before the night of the accident? Wasn't that fun?"

"Sure. It was good."

"Any hot guys?"

"Wall-to-wall baseball players."

"I keep telling you, your no-athletes rule is dumb. You're not your mom. And some of those Saints players are pretty hot," Em said, grinning widely.

"Um. No. We discussed this, remember? Operation Nice Guy is in full swing. No Wall Street billionaires. Definitely no baseball players." Which begged the question why she'd had so much fun just sitting with Oliver last night playing word games over the Internet.

Em grinned. "That's your plan, I never said I was on board with it. What's wrong with a nice billionaire? He can sweep you off your feet and take you away from it all."

"Not sure there are many nice billionaires. I think becoming a billionaire requires a fairly ruthless streak. And I'd imagine that landing one requires a fairly ruthless streak, too."

"But think of the private jets," Em said teasingly. "You want to travel. Just imagine how handy a private jet would be."

She didn't want to think about it. It sounded wonderful.

"Come to think of it, baseball players travel a lot, too," Em said.

"They travel between U.S. cities and probably don't get to do much more than see airports, buses, baseball fields, and hotels," Amelia said. "That's not my idea of a traveling lifestyle."

"They go to Toronto, too," Em said.

"To the baseball stadium. Besides, Canada isn't that exotic."

"You're no fun," Em said.

"That's me," Amelia said cheerfully. "All work and no play."

"Okay then, tell me about work. How's the Ice Man?"

Amelia glanced guiltily at the glass wall of her office, expecting to see Daniel Carling walk past as if summoned by the mere mention of his nickname. "He's fine."

"He is, indeed," Em said with a sigh.

Em, inexplicably, found Daniel attractive. She'd met him once when she had been meeting Amelia for lunch on one of her visits to Manhattan and declared him hot. So it was just as well that she lived in Chicago. Her best friend dating her boss was pretty much a nightmare scenario.

"Enough about me," Amelia said. "Finn said your folks are coming to see him play."

Em nodded. "Yes. They're flying to Boston today and then coming down to New York on Friday. I thought Mom would have called you by now," Em said. "You know they'll want to see you."

"Finn asked me to the game on Saturday, so I'll probably see them then," Amelia said. She always saw the Castros when they came to New York and when she came home to Chicago.

"Is your mom coming?"

Amelia sighed. "No. I offered to fly her out, but you know Mom."

"Still won't fly?" Em sounded unsurprised.

"Nope. And she didn't want to do the train trip." Her mom didn't like to travel.

Em frowned. "Is she feeling okay?"

"Yes, she's fine. She just had her annual checkup with her oncologist a few weeks ago. All good. No sign of anything." Amelia smiled, unable to help herself. Every year, her mom's checkup freaked her out. Even though she'd been in remission from the cancer and the aplastic anemia that had developed after all her chemo for six years now, it was still hard not to worry about a recurrence. Most of the time she managed to not think about it, but the checkups brought back too many hard memories. "What about you? Are you going to come see him play?"

"I'm not sure. We'll see how today and tomorrow go in court. This case is brutal. Not really a good time to go running off to New York for a weekend."

"I thought that partner you always work with was a baseball fan."

"He is. But he's a Cubs fan. So as far as he's concerned

the season is done. Plus he's not that interested in Finn now that he's not playing for the Cubs anymore."

"Try and work your magic. Bat your eyelashes at him or something," Amelia said. "It would mean a lot to Finn. And I'd love to see you. It's been way too long." She tried her own version of puppy-dog eyes. "C'mon, one weekend would be great. Even one night."

But she didn't see Em's reaction—a notification popped up on her screen, obscuring her friend's face.

A notification from the word game app. From Oliver. A smile spread across her face even as she tapped the screen to dismiss the notification.

"What's that smile for?" Em said.

Amelia blinked. Damn, she'd forgotten that Em could still see her even when the notification was blocking Amelia's view. "Just happy at the thought of getting to see you."

"I don't think so. I saw you. You were reading something on your screen. Is someone sexting you, Milly? Have you got a secret guy you're not telling me about? A late-night booty call?"

"Why would a late-night booty call be texting me at one p.m.?" Amelia asked, trying to stall for time.

"Maybe he thinks you're awesome and he can't wait for the next late night," Em said, laughing. "'Fess up, Amelia, have you been holding out on me?"

Amelia summoned her best innocent face. It rarely worked on Em, who was annoyingly good at reading people. Part of the reason that she was such a good attorney. "Not holding out. Nothing to report. Just a notification. I'm playing a game with one of the girls in the Hong Kong office."

"Game? What game? Oh God, Finn hasn't gotten you hooked on one of his video games, has he?"

Em was not a fan of video games. She claimed they made her motion sick and always got cranky when Amelia and Finn decided to battle it out onscreen.

"Finn's limiting his screen time, remember?" Amelia said. Bringing up Finn seemed like the best option at this point. It was guaranteed to distract Em.

"He's supposed to be limiting it. I know my baby brother. I bet he didn't. Idiot."

"Twenty-five-year-old idiot," Amelia said, tentatively. "Big enough to decide for himself."

"He needs someone to talk to him," Em said. "You're too nice to him, Milly."

Amelia rolled her eyes. Em liked to think she was tough but she was just as much a Team Finn sucker as her parents and Amelia. "If you want to deliver tough love, come out here to Manhattan and deliver it yourself."

Her phone pinged as another notification flashed up. She ignored it. "Look, I have to go, I have a meeting in fifteen and need to finish printing some stuff. Let me know if you are coming. You can stay with me if you want."

"We'll see," Em said. "I might just have to take a red-eye back here if I do get away."

"What if there's a game on Sunday as well?"

"You really think the Saints have a chance against the Red Sox?" Em asked.

"They've been playing really well this year," Amelia said. So had the Red Sox. "So who knows?"

"Well, win or lose I doubt I could pull off staying for Sunday. But I'll let you know if I can figure Saturday out. Smooches. Gotta get back to court."

The screen winked out. Em had never been big on good-byes.

Without Em's face in the background, the notification from the game was stark against her screen.

She should ignore him. She had work to do.

She opened the app anyway.

And noticed the little message notification. Damn. She'd forgotten there was a chat function. She opened the message.

Sitting around all day is boring.

She rolled her eyes. Sitting around all day with no responsibilities sounded pretty good to her. But she wasn't a professional athlete.

Read something, she replied.

You're no fun, Amelia.

The response came back so fast she had to wonder if he was just sitting there waiting for her to reply. That seemed unlikely. But the thought made her smile.

Then why are you messaging me?

To remind you that you should be fun.

All fun and no work makes Amelia a poor girl.

The phone on her desk rang. She hit the speakerphone button. "Amelia Graham."

"I think the saying is all work and no play," Oliver said in a low voice that made her want to purr.

She ignored the swift flash of pleasure as she grabbed the handset to take the call off speaker. "Maybe I believe in balance."

"Says the woman who works on Wall Street."

"That may be a case of the pot calling the kettle black. Baseball doesn't allow for lots of spare time, does it?" she said then realized what she'd just said. Oliver had nothing but spare time right now. "Sorry, I meant—"

"It's fine," Oliver said though his voice had lost a little of its teasing tone. "Though if you feel bad about it, then you can make it up to me."

"How?"

"Come over tonight."

She looked at the document open on the screen in front of her. The list of issues with the latest version of the model the IT guys wanted to discuss with her in the morning. It was long. And she needed to be up-to-date with it and have suggested solutions. It was going to take her hours. "I—"

"Don't say no." There was something a little too raw in that statement. Something lost in his voice that made her stomach curl.

Made her want to soothe that pain away. Though she had no idea how. Tonight he should be in Boston with the rest of his team, playing the sport he loved. But he wasn't. Her fingers tightened around the phone. "There must be someone else you can hang out with."

"Amelia, ninety-nine percent of my good friends are in Boston right now."

Where they would be playing—or watching people play—the game he couldn't. That had to suck pretty hard. She didn't like the thought of him sitting on his big sofa alone while that happened. Though she wasn't entirely convinced that he had no friends left in New York. She was pretty sure he could open up whatever his equivalent of a little black book was and have some female company in two seconds flat.

But he'd asked her.

And it seemed she wasn't very good at resisting Oliver Shields asking her for things. "It will be late again."

"I'll send you the details of my car service. Just call them when you're ready."

"I can take a cab."

"I know you can. But you're doing me a favor here, Amelia. Let me do you one in return."

It was hard to argue with that. "I'll take the car," she promised and hung up.

Chapter Five

Oliver put the cell phone down reluctantly. He'd paid the nurse who'd come to check on him to go and buy him a new phone with some prepaid credit. For the sole purpose, as near as he could tell, of giving him a way to play the word game with Amelia. He'd get himself set up with a new iPhone and a new number soon but right now, it seemed like too much hard work. He just needed something so he could call a few select people. And play Words with Friends apparently.

He'd told himself that he wouldn't bug Amelia at work. So that was a fail.

Apparently he was crap at sitting around doing nothing. Even though he still felt like he'd been run over by something large and tanklike—and come to think of it, being hit by a Hummer was probably as close as you'd get to a tank outside of the military—he was rapidly driving himself nuts.

Normally in his downtime, he was studying the Saints, or studying other teams, or, at worst, watching some other sport. If he took vacations, they were active ones with some of his Saints buddies. Skiing or hiking or making a beeline for somewhere warm where they could swim and Jet Ski and windsurf by day and party by night.

But right now knowing that the Saints were playing in the divisional series and he wasn't was an acid burn in his gut. Any thought of sports—any sport—just made it worse.

So his usual distractions were out. He'd tried to read and watch movies but his concentration was shot.

The only thing that made him feel better was Amelia.

Who'd kicked his ass soundly at four games last night before she'd insisted it was past her bedtime and left him alone. Now she was at work and the day loomed before him in a big ugly stretch of nothing to keep him from having to face his current reality.

His current reality sucked balls.

He didn't want to think about it. Didn't want to be in it.

Hence the phone call. Because if he couldn't have Amelia sitting on his sofa, smelling delicious and smiling at him with those pretty blue eyes, then he wanted to at least hear her voice.

Which maybe was the most pathetic thing about his situation.

It was Thursday. He'd met her Sunday night. Then his world had been wrecked. Literally. Less than five days and she was already the high point in his day. Which seemed crazy.

He didn't know which was the scarier option: that it might be the truth and he'd finally met someone who could hold his interest, or that it was just the trauma of the situation and his brain choosing Amelia to fixate on rather than facing reality.

The first one seemed ridiculous. The second one made him a jerk. But he didn't know how to find out which option it was other than to see it through.

Which left him with nothing to do but sit here and

know that he was missing out on what would have been the biggest game in his career. All because of Finn.

Fucking Castro.

Who might well be playing Oliver's goddamn position today. He hadn't been able to bring himself to ask. Maggie had called earlier on her way to Boston and he'd wriggled his way out of a conversation in about thirty seconds flat by pretending the nurse was at the door. Anything to avoid hearing details about tonight's game.

Pretty damned weak.

He dropped his head back against the sofa, his left hand balling into a fist. His right hand twitched in sympathy. Which hurt.

Fuck it, maybe what he really needed was to start drinking. Maybe then he'd sleep until Amelia arrived.

Oblivion sounded damned good about now. And it wasn't as if the weak-ass painkillers he was taking could interact badly with alcohol.

Pushing up off the sofa with his good hand and leg, he fumbled for the walking stick propped beside him with every intention of finding himself a big glass, some ice, and pulling out the bottle of fifty-year-old scotch that Maggie had given him for his thirtieth birthday.

His plan was interrupted by a knock at his door.

Fuck. Who was bothering him? It better not be a fucking reporter—if one of them had managed to sneak past Tony then he was going to tear someone a new one.

But when he peered through the peephole in the door, he was confronted not by an eager reporter but by the immaculately dressed form of Lucas Angelo. With his wife, Sara, at his side.

"Aren't you two supposed to be in Boston?" he said as he threw the door open.

"Hello to you, too, Ollie," Sara said. She stood on tiptoes to reach his cheek to kiss him hello. She smelled, as always, faintly like engines as well as the light flowery scent she wore.

"Hello," he replied, smiling at her.

He was in a crap mood but he wasn't going to take it out on Sara, who was a complete sweetheart. Not to mention Lucas would probably kick his ass if he did. Or Maggie would. Hell, most people involved in the Saints would line up to smack him upside the head if he upset Sara.

"Lucas," he added, stepping back to let the Angelos in. "What are you doing here?"

"You have a checkup with your surgeon this morning," Lucas said. "Did you forget?"

"No," he lied. Crap. He'd known about the appointment. So his little scotch plan would've been a disaster. "But my driver is picking me up at eleven for that."

"Well, now it's us and my driver," Lucas said.

"I'm a big boy now. I can go see the doctor by myself."

"Maybe. But I'm in charge of player well-being on this team and that means I'm coming along to hear what George has to say about your hand."

"If you're in charge of player well-being, you should be in Boston," Oliver retorted.

"Which I will be about two hours after we're done with you," Lucas said. "Sara's flying me there."

Sara nodded then disappeared into the kitchen. Oliver looked at Lucas somewhat warily. Lucas, who really didn't like helicopters despite being married to a woman who flew them and having to spend more time in them than most people due to his punishing schedule. But Oliver had never known him to take one when there was a non-airborne transport method available. Like a train, the team bus, or a car in the case of Boston. So he must be worried to show up here today and subject himself to a helicopter flight because of it.

"Checking up on me?" he asked, feeling suddenly nervous. Had Lucas already spoken to George? "I was going to go to the appointment. I don't want to fuck up my recovery."

"Good," Lucas said. "I don't want you to fuck it up, either. But no, not checking up. Like I said. I want to know what George has to say. Easier to get it from the horse's mouth." He looked Oliver up and down. "Why are you answering the door, isn't the nurse here?"

"Been and gone. Besides which, I'm allowed to walk short distances."

"Short. When you need to. You're still supposed to be resting." Lucas jerked his head toward the living room. "We're early so how about I take a look at your ankle while I'm here?"

"Alfie—the nurse—rebandaged it this morning."

"I'm sure he did an excellent job. But Alfie isn't a doctor. I want to see it for myself."

Oliver couldn't find an argument to that. Lucas was his boss and one of the best orthopedic surgeons in the country. If he wanted to check out a sprained ankle, Oliver wasn't going to stop him. He turned and limped back to the couch, taking as much weight as he could on the stick.

"Are you getting sore in the hips at all?" Lucas asked, following him.

"All of me is still sore," Ollie pointed out. "I was in a car accident."

"Funny man," Lucas said. "I'm serious. Using a cane and wearing a boot puts your hips and back out of alignment. You could still be taking something stronger, you know. I'm happy to call in a prescription for you."

Ollie shook his head. "No, I'm good."

Lucas grinned at him.

"What?"

"I told Maggie you'd say that. She said to tell you you're an idiot."

"I'm used to Maggie telling me I'm an idiot." Ollie eased himself back down on the sofa. Lucas dragged the coffee table forward so he could sit on it and lifted Ollie's injured foot. "You know," he said, as he expertly stripped off the walking boot and began unwinding the bandage, "taking the painkillers for a week or so isn't going to kill you."

"Not taking them isn't going to kill me, either," Ollie said, gritting his teeth as Lucas unwound the last part of the bandage.

His foot was several dark shades of purple and green and still very swollen.

Lucas studied it then started probing gently with his fingers. "Flex your foot—carefully—" he said.

Ollie obeyed. It hurt. He gritted his teeth.

"Are you icing it regularly?"

"Yes. Following doctor's orders," Ollie said.

"Good. It looks less swollen than it did Tuesday, so that's good. Keep the boot on for a few more days and I'll check it again when we're back from Boston." Lucas rewrapped the bandage. "Ice, elevation, you know the drill. Like I said, if your hips or back get sore, tell the nurse. He can organize a massage for you. Using the boot and the stick is going to throw your gait out and we want to keep any change under control, get your ankle back to normal as soon as possible."

"I've sprained my ankle before," Ollie said. "I know the drill."

"I know. But this is a bad sprain. Frankly, you're lucky you didn't snap the tendon completely," Lucas said. "And you already have a weakness on your right side from your ACL."

As if he needed reminding about that. But ankles

and knees could be managed. Braced. Strapped. Pampered. The important thing was getting his hand back. He looked down at the plastered blob of it where he was resting it on his leg.

Lucas's gaze followed his. "How does it feel?"

"Hurts. The stitches are itchy."

"Itching is good. Itching is healing. Don't try and poke something under the plaster to scratch. That's never a good idea. Keep it elevated as much as possible, too."

"Thank you, Doctor Obvious. Do you think Dr. Banks will let me lose the plaster? I feel like I've got a fucking mummy hand."

Lucas shrugged. "Maybe. It's a balancing act between protection and you being able to start physical therapy. Right now, it's early and your hand will still be swollen and bruised. And if you move it the wrong way you'll tear your external stitches. Or worse, the internal ones. Which would mean more surgery. But the longer it's completely immobilized, the longer your recovery will be. So it's George's call. He's the expert." Sympathy was clear in Lucas's bright-blue eyes. "I know it's frustrating, working with only one hand. If you need more help—"

"No," Ollie said. "Alfie's enough. I can manage."

"If you change your mind, you just have to yell," Lucas said. "We can afford all the help you need."

He didn't care about the cost. He could afford a full-time housekeeper if he wanted. He had money. But money couldn't guarantee him a fully functional hand. Nothing could.

Which made him suddenly want that scotch all over again.

It was nearly half past eight by the time Tony called up to let him know that Amelia had arrived.

Finally.

The game had started half an hour ago and he'd been sitting on the sofa for the last hour arguing with himself about whether or not to turn on the TV, desire to know what was happening warring with the raw burning anger that he wasn't there.

He made it to the door before Amelia knocked, priding himself on his increased speed with the boot and his stick. Amelia looked surprised to see him when he pulled the door open.

"Are you supposed to be opening doors yourself?"

"My ankle is improving," he said. "So yeah. Hello, Amelia."

She smiled up at him. "Hello." She held up a plastic bag. "Have you eaten? I got takeout. Italian. Lasagna. Tell me you like lasagna."

"Yes, Amelia, I, like most guys, like lasagna. And no, I haven't eaten."

He still didn't have much of an appetite so he'd waited, figuring she'd need to eat.

Her smile widened and some of the tension he'd been carrying all day melted away. Good call, inviting her over. If anyone was going to get him through tonight, it would be her.

"Great," she said. "I'll get some plates and things."

He stepped back from the door to let her in. Saw the moment her eyes clocked the sling around his neck and her smile faltered.

"Don't frown, Amelia," he said. "The sling is a good thing. Or a compromise, maybe." He rotated his hand in the foam padded strap gingerly. "I saw my surgeon today. He doesn't want me using my hand but he agreed to take me out of the plaster. So sling it is." The black plastic splint he now wore made his hand look kind of like a robot, which wasn't really that much improvement over a mummy. But the plastic was far more comfortable than the plaster, so he was trying to be grateful and obey Dr. Banks's strict instructions about avoiding too much movement.

Her eyes were on his hand, at the bruised tops of his fingers—now starting to turn interesting shades of green—visible above the top of the splint. They were still slightly swollen but at least looked like fingers.

Then she looked back up at him, smile firmly back in place, if a little less believable than it had been a minute ago. A worrier. But apparently she wasn't going to grill him.

"That must be a good sign," she said. "Am I allowed to ask what else he said or is that something you don't want to talk about?"

He didn't want to talk about it. George Banks had been thorough and brisk and declared it too early to know much about what was going on with Ollie's hand function. Still, Ollie had caught the look that Lucas and George had exchanged when he'd struggled to bend his fingertips more than a quarter inch or so. But it wasn't fair to take his crappy mood out on Amelia.

"He said it's too early to tell much," Ollie said. "But I start seeing a hand therapist next week."

Her smile this time was genuine. "That's great! Though sympathy on the physical therapy. It always seems to hurt like a son of a bitch."

"I'll take pain over a hand that doesn't work."

"Smart man." She nodded to the kitchen. "I'll go deal with the food."

By the time he'd made it back to the sofa and settled himself at the far end, propping his foot up on the brand-new ottoman that had arrived that afternoon with a note from Sara saying it would give him more options to support his leg, Amelia reappeared with napkins, a plate of garlic bread, and glasses.

"Nice ottoman," she said.

"Sara Angelo sent it. Her dad smashed up his knee pretty good a few years ago and she said he had one."

"Gives you more ways you can sit on your sofa," Amelia said. "Smart."

He wondered if she'd noticed that he'd strategically had the ottoman placed at the far right end of the sofa, so that he could sit with his leg up, his bad hand resting on the arm of the sofa if he wanted out of the sling and his good hand free to . . . well, do other things if he could coax Amelia to sit next to him now that he wasn't taking up the length of the sofa.

"Eat," she said, offering the garlic bread. "I'll be back with the pasta. Do you want something to drink?"

"There's beer in the fridge. I'll take one of those."

That earned him another studied look. But no more questions. She just went back to the kitchen, returning a few minutes later with two plates of lasagna and salad balanced on one arm and two beers in her other hand.

"Nice skills."

"I used to waitress during high school and college," she said. "Comes in handy sometimes."

Beers and food were distributed with easy efficiency, which made him think she'd probably done pretty well as a waitress. Then, to his delight, she sat next to him on the sofa.

He sipped beer and watched as she started eating. Two pieces of garlic bread had taken the edge off his shaky appetite. But the beer tasted good. Cold and sharp.

Amelia forked up salad for a minute or so, eating enthusiastically.

"Long time since lunch?" he asked.

She nodded while she chewed, then swallowed before putting her fork down. "Busy day. How about you?"

"Well, the highlight was the trip to the surgeon, which gives you some idea about the level of excitement I'm dealing with."

"Must be frustrating," she said. She glanced toward the dark screen of the TV. "Not watching the game?"

He shook his head. "No."

"Understandable . . ." She hesitated a moment. "Do you mind if I check the score on my phone? It's Finn's first play-off series."

Muscles along his jaw tightened—it should have been his first time—but he managed to nod. "Just don't tell me. I'll find out later. One of the guys from the team will call me if it's good news."

"Okay." She made no move to put down her food.

"You're not going to check now?"

"We're eating. Or rather, I'm eating and you're not." Her frown was directed at the untouched food on his plate.

"I'm fine. I already ate garlic bread."

"Exactly two pieces," she said. "Are your meds—"

He held up his left hand to cut her off. "I'm eating okay. Just not super hungry yet, which my very expensive surgeon tells me is normal. As does my equally well-qualified boss. So I'm going to enjoy some of this beer first and you can eat your dinner." He took another swig of beer. The alcohol was already making a good warm burn in his stomach, which told him that it wouldn't be wise to have another. He didn't drink a lot during the season and between that, not eating much, and, he guessed, the various meds he was taking, he didn't want to end up wasted.

Her lips pressed together. "Okay. I get it. I'm not your mom. No nagging."

"I like that you're worried about me. Just letting you know that you don't need to be."

That earned him a smile. "Yeah, okay. But you know how I told you Finn's sister is a worrier?"

"Yes."

"Well, maybe a little of that rubbed off on me."

"I figured that part out already." He smiled at her. "But you have plenty of other things to worry about, I'm sure. Like whatever is keeping you so busy at work."

"It's Wall Street. Long hours."

He tipped his head at her. "I thought we talked about this. I want to know about your day."

She reached for her own beer. "If you insist." She took a swallow. Hitched a shoulder slightly. "Right now my major project is developing a new model for predicting movements in currencies in Southeast Asia."

He had no idea what that might involve. But he liked how smart she sounded when she talked about her job. He didn't like that other guys had apparently made her feel like she was boring. So he was happy to let her explain it to him. "And how exactly do you do that?"

"You really want to know?"

"I do."

Which earned him a very approving smile and then a ten-minute lecture on the project and hedging and capital management for banks, most of which he didn't understand. He kept a vague eye on the stock market but he left the management of his money largely to the financial advisers that Alex had pointed him to when he'd asked about it. What was good enough for Alex was good enough for him. And so far the reports he received every month had proven that theory right. The new guys were better than the advisers he'd had before.

But understanding a profit-and-loss statement was a

long way from understanding the stuff that Amelia was talking about. Not that he cared. He'd known she was smart from the get-go. What mattered was the way she looked so happy talking about it. It made her big eyes glow behind the retro glasses. He'd had a dream about her and those glasses the night before. The hot librarian—or hot economist, really—look worked for her. And stripping her out of her hot economist clothes had definitely worked for his subconscious. He'd woken sweaty and horny—though rolling over in bed too fast to reach for his bedside lamp when he'd woken and banging his ankle in the process had killed the horny part.

What it hadn't killed was the idea that he'd like to see what getting her out of those clothes would be like in real life. She wore another one of her curve-hugging serious business suits today. This time it was a deep blue that made her skin look like moonlight and her eyes look even bluer.

So he listened while she talked and tried to make intelligent noises and watched her. Hoping that what he was really thinking about didn't show on his face. Particularly not when he wasn't entirely sure how he would manage to do anything about those thoughts with a walking boot and one hand in a sling.

She talked on for another few minutes and then he saw her glance at her phone, lying next to her abandoned pasta.

"You really want to know what's going on, don't you?" he asked.

"Don't you?"

"Part of me does," he admitted. Between Amelia and the beer he'd almost finished now, the sting of missing out wasn't quite so sharp.

"What about the other part?"

"That part is pretty pissed off that I'm not there. Go ahead. Turn on the TV. But how about we compromise and turn the sound off?"

"We can do that," she said and reached for the remote. She found the game and killed the volume, then leaned forward eagerly, studying the screen. The Sox were batting judging by the image on the screen. He moved his gaze back to her, watching the play of light on her face. She watched for a minute or two, her focus intense, as if she could will the outcome of the game to go her way.

He knew the feeling.

Knew it was pretty futile, too.

"You care about Finn, don't you?" he said as her expression fell when the Sox batter connected solidly and sent the ball arrowing out deep.

Amelia turned back to him. "Yes. Like I said, his sister—Emma—and I are best friends. Her mom and dad are like my second family, really. They've always been there for me." There was a flash of something in her eyes that he couldn't interpret.

"What about your own family?"

She shrugged. "My mom worked a lot. The Castros lived on the next street over from the apartment block where we lived. So once Em and I became friends, they used to let me hang out at their house."

Her mom. Not her dad. "What did your dad do?"

Her expression went guarded. "Mostly he left," she said, eventually. "When I was six. Which was why my mom had to work."

"And the Castros looked after you?"

A nod. "They kind of saved me. Gave me somewhere to be. Cared about me. God knows what might have happened to me if I'd had to grow up with babysitters or being left home alone."

He didn't want to think about it. About a smaller version of her, vulnerable and alone.

"Don't get me wrong," she said quickly. "I love my mom. What she did for me. She always worked so hard to make sure we had a roof and food on the table. But that meant she couldn't be around so much. But I had Emma and Finn and Eddie and Mari. They took me in. They never made me feel bad because my mom worked or we didn't have a lot of money. And when my mom got sick—"

"Wait, your mom is sick?"

"Was. She had breast cancer when I was fifteen. But she made it through. I lived with the Castros on and off for nearly eighteen months when she was going through treatment. Whenever she was in the hospital. She had a few rough patches along the way. The Castros helped us out a lot. Mom couldn't work for a long time and they let us use their garage apartment. Other stuff."

What exactly was "other stuff"? There was obviously more to the story, but they hadn't known each other long enough for him to push. "They sound like good people." Which raised the question of how they'd raised a jerk like Finn but sometimes that happened. One thing was clear. Amelia was tightly wrapped up in that family. And felt indebted to them. She might as well be Finn's actual sister. So he needed to be careful about this. Because maybe, if push came to shove and Finn really got his nose out of joint, Amelia might just pick family loyalty and walk away again. The way she had back in the bar.

"They loved me. That means a lot when your dad walks out of your life without a backward glance." She looked away.

"Do you know why he left?"

A second shrug, this one with a defensive hunch that

told him it still hurt. "My mom got pregnant, that's why they got married. Turned out he couldn't handle family life. Stuck it out for a while but then he bailed."

"You don't have any contact with him?"

"He sent a few birthday cards for the first couple of years. But no. I haven't seen him since he left." She shrugged again. "Which is okay, we did just fine without him."

Just fine seemed like an overstatement. It had obviously been tough for her. She'd worked hard to get where she was. So she was okay. But that didn't stop him wanting to punch the man. Dick move to walk out on a kid. Then again, if her dad was that much of a dick, maybe Amelia was right, maybe she was better off without him in her life. "I think you're doing better than fine," he said. "Look at you. Wall Street. Brain full of all kinds of brilliant ideas. He has no idea what he's missing out on."

She blinked at him, looking startled. Then ducked her head. "How about I clear these plates away?" She was up and whisking his plate off his lap before he could say anything more. Crap, had he upset her? He stared at the screen in front of him. Just at the moment when the damned camera chose to zoom in on first base. Showing him Finn's face, eyes intent on the pitcher, every inch of his body ready to move when the hit was made.

Fucking Finn.

Someone else who wasn't above pulling the odd dick move. But apparently Oliver was going to have to learn to deal with Finn if he and Amelia continued down the path they seemed to be on. He shifted on the sofa, eyes glued to the screen. The Sox were winning. By a lot. Damn it.

"I thought you didn't want to watch the game?" Amelia said from the doorway.

He looked up. "I was just waiting for you."

"Who's winning?"

"Not us."

"Crap," she said. "Are you okay?"

"Pissed off," he growled, then tried to lighten his tone.

"Pissed off because you're not there or pissed off because they're losing?"

"Does it have to be one or the other?"

"So it's both?" She was watching curiously.

"I'm thinking that's a question that I barely know the answer to. It's complicated." He reached for the remote, turned off the TV, and slumped back on the couch. The loss of the light from the screen turned the room dim and turned Amelia into a backlit silhouette in the doorway. A silhouette that was killer curves and long legs and did very good things to his heart rate.

"Do you know what you want to do after baseball?" she asked.

It felt like she'd punched him. Just because she'd asked the obvious question. The one he'd worked very damned hard to avoid every day since he'd been seventeen. But she'd told him some of her truth, so he could maybe tell her part of his. "Not really."

"You've never thought about it?"

"I've thought about it. Just never come up with a very good answer. It's always seemed a long way off." Until now. Now it felt far too close. Not that the feeling had brought any blinding insights into what he should do next with it.

"I guess it is a long way off when you're seventeen. Seventeen-year-old baseball players think they own the universe."

"What do you know about seventeen-year-old baseball players?" he asked.

She tilted her head. "Oh, I know a thing or two about jocks."

He wished he could see her face. But she was hidden by the shadows across her face. "Because of Finn?"

"Finn isn't the only jock I've known in my time."

Something in the sudden purr in her voice caught at him. Set his blood racing again. That was flirting. Definitely. "Oh really?" He patted the sofa beside her. "Were you one of the good girls off under the bleachers with the jocks after the game, Amelia? Why don't you come over here and tell me all about it?"

One corner of her mouth lifted. "Why? So you can relive your seventeen-year-old glory days?"

"Trust me, Amelia, seventeen wasn't my glory days. I've learned a lot since then."

Chapter Six

She had no doubt that he had. And no doubt, from the sudden heat between her legs, she wanted to know exactly what he had learned since then. What she wasn't so sure about was how the conversation had taken this turn and how, with a few words, he'd managed to turn her from worried about his mood and what was happening between them to being a mess of wanting, ready to throw herself at a guy who was two days out of the hospital.

His eyes were very dark across the room. Intent. Watching her like he was concerned she might just vanish.

She wasn't so sure that vanishing wouldn't be exactly the correct thing to do here. Not to mention the smart thing.

But staring across the room at Oliver, waiting for her answer with those dark eyes and that damned beautiful face, she knew she wasn't going to vanish.

She could no more have moved toward his front door and relative sanity than she could have grown wings and flown away.

So she took the only path left open to her. Toward Oliver. To danger.

To possibility

To recklessness.

She stopped when she reached the sofa. Looked down at him, not knowing exactly what happened next. Her pulse hammered in her ears so loudly that she was pretty sure even his neighbors could hear it. Otherwise the apartment was very quiet. Very still. He hadn't closed his blinds, and the glow of the city lights came through the windows behind the sofa, shedding golden light softly into the room. It wasn't enough to break the illusion of darkness, of the two of them suspended here together somewhere outside the rest of the world. Caught in their own private bubble. Nothing to worry about.

Except, perhaps, how long she was going to stand here before she gave in to the inevitable and let herself find out exactly what Oliver Shields had learned since he was seventeen.

The thought made her shiver and she lost her nerve and looked up and away, over his shoulder and out the window. The mostly dark expanse of the park across the street and the reflections of the lights of the buildings beyond were breathtaking. But not as breathtaking as the man himself.

Who was waiting, silent. All she had to do was give in to what she wanted. Take what he was offering. She turned back. Managed a lopsided smile despite the churn of need and nerves buzzing through her body. "I don't remember the bleachers having this sort of view."

"Neither do I," he said, in a voice suddenly rough with tension that told her he was as unnerved by the moment as she was.

"You never took a girl under the bleachers at seventeen?"

He grinned then. "Never one who looked like you."

She laughed, the sound bubbling up unexpectedly and

chasing away her nerves. "Well, you've definitely learned to be good with a line since then."

"Seventeen-year-old me never was good with words. Always been more sort of hands-on."

"Oh, so you did try it under the bleachers?"

"Pretty sure seventeen-year-old me would have had a heart attack if he'd gotten you under the bleachers. I'm also dead certain that current-day me is going to have a heart attack if you don't let me put my hands on you in the next few minutes."

"I'm amending that to very good with a line," she said, wondering how her knees, which were beginning to feel a lot like they'd been replaced with Jell-O, were holding her up.

"It's only a good line if it works."

"Oh, it's working." God. She wanted to kiss him. But she didn't want to hurt him in the process and she wasn't exactly sure how the logistics were going to work.

"Amelia, if you don't get down here on this sofa with me, then I'm going to have to stand up and come to you." He lifted his good hand and crooked his finger at her. She gave up on trying to work out a perfect solution and moved without thinking. Which was how she found herself straddling his lap, one knee on either side of his legs, the heat of him practically scorching her thighs. She didn't lower herself completely, just held herself above him, looking down. His eyes were nearly black now. She didn't know if it was the dim lighting or whether he was as frantically turned on as she was. She swallowed, sucked in a breath, trying to think. Saw his chest rising and falling a little too fast as well. And they were hardly even touching yet.

Madness.

"You're still a bit too far away for my liking." He settled his hand on her waist. His big hand curled easily around her, fingers splaying across her back. Each one a line of heat licking at her through the wool of her jacket. She tore at her buttons as heat flared through her and shrugged out of it, tossing it behind her without looking.

Oliver smiled. "I like your thinking. Come here." His hand pressed gently, urging her closer. She let herself give in to the tremble in her thighs and lowered herself until she was hard up against him. Belly-to-belly. Chest-to-chest.

He was hard between her thighs which felt too damned good—but that wasn't the part of him she was interested in right now. Not yet. Not now. Right now, she couldn't look away from his mouth.

"Hi," she said, nervous all over again.

"Hello." The word was soft. Enticing. "You feel good, Amelia."

She was pretty sure she was red-faced and wild-eyed. Hardly sexy. Except the look in his eyes told her that he thought she was. And with him so close. So *there*. So obviously willing to let her do whatever she wanted to him, she couldn't bring herself to care too much that she was blushing.

"You feel pretty good yourself," she said, letting her knees sink just that little bit farther forward so that she rested more tightly against him. He groaned and she froze. "Did I hurt you?"

"God, no," he said. "Don't you dare move an inch."

"But if you don't let me move I can't kiss you."

A laugh rumbled through him, and the vibrations set off some rumbles deep and low in her own body. "You really would have been the death of seventeen-year-old me."

"Probably," she agreed. "So it's a good thing that you're not seventeen anymore, isn't it?"

"Definitely," he said. His hand slid up her back to

cradle the back of her head. She never would have done this at seventeen. Never let a baseball player near her. Particularly not one as gorgeous as Oliver. Too scared of ending up like her mother. But Oliver made her feel safe, not scared. So she forgot about seventeen and her mother's fears and let herself feel. Let herself give in to what she wanted.

And without her quite knowing how or when they'd moved, his mouth was finally on hers.

Soft at first. Questioning.

She knew the answer to that question. Curled one arm around his back and the other hand into his hair and kissed him back. Opened her mouth to him and let him take her like the pirate he was.

Pirates, it seemed, kissed gloriously.

Beyond gloriously.

His lips and tongue took her and tumbled her into heat and darkness and longing. She pressed herself against him and went willingly. Because there was really nothing else she could do. The world arrowed down to a single place, to the few inches of his mouth and hers, and the rest blurred to pleasure. If any seventeen-year-old had ever kissed her like this under the bleachers, she wouldn't have been a virgin until she was nineteen.

These kisses were the real deal. One hundred percent raw longing and need. One hundred percent guaranteeing that she wanted more. Wanted the rest of him. Wanted his hands on her and his weight above her. Wanted flesh on flesh and the slide of hard against soft.

The hand she'd pressed to his back grabbed a handful of his T-shirt and yanked it upward until she could get to bare skin. His skin. Hot under her touch. As hot as hers felt. The combination was near scorching. As she slid her hand over his back, his muscles tightened and trembled, and then he yanked his mouth away from hers.

It took her a second to come back to herself. To dull the roar of lust through her body and get her brain to re-engage.

He'd stopped kissing her. So mostly what she was able to think was that she didn't like that fact very much.

"Did I bump your ankle or something?" she asked, doing a hasty inventory of where her hands and feet were. Nowhere near any wounded parts of him as far as she could tell. Which brought her back to why had he stopped kissing her?

"No," he said. "But I think we need to stop."

"You want to stop?" Her body didn't want to accept that message.

"I said 'need' not 'want,'" he said, sounding suddenly cranky.

"But—"

"Amelia, I think we both know where that kiss was heading. And as much as I like that direction, I think I have to call a time-out."

She had liked the direction, too. She wanted all of him. Naked. In her. So much it was hard to think. "Did the doctor tell you not to?"

He laughed at that. "No. But he probably didn't think he needed to."

"I did hurt you."

"No. You didn't. Well, only in a good way."

"Then what's the problem?"

"You only met me on Sunday."

That startled a laugh from her. "You think it's too soon? I think your seventeen-year-old self just voted you off the island."

"Yeah, well my seventeen-year-old self was a bit of an idiot. I liked kissing you, Amelia. I liked it a lot. I'd like to do other things to you even more, but you have to go to work in the morning and I'm kind of playing with a handicap here." He lifted his bandaged hand. "So I'm just suggesting we take this slow. I don't want you regretting anything. I want you sure."

She could feel him hard against her still. Every inch of her wanted to feel more. "I'm sure. Unless I'm mistaken, you feel pretty sure, too."

"Trying to think with the bigger brain here," he said, determination underscoring his words.

There really was going to be no persuading him, she realized. Damn it. "Your bigger brain sucks," she grumbled, but she eased herself off him and onto the empty space on the sofa on his other side. "Happy now?"

"Not particularly," he said.

"Me neither."

"Me and my great ideas," he said. "So . . . want to play Words with Friends?"

If she drank one more coffee she was probably going to make her brain explode. Nevertheless she was going to drink it. She'd stayed at Oliver's until close enough to midnight, until he'd begun to yawn and look exhausted and she'd made her excuses and stolen away. Then when she'd gotten home she'd watched her recording of the game. Because there was no way she'd be able to face Finn, Em, or their parents if she hadn't watched it. So she was operating on about three hours' sleep, a body humming with frustration, and a mood not improved by the fact that the Red Sox had beaten the Saints. Putting them one up in the series. Two more games like that and the Saints' chances would be over.

Which might make things easier on Oliver. Maybe. He was obviously pissed about having to watch the Saints from the sidelines but she had no idea if that meant he'd prefer them to lose. What she did know was that Finn wouldn't take losing the divisional series well. He loved to win. Pushed himself relentlessly to win. To be the best at what he did. Which was why everybody had tended to let it slide if he sometimes chose to blow off some steam. But with Oliver out of the picture, Finn would be trying to prove himself more than ever. Go after what he'd decided was his. She had no idea how he'd cope if it didn't work out.

Baseball. Who knew it could cause so much drama in her life? She'd made a choice of a sort last night by going to Oliver. By kissing him. Finn might well see it as a betrayal. So that needed to be handled carefully to avoid even more drama. But not as much drama as Daniel would cause if she screwed up this project. Which was why she was on her fourth coffee of the morning and wishing desperately that Pullman Waters was the sort of workplace that let its employees take nap breaks.

The only thing a nap break would get her here would be fired. She tipped extra sugar into the coffee she normally drank black and unsweetened and carried the mug back to her desk, trying to not to think about how many hours it was going to be before she could sleep. Also trying not to wonder if Oliver was going to call her. It was still relatively early, just on eleven. Maybe he was sleeping late. There hadn't been so much as a move in their word game all morning.

Which was making her nervous.

Maybe he'd stopped kissing her last night because he hadn't liked it.

Her body voted no on that theory. There was no way kisses that had made her want to peel off his clothes and drag him to bed, that had left her hot and wanting hours later, had meant nothing to him. He'd been just as frustrated as her last night after he'd called a stop to their make-out session. She could tell by the way he'd watched her and by his restless movements as they'd played their silly word game.

In retrospect, he'd done the smart thing. They were going too fast. Crazy fast. Logically she knew that. He was being sensible. Which the parts of her not currently feeling stupidly horny appreciated.

But why hadn't he called?

Maybe he had another medical appointment.

And maybe she was just going to drive herself nuts trying to figure out what was going on and she should just call him.

Woman up. It was, after all, the twenty-first century. No one had to sit around waiting for a guy to call if they didn't want to.

She definitely didn't want to. She slurped down more coffee and reached for her phone. Then nearly dropped it when it vibrated to life in her hand.

But the name on the caller ID was Em's, not Oliver's. A pang of disappointment rolled through her. Chased swiftly by guilt.

"Hey, Em," she said, trying to sound awake.

"Hey yourself," Em said. "Did you watch the game last night?"

"Of course." It wasn't a lie. She just hadn't watched it live. No, instead she'd made out with Finn's archrival. Information she wouldn't be volunteering to Em. "Finn played well."

"Still lost, though."

"It's the Red Sox. They've got a lot more experience at play-offs. I'm sure the guys will settle down to the job tonight."

"I hope so," Em said. " 'Cause the judge hearing my case decided he wants a long weekend or something because he's adjourned until Monday."

A smile spread over Amelia's face. "Does that mean you're going to Boston for the game?" She hadn't been happy with the thought that Em wasn't going to get to see Finn play.

"No. The earliest flight I could get to Boston last-minute was the seven-thirty flight tonight. I'd miss most of the game."

"Oh. Finn will be disappointed."

"No, because I'm booked on the seven o'clock flight to New York instead. So I can see him play tomorrow at Staten Island." Em sounded gleeful.

"You're coming here? Tonight?"

"Yes. I can still stay with you, right?"

"Of course," Amelia said, happiness at the thought of seeing Em dampened a little by the fact that a house-guest meant she wouldn't be able to go see Oliver tonight. "What time does your flight get in?"

"About nine thirty, if everything goes well. I'll just get a cab to your place. Don't come meet me."

"Are you sure?" Was it bad that she felt relieved? The thought of battling her way out to JFK sounded pretty crappy. Particularly when she was so tired.

"Absolutely. Friday nights are always a zoo at airports. Stay home and mix us up a batch of margaritas."

Amelia grinned. Friday-night margaritas with Em sounded pretty good. Even if Em wasn't tall, dark, and handsome. "I can do that." If Em was landing at nine thirty, she wouldn't be at Amelia's until well after ten thirty. Maybe even after eleven. Which meant Amelia might even get in a nap.

"Cool," Em said. "Don't tell Finn if you talk to him. I want to surprise him and my parents."

"My lips are sealed," Amelia said. She'd left Finn a "good luck for tonight" message earlier, carefully avoid-ing any mention of the loss to the Red Sox. But she hadn't had a response. She wasn't really expecting any. He needed to focus on the game ahead.

"Awesome. I have to go, our recess is almost over," Em said. "See you tomorrow night."

After Em hung up, Amelia put her head down and worked. She needed to get shit done if she wasn't going to have to work half the weekend. With Em in town and two baseball games, she didn't want to do that. So *Ignore the lack of sleep and just do it* was her new motto of the day. She'd done it before and would do it again. In fact, she got so lost in the work that when Daniel knocked on her door, she realized it was nearly two and her self-imposed deadline to hear from Oliver had passed.

"How's it going?" Daniel asked.

"Good," Amelia said, hoping she looked more alert than she felt. "Just knocking some things off the issues register, then I have another meeting with IT this afternoon."

"And the Singapore analysis I wanted?"

"Will be on your desk by the end of the day."

"Good."

She smiled, trying to decipher the expression in his pale eyes. "Are you going to the Hamptons this weekend?"

"Yes," he said.

She tried not to let pleasure at the news show on her face. When Daniel went out of town for the weekend, there were far fewer weekend emails that needed attention from his team before Monday morning.

"What are your weekend plans?" he asked.

She waved at her desk. "I've got a few things to work on but actually I have friends in town. We're going to see the Saints play tomorrow."

"Ah. Yes. You have a friend who plays baseball, don't you?" Daniel said.

"Yes. It's his first play-off series, so it's pretty exciting."

He arched an eyebrow. "The Saints are a terrible team, aren't they? Seems unlikely they'll win."

Was he trying to annoy her? Or was he just being his usual straight-to-the-point-regardless self? "Actually, since the owners changed a few years back, they've been doing better each year. They might just surprise you."

He looked like he doubted it. "To each their own," he said eventually. He was studying her again. She wished she'd had time to go digging as to whether there was an opportunity in Hong Kong coming up. Otherwise she wasn't sure why he kept turning up in her office. Twice in one week was unheard of. It was making her nervous.

She nodded at her computer. "Was there anything else you needed me to do?"

"No," he said. "Just make sure I have that report before you leave tonight."

"Not a problem."

She needed more coffee. Or maybe a Coke. Easier on her stomach. She leaned back on her desk chair and stretched. It was nearly four and she had to do her final pass on the report for Daniel and come up with a brilliant solution for one last issue with the Australasian model and then she'd be done. Or as done as she planned to be. She could try to work later tonight but she desperately needed a nap. Her head was starting to ache and her eyes were burning from staring at her monitor practically nonstop since seven thirty.

Oliver still hadn't called. At least, she didn't think he had. She'd turned her cell off after lunch, not wanting to be interrupted. But he'd called her landline before, so she hadn't thought getting her voice mail on her cell would stop him getting to her if he really wanted to.

Caffeine and sugar first, though. She snatched up her purse and her phone and decided to hit the coffee cart outside the building to get some fresh air. As she stepped into the elevator, she switched her phone on.

No message alerts.

The tension in her stomach shifted from too much caffeine to sheer nerves.

"Pull it together, Graham," she muttered to herself as she hit the first floor and headed outside. It wasn't as though she and Oliver were officially dating or anything. She'd spent time with him exactly four times and kissed him for a few minutes. They'd been a few fantastic minutes but she needed to keep her cool.

The October air—still colder than usual—slapped at her as she left the building. The sting of it actually woke her up a little, and she tried to breathe it in more deeply as she reached the coffee cart and placed her order.

Five minutes. Five minutes out in the fresh air and she'd go back to her desk. She sipped her mocha—combining the chocolate and caffeine just seemed easiest at this point—and found a seat.

And, fortified by a fresh hit of caffeine and the cold, she dialed Oliver.

Oliver jolted awake when the phone rang. Crap. He'd fallen asleep again.

Who was calling him?

He blinked, trying to think. How long had he actually been asleep? He'd slept late that morning already. Gone through his routine with Alfie of having his splint taken off and his hand taped in a bag so he could shower. The dressing on the wound was apparently waterproof, but rebandaging the whole thing and getting the splint back would be nearly impossible on his own and Alfie had sensibly pointed out that it would be less painful to him if he had the splint on in the shower in case he knocked his hand somehow. Then there'd been the post-shower icing and dressing changing and rebandaging of everything.

Hardly a jam-packed morning. So he shouldn't be tired. But apparently he'd fallen asleep again at some point during his exciting afternoon of watching *Justified* reruns on TV. Surgical recovery sucked.

He managed to grab the phone before it stopped ringing, his brain finally clicking into focus when he saw Amelia's name on the screen.

"Hey," he said.

"Hey yourself," Amelia said.

She sounded . . . tired? Or just stressed. He leaned toward tired and then felt vaguely guilty that he'd kept her up late. Not too guilty, though, because kissing her had been too damned good to feel guilty about.

"I was going to call you," he said. "But I've been—" Sleeping sounded lame. He didn't want her thinking of him as the injured guy. Helpless, in need of cosseting. Less than whole. But she'd seen him at the hospital, the day after his surgery. She probably did see him that way. But that didn't mean he had to reinforce her impression.

"Resting, I hope," Amelia said. "Or at least following doctor's orders."

If one more person mentioned following doctor's orders he was going to lose it. But Amelia sounded worried when she asked, so he was giving her a pass. Besides, she didn't seem to be pissed that he hadn't called yet, which was more than he deserved. He'd meant to call her as soon as Alfie left but had been distracted by a call from his agent, checking up on him.

"I have been an excellent patient all day," he said. "Which is why I'm hoping you might come over tonight. I've earned a reward."

She laughed. "Most people get a lollipop when they're a good patient."

"Amelia, you taste way better than any lollipop I've ever tried."

Her breath caught. He heard it clearly. A sudden indrawn breath. It made him hard. Damn it. Why had he been so freaking sensible last night and sent her home? He wouldn't be feeling like a teenager with his first taste of a woman if he hadn't sent her home. Sure, he might not have been able to pull off actual sex with his arm in a sling, but there were plenty of other things they could have done. And he might have heard Amelia make a whole array of sexy noises like that little sucked-in breath.

"Still there?" he said softly when she failed to speak.

"Yes," she said, sounding just that little bit foggy. He knew how she felt.

"So, are you going to make me happy and come on over?"

"I'd love to," she said and he almost did a fist punch of victory with his good hand . . . only he was using it to hold the phone.

"But I can't," she continued.

His happy sense of victory deflated like a balloon hit with a sledgehammer. "Can't or won't?"

"Can't," she said quickly. "I have a friend coming into town. She's staying with me."

"Tell her you're having your apartment sprayed or something. Send her to a hotel."

She laughed. "I can't. I already invited her over."

He sighed. "Let me guess, it's Castro's sister, isn't it? Your best friend?"

"Yes." She sounded regretful, which made him feel slightly better. Slightly. But he knew better than to try to fight against the best-friend code. Nothing good ever came of trying to do that. And Amelia's best friend was also Castro's sister. Which only complicated things even more. The smart thing to do would be to be the easy part of the equation.

"When is she arriving?"

"Tonight. Nine thirty. But I have to work late again. I need to clear my desk so I can—" She broke off.

"Go to the game tomorrow?" he said. "Don't worry, I pretty much assumed that you were going to go see Finn play."

"Are you going to go?"

He hadn't planned on it. Maggie had already asked him if he wanted her to organize a driver to bring him to Staten Island but he'd put her off, claiming he didn't think he was up to it yet. Didn't think he'd fooled her about the real reason, either. But she hadn't called him on it. That might change if the Saints lost again tonight. Then he figured he'd be asked to come down for team morale. He hadn't decided whether or not he'd say yes. "That's another one of those complicated questions."

"Which means you haven't decided?"

"Which means I'm probably going to say no," he said. "Not sure I want to see them lose. Not entirely sure I want to see them win, either. And trust me, I know that makes me a crappy teammate."

"I think it makes you human," she said. "No one likes to stand by and watch while something they've worked hard for is taken away from them."

"Maybe," he said. "Not sure the guys on the team will see it that way."

"Well, you still have time to make up your mind," she said. "See how you feel tomorrow."

"If I did come, would I get to hold your hand?"

"I . . . I don't know," she said. "Isn't it a bit early for that?"

"You tell me."

She went silent again. "I think it's a complicated question. And I think that neither of us wants to make waves at a time when the team all needs to be focused on the game."

"You mean Finn."

"Yes," she said.

"You think he's going to take you and me badly?"

"He's hardly your biggest fan."

That was tactful of her. "I'm not his biggest fan, either. And I'm not willing to give you up to keep him happy."

"I'm not asking you to give me up. I don't want you to give me up. But does it really hurt if no one knows about us for a little bit longer? After all, do you even know what this is yet?"

"I know I liked kissing you," he said. "I know that kissing you again is just about all I've thought about today."

She made another little sexy noise. "Good answer. And right back at you. But let's be a little more sure where this is going before we drop any bombshells. After all, you might get sick of kissing me."

"I really don't think that's likely."

"Good to hear. So, are we agreed? Just between you and me for now?"

"Fine," he said. "But you owe me."

"Oh really? Owe you what?"

"I'll think of something."

"Something good, I hope." Laughter bubbled through her voice again. Sexy laughter.

"It will be. Are you sure you can't come over tonight and find out what it is?"

She sighed. "Yes. Which sucks."

"Can't argue with that. How long is Em staying?"

"She'll have to fly back Sunday, I think. She's in the middle of a big case."

"She's a lawyer?"

"Yep. Good one."

"Huh." He hadn't exactly bothered to find out anything about Finn's family. He normally tried to help new guys settle into the team, but Finn had made it clear he didn't want anything from Oliver other than his first-base slot. So Oliver had steered clear as much as possible. Other than when he'd had to squish the kid a few times. Pity. If he had, he might have met Amelia sooner. But that aside, he hadn't pictured Finn having a lawyer for a sister.

"Finn's pretty smart, too," Amelia said. "He actually had an offer for an academic scholarship, before he got an athletic one, at college. I'm pretty sure if he hadn't loved baseball so much he might have gone to med school or something."

Finn Castro, GP. Nope. His brain wouldn't go there. GPs were meant to be concerned about other people, weren't they? As far as he could tell, Finn Castro was mostly the number-one fan of Finn Castro.

"You don't say," he said, trying for the diplomatic response. "Good for him."

"Maybe it would have been," she said. "He loves baseball, though."

"He's got talent," Oliver said. "No reason he can't have a good career if he keeps his head screwed on straight." And learned not to party at every opportunity. Most young guys went a little nuts when they got to the majors, but Finn wasn't as young as some. He'd spent a couple of years in a minor-league team out of college before the Cubs had drafted him. They'd sold him a year later. He should have wised up right about then.

But that wasn't a talk he was going to have with

Amelia. "I'll let you get back to work. How do you feel about Sunday night?"

"I've always been a fan," she said. "But we have to wait and see what happens. If the Saints are still in the running then Finn's mom and dad are going to be in town. If not, well, won't the team be throwing some sort of end-of-season event?"

Commiseration party, she meant, even if she was too tactful to say so. Damn it. He'd forgotten about that. Cock-blocked by his own goddamned team. The universe definitely had it in for him right now. "I guess we'll have to wait and see. But I'll let you get back to work."

"Thanks for understanding."

"You're worth waiting for," he said and hung up the phone.

Chapter Seven

"Pass the tequila, woman," Em said, waving her empty glass in the air.

"Have you developed a secret booze habit in the last few years?" Amelia said with a half groan as she reached for the nearly empty bottle of Cuervo. "You're drinking me under the table."

"I'm part Irish. Good head for liquor."

"Don't give me that, I'm more Irish than you are." They'd done the math once. Amelia's grandfather on her dad's side was Irish. Whereas Mari Castro's mother had been half Irish, half English.

"You're obviously not training hard enough," Em said. "You need to let Finn take you to a few more of his baseball parties. Lots of free booze."

"I think Finn needs to lay off the free booze, not drink more of it," Amelia said without thinking as she grabbed a handful of tortilla chips to help soak up the alcohol. She was halfway to smashed despite having slept for two hours when she'd gotten home. No more for her. She was switching to club soda as soon as she finished her glass.

Em straightened on the sofa, swinging her legs down

from their perch hanging over the arm. "What's that supposed to mean?"

Amelia froze, trying to remember exactly what she'd said. Something about Finn and drinking. Right. "Well, he did get into the accident because he'd been drinking."

Em's eyes, the same unfairly green shade as her brother's, narrowed. "He wasn't driving. It wasn't his fault."

"Easy there, counselor," Amelia said. "I didn't say it was his fault. I said he'd been drinking."

"What's that got to do with it?" Em said.

Had Finn not told her exactly how the accident had happened? Amelia put her glass down carefully. "Finn was in the car because the Saints were sending him home from the party because he was wasted."

"He was celebrating."

"Em, he drank so much at a team party they sent him home," Amelia said. "That's like you or me getting tanked at a work function."

"So? Everyone is allowed to do stupid things from time to time."

Not when they started involving other people getting hurt. She wasn't sure this was the right time to have this conversation with Em. But she wasn't going to let Finn get away with giving his family the impression that everything was going swimmingly in New York. "Finn is still new at the Saints. He needs to be careful, that's all I'm saying. I don't want him to screw up his chance here."

"And you call me a worrier," Em said, waving a hand. "I'm sure he's fine. It was just a fender bender."

"It was a little more than that. Finn got a concussion, don't forget. And the guy who was taking him home got his hand sliced up. He had to have surgery. That's pretty serious for a baseball player. It could end his career."

Em's expression went shuttered for a moment, then her

eyes focused like lasers. "He doesn't have a case against Finn."

"I didn't say he did. Or that Finn was going to get sued over this. I'm just saying it wasn't just a minor accident." She lifted the bottle and refilled Em's glass. This conversation wasn't going the way she hoped. Em was too wound up from her case and, most likely, from being nervous about the play-offs to react well to a heads-up about her baby brother's fondness for enjoying himself a bit too much. Time to try again in the morning. "Anyway, enough serious talk. Tell me about Chicago. Any hot lawyers appearing on the scene?"

Em shook her head, dark bangs falling into her eyes. "Nope. None worth taking out for a trial run, anyway. The city's a wasteland, I tell you. A wasteland." She fell back on the sofa again.

"Is the definition of *wasteland* 'Emma Castro works too hard and doesn't take time to have any fun'?" Amelia teased.

"Hello, pot, meet kettle," Em shot back.

"Hey, I have fun," Amelia said then bit her lip. 'Cause there was no telling Em about her latest piece of fun. Not yet. If Em had gotten prickly at the suggestion that Finn was drinking too much, she wasn't going to take very well to the news that Amelia was having an attack of flaming hot pants over the guy who'd been in the accident with him.

"Economic modeling doesn't count as fun for normal people."

"Neither does reading legal briefs until one a.m."

Em groaned and put a hand over her eyes. "We are too hot to have love lives this sad. How did this happen?"

"No idea," Amelia said. "Obviously it's all the fault of the men in these cities."

"I'll drink to that," Em said. "I'm starting to think I'm going to try the online thing again."

"Oh yeah, because that's worked well in the past." Em's tales of Internet dating disasters were legendary.

"Well, I could try Tinder. At least get some sex."

"I'll buy you a new vibrator," Amelia said. "How do you know some random guy you meet on the Internet isn't an ax murderer?"

"How do you know a random guy in a bar isn't?"

She was pretty sure that Oliver Shields wasn't an ax murderer. Maybe a sanity killer, but not an ax murderer. "You at least talk to the guy in the bar first."

"Talking's half the problem. Too many of them ruin it when they open their mouths." Em smiled suddenly. "How's your boss with the divine accent?"

"Still mostly an ambitious asshole," Amelia said.

Em looked wistful. "Maybe asshole isn't so hard to take when he sounds like that."

"Trust me, the charm of the accent wears off fast. And I'll sign you up for online dating myself before I let you date Daniel. Besides, you live in different cities."

"Who said anything about dating? Is he in town this weekend?"

"He goes to the Hamptons," Amelia said. "Don't even think about it."

"Damn."

"If you're that desperate, maybe you're the one who should be going to Finn's baseball parties," Amelia said. "Move to New York. They like lawyers here."

Em wrinkled her nose. "Baseball players are your kink, not mine."

Sadly, that was true. Not that she'd ever succumbed to that particular preference. Nor had Em ever fallen for the charms of any of the hot-bodied guys they'd come across in their teens thanks to their attendance at Finn's games. Finn, who'd always been a bit of wunderkind and subsequently usually ended up playing with guys a few years older than himself. Aka, exactly Amelia and Em's age.

It really was a miracle neither of them had ever dated a jock. But Amelia had been too well indoctrinated by her mom, and Em had gone for the bad-boy type instead. The guys with guitars or motorcycles or rumored drug habits. Which didn't explain her weird fascination with Daniel, who was straitlaced as only a Brit could be. At least as far as Amelia could tell, he was.

She shook herself, trying to clear the tequila fog from her brain. This conversation was straying into dangerous territory again. "I do not have a baseball player kink. I've never dated a jock."

"And look, you're still single. Face it, Milly, you have a little thing for guys in tight uniforms."

"Remind me not to give you margaritas again," Amelia said, sticking her nose in the air. "It makes you regress to seventeen."

"Maybe if you let your inner teenager out you might have more fun."

"Who needs men for fun when I have you?" Amelia said. "Now, is it time for ice cream?"

It wasn't the first time she'd watched a game from great seats. Finn had gotten her tickets at Deacon Field, the Saints' home stadium, a few times over the season, and the players' families had prime positions. But watching from the owners' box—and she still wasn't sure how Finn had pulled off four seats in the box when there must be a cast of thousands wanting to sit up there for the Saints' first home game of the series—was a whole other experience. Food handed around by waiters, ditto drinks. Cushy leather seats. Not to mention the box was far warmer than the cool October evening. High-definition flat screens on the walls showed different angles of the game and the crowd, if actually gazing out the floor-to-ceiling glass window that looked out on the field was too much effort.

It was luxurious and not a little glamorous.

It was also the most tense place Amelia had been in a very long time. Including the trading room at Pullman.

Everyone at the Saints was taking this game very seriously. Very, very seriously. Which made her nervous. Two down in a play-off series wasn't a great place to be for a team inexperienced in handling this kind of pressure. She wasn't sure she wanted to be a firsthand witness to the disappointment of everyone in the room if the Saints lost this game and the series came crashing to a halt.

The atmosphere was already enough to make her feel vaguely queasy, and the game hadn't even started yet.

This was going to be an interesting evening.

She glanced at Em, seated next to her. Mari had her daughter's hand in a death grip as they both stared down at the field where the Saints dance squad, the Fallen Angels, were nearly done with their trademark opening routine, the white of the huge feathered wings they wore brilliant against the green field.

On Mari's far side, Eduardo Castro looked like he just wanted it to be over already, his face grim as he stared equally intently down at the diamond.

Normally she'd crack a joke to try to lighten the mood. But she had the feeling that any joke was likely to land as gracefully as a lead balloon.

So she stayed silent, sipping champagne and wondering what Oliver was doing. Was he alone in his apartment? Sitting through the game with nothing to distract him?

She'd spoken to him earlier when Em had made a side

trip to the Met, but there'd been no time to sneak away to see him. Em was staying the night and then flying out in the morning, back to Chicago. So there would be no sneaking out after the game, either. And if by some miracle the Saints won and kept their chances minimally alive, the Castros would be in New York another night. That meant she'd have to hang out with them and go to another game on Sunday.

All while she really, really wanted to be with Ollie again. To kiss him again. To do more than kiss this time if she had her way.

She'd been hoping to see him, if only across the room, given their agreement not to go public yet. But apparently he'd decided not to come to the game.

Sigh.

She was just going to have to be patient. If the Saints won both their home games then the final game would be back in Boston. So really she only had to survive another day and a half at worst.

Thing was, she wasn't sure how she was going to do that without going crazy. Or tripping up and mentioning Oliver's name to Em, Finn, or the Castros. It had been on the tip of her tongue a few times last night under the deadly combination of tequila and not enough sleep but she'd managed to stop herself, even when Em had started grilling her about her love life for a second time.

Down on the very green grass, the Angels were wrapping up their routine. The noise of the crowd grew louder and louder and the nerves in her stomach twisted tighter with each roar.

The stadium stands were a sea of blue, white, and gold, punctuated with swaths of red-and-white-clad Sox fans who'd made the trip from Boston to watch the game.

She figured the ratio was probably two to one Saints fans to Sox supporters. Which made sense. The Saints fans hadn't had a chance to see their team in a divisional series for decades. They must have been just about willing to commit murder to get their hands on tickets.

She could relate to that feeling. She felt much the same way about getting her hands on Oliver Shields.

Just thinking about him made her hot and needy and unable to sit still, like her skin was buzzing and her blood too warm. Her foot was tapping now, trying to burn off some of the nervous energy. She knew that she wasn't going to be able to just sit quietly through the singing of the National Anthem and the other ceremonies that went before the actual first pitch.

Murmuring an excuse to Em, she left her seat and headed out of the box to the bathroom. The air felt several degrees cooler in the corridor outside the box but she figured that was probably due to the lack of tension.

Running cool water over her wrists helped her feel calmer and she stayed in the bathroom, staring at the mirror a little too long. Her phone was in her bag. She could call Oliver.

She wanted to so badly it made her palms itch. But it seemed like madness. She should be able to wait to talk to the man, for God's sake. Instead of having to fight the need to talk to him.

Besides which, she was surrounded by people who actually knew Oliver. What if one of them overheard her saying his name or something? She knew that if this thing between them continued, she was going to have to face his friends and teammates and the Castros eventually, but she wasn't ready for that to happen just yet. No, she needed it to be a secret a bit longer. Something just for her.

Something no one else wanted or needed from her. Something she was doing purely because she wanted to.

It felt like way too long since she'd done something selfish.

Something foolish.

None of the Wall Street guys had felt like this. They'd been scratching an itch maybe.

Oliver wasn't an itch.

No.

He was already more like an addiction.

Which should worry her but right now, like any good addict, she was more focused on getting her fix than where her addiction might lead her.

She could hold off a little longer. No calling him.

Instead she reached into her bag for her lipstick, repainting the deep coral she'd chosen to go with the royal-blue top she'd donned under a white jacket. Hammered gold hoops in her ears and a matching long loop of hammered gold and silver links around her neck were the best she could do to make up the Saints' team colors without resorting to a cap or a team jersey—which was in no way suitable to wear in the owners' box. She'd paired the jacket with skinny black jeans and spike-heeled boots. Dressy but not too outright fussy.

Her instinct had been right, as it turned out. The other women in the box wore subtle hints of team colors but were otherwise dressed similarly to her. Expensive jeans or short skirts or sleek dresses.

She fit right in.

Which was a pretty odd thought.

Lipstick restored, along with a measure of calm she hoped, she made her way back to the box when she heard the last few lines of "The Star-Spangled Banner" echoing across the PA system and the crowd start to cheer again.

Please don't lose, please don't lose, please don't lose.

She wanted it for Finn. They'd seen him for a few

minutes earlier but he'd been tense and distracted. Amelia had coaxed the Castros and Em away, and he'd given her a grateful smile over his shoulder as he'd disappeared back into the locker room.

The last thing she was expecting when she stepped back into the box was the sight of Oliver, leaning on a walking stick and talking to Maggie Winters at the rear of the box. Maggie was grinning at him, clearly delighted that he'd turned up.

Amelia fought her own cheek muscles to keep the grin that wanted to take over her face at bay. There would be no grinning goofily at the pretty baseball man. Not while Em and the Castros were in the room. Still, she couldn't help shutting the door with a little more force than was strictly necessary. There was enough noise in the room that she didn't think anyone was really going to notice, but Oliver's head turned toward her like she'd shouted his name.

He gave her one fast smile, dark eyes approving, before he turned back to Maggie.

Which left her feeling vaguely put out.

Idiot.

She was the one who had told him to play it cool in public. Couldn't blame him for sticking to the plan. So she needed to get back to her seat and focus on the game before she blew said plan for both of them. But there were several important-looking guys in expensive suits blocking her path, and she didn't want to just barge her way through. Not when she didn't know exactly where she was. So she stayed put, looking for an alternative route and definitely not looking at Oliver. No sir. No looking. Looking was bad. Looking made her forget important things.

Like her inhibitions.

Unfortunately she hadn't counted on Maggie Winters.

Who spotted her hovering by the door and arrowed over to her with a smile of welcome.

"Hi. You're Amelia, aren't you?" Maggie said. "We met at the hospital."

"Yes. I am. And you're Maggie. I remember." Not exactly the smoothest opening but it would do. She focused on Maggie's face, determined not to look past her to Oliver.

"Are you sitting with Finn's parents?" Maggie said. "They must be nervous. You must be nervous. Can I get you a drink?"

"I'm fine," Amelia said. She wasn't sure whether Maggie's rapid-fire conversation was her normal hostess style or whether the truth was that Maggie herself was nervous. "Big day for all of you.

"Yes." Maggie swallowed hard then shook her head. "But we're going to win, so it's all fine. Hey, did you see Oliver was here? He got out of the hospital a few days ago. Did he tell you?"

"Um, no." Amelia said. There. Nice and noncommittal. Maggie could draw her own conclusions about what exactly she was saying no to.

"Come say hi. I'm sure he'd like to see you. It was nice of you to visit him in the hospital." Maggie put a hand on Amelia's arm and headed toward Oliver. There was no way to politely stay where she was, so Amelia went with her, making pleading eyes at Oliver who was watching them now, his expression politely interested.

"Ollie, you remember Amelia, don't you?" Maggie said. In front of them, the crowd suddenly roared and Maggie's head snapped around to the field like a dog catching a scent.

"First pitch," Oliver said. "Go sit with Alex. I'll find a seat."

Maggie nodded absently, attention still riveted to

the field. "Okay." She smiled at Amelia then turned on her heel and left them alone.

"Don't you want to sit down, too?" Amelia said, trying to think of something casual to say. But all that she could think was that Oliver was here. With her. So close she could smell him. Dressed in a dark jacket, white shirt, and dark pants that fit him like a glove. Put a gold hoop in his ear and he would be the perfect modern pirate. And she suddenly desperately wanted to be plundered. Damn it.

"I'll wait until everyone settles down a bit," Oliver said. "Easier to maneuver once everyone else is seated." He sounded casual, too, but the look in his eyes was hot.

"It's pretty crowded in here, isn't it?" Amelia fanned her face, hoping everyone in the room would think the heat in her cheeks was due to the excitement of the game.

"Definitely more crowded than I'd like right now," Oliver agreed with a half smile.

She narrowed her eyes at him. "Do not flirt," she said in a fierce whisper. "Flirting is not part of the plan."

"Amelia, right now we could probably make out and most of the people in this room wouldn't notice. They're all watching the game."

"Don't even think about it." Now she was thinking about it. Crap. "As far as these people know we've barely met, remember?"

"They'd just think you'd fallen for my irresistible charm." His grin widened. She resisted the urge to smack him. Because he was injured. And it might cause a scene.

"I'm feeling an irresistible urge to go find my seat," she said sternly. "After all, there's a game on."

His grin vanished. "Don't go. I'll behave. Scout's honor."

"I'll bet you were too busy playing baseball to be a scout."

"Busted. But I'll behave. Stay here and talk to me. Just for a few minutes. I've missed you."

Well, that was unfair. How was she meant to be sensible and go back to her seat when he said things like that to her? "All right. But only for a few minutes."

She looked up at him, suddenly unable to think of anything to say that wasn't *Let's get out of here, to hell with everybody.* Double crap. She had it bad. Em was right. Baseball players were apparently her kryptonite. Or this particular one was.

"Did you have fun with Em last night?"

"Yes." She paused. "Did you watch the game?" The Saints had lost. Which put them two down. So today's game was all or nothing.

"A little," Oliver said. "Until it became clear what was happening."

The Saints had played well for the first two innings but then the Red Sox pitcher had taken two outs with two pitches and everything had gone to hell in a handbasket. "How about you?"

She'd watched every minute from the time she'd woken up after her nap to Em knocking on her door. At which point, like Oliver, she'd given up, too depressed to watch the inevitable. She'd recorded it, though, and watched the highlights while she'd done the work she'd brought home with her after breakfast. But she didn't think Oliver really wanted to rehash the game.

"Do you think they can pull it off today?" she asked.

Oliver shrugged. "They can play well enough to do it. It's mostly a matter of whether they let the situation get to them. If they do that, they're toast."

"Remind me again why baseball is meant to be fun?" Amelia said, feeling queasy all over again.

"Well, for one thing, it's the way we met, sort of," Oliver said.

She shook her head. "Not sure that counts." She lowered her voice. "And that's getting back to things we aren't talking about here." She glanced down to the front of the room where Em and the Castros were sitting. "I need to get back to them. They're going to wonder where I am."

Oliver nodded. "If you have to." He reached into the pocket of his jacket and pulled out something wrapped in brown paper. A suspiciously small package. Casually he reached over and dropped it into the pocket of her blazer. "That's for you."

"What is it?"

"Something best not talked about here," he said. "Go sit down, Amelia. We'll talk later."

Chapter Eight

It was late by the time they got back to Manhattan. Despite the fact the Saints had pulled off a win, Amelia mostly felt exhausted rather than elated. Though part of her still seemed to have the energy to wish she was at Oliver's rather than here in her own apartment with Em.

She pulled off her jacket and the small parcel he'd given her fell to the carpet. Damn. She'd forgotten about it in the excitement of the game and its aftermath. And now it was lying on her rug, a mystery, daring her to open it.

Em was in the bathroom, brushing her teeth. The sound of water running and Em clattering around meant the coast was temporarily clear.

The paper came off easily and all too soon she was staring down at a bright silver key. A house key. Or rather, in this case, what she could only think was the key to Oliver's apartment.

What the hell?

"Whatcha got there?" Em said from the doorway. Amelia jumped. The key, predictably, went flying, landing halfway across the room. She dived for it, scooping it up again before Em could grab it.

"Jumpy," Em commented.

She'd donned pajama pants printed with Wonder Woman and a Saints sweatshirt, piling her dark hair up in a messy bun. She still looked gorgeous. Really, the Castro genes should be illegal.

"Whose key is that?" Em asked.

Amelia thought fast. "Um, one of the neighbors. Wants me to feed their cat next week when they're away."

"So why were you staring at it like you'd seen a ghost?"

Because Oliver Shields had given her the key to his freakin' apartment. "I had a moment where I couldn't remember if it was meant to be this week I was feeding the cat," she lied. "But no. Next week. So it's all good."

"Too much excitement today scrambling your brain," Em said. She came over and climbed onto the bed next to Amelia. "I thought I was going to have a heart attack during the final inning. I can't believe they won by one run. And that Finn got the out." She bounced on the bed. "He did so well. One run. Amazing."

"Bet the Red Sox can't believe it, either," Amelia said.

"Yeah, well, the Red Sox can suck it," Em said. "My baby brother lives to play another day. At first base." She held up her hand for a high-five and Amelia hit it. Part of her felt uneasy with the knowledge that Finn was playing Oliver's position, but it wasn't as if she could go back and change what had happened the night of the accident. And maybe Finn getting the chance to play in the position he wanted would ease whatever it was that had been making him edgy the last few weeks.

Em bounced a second time, almost making Amelia drop the key again. She tossed it into the little container of change on her nightstand then hugged Em with an arm. "I'm glad we got to watch the game together. Felt like old times." When they'd gone to high school baseball games pretending to hate it but secretly enjoying every minute. When they didn't live in different cities and had to make appointments to Skype.

"I can't believe I can't stay and watch the game tomorrow," Em said, squeezing her back before she sighed. "Whose bright idea was it to become a lawyer?"

"Yours when you were about twelve," Amelia said.

"Twelve-year-olds know nothing. I really want to stay and watch Finn play." She sighed again. "But that's just not going to happen."

"We're still having brunch with him and your folks before you leave, though. So you can tell him to break a leg or whatever."

"No breaking legs. Breaking legs would be bad." Em sighed. "Unless it's a Red Sox player. Is that terrible of me?" She flopped back on the bed, scowling. "I'm never going to get to sleep. I'm still wired from the game." Her expression brightened. "Hey, I'm starving. Can we make grilled cheese or something? Watch a movie?"

Amelia was pretty sure she had cheese and bread in the fridge. She'd been working such crazy hours lately that she hadn't stocked up on groceries. But she definitely had DVDs and they could always order pizza if her fridge failed to provide any food. Em wouldn't mind if Amelia fell asleep on the sofa during a movie. "Sure. Just don't blame me if cheese before bedtime gives you nightmares."

Em bounced off the bed and headed into the kitchen. Amelia stood to follow her but heard her phone vibrate on the nightstand.

She snatched it up.

The text was from Oliver.

Did you open it?

Yes.

Are you freaking out?

It's a key, Oliver.

You are freaking out. Don't freak out.

Easy for him to say. *I can't talk now*, she sent back. *Em's here.*

Okay. But don't freak out. I'll see you at the game. Sweet dreams, Amelia.

She was quite tempted to hurl the phone across the room. Sweet dreams. After he'd given her a key without any warning? More like lying awake staring at the ceiling wondering what the hell was happening.

They'd kissed once. He shouldn't be giving her a key. That was way too serious.

And made her way too happy.

"Did you fall asleep in there?" Em yelled from the kitchen. "No sleeping. Sleeping is for losers. Get your ass out here and help me find your frying pan."

Grilled cheese. She could do that. Grilled cheese was simple. Unlike keys and Oliver Shields.

"Coming," she yelled and shoved her phone and the key into her purse, where neither one could bother her until morning.

"Your mom says to say hi," Mari said as she reached for water at brunch the next day.

Amelia grinned at her. "Don't try to guilt-trip me. I talked to Mom yesterday."

"Talking isn't the same as seeing her," Mari said. "You haven't been home since Easter."

"We Skype a few times a week. She sees me," Amelia protested, shoving down the pangs of guilt. Usually she managed three or four trips back to Chicago in a year, but work had been so crazy this year she'd only managed to get away once.

Plus every trip back ate into her carefully hoarded vacation days. She tried to take as few as possible. Pullman was generous to employees, but she wanted to save hers. Because one day she was going to get that overseas job and at the end of that, she was going to take as much time as she could to travel. See the world. Not just New York and Chicago. Get on a plane and just go. See what was out there. Not be her mom and miss out on so much.

"I'll be home for Christmas," she said. "I tried to see if Mom wanted to come and see Finn play but you know how she is about planes. I'd see her more if she would just fly."

Mari rolled her eyes at her but Eddie Castro, seated next to his wife, patted Mari's arm. "Stop nagging, Mari," he said. "Or she won't come visit us when she does come home."

Em snorted. "As if that's going to happen. She's addicted to Ma's Christmas cookies."

"Me?" Amelia tried to look innocent. "It's Finn who eats all the cookies."

Finn, who was uncharacteristically quiet, shook his head at her. "I don't think so."

"You can deny all you like," Amelia said. "But I know you raid the secret cookie jar."

"How do you know there's a secret cookie jar if you don't raid it yourself?" Finn shot back. But he smiled and Amelia leaned back in her chair, happy to have distracted him for a moment or two. She'd expected him to be full of excitement, still riding the high of the previous night's win, but he'd been very quiet since they'd picked him up. Nerves, she supposed. God. She couldn't imagine how nervous he must be right now.

"Em must have told me," Amelia said. "I'm pleading the Fifth. I know nothing of cookies. Only bacon." She stole a piece off Finn's plate. They were having brunch extra early because he had to report to Deacon Field before midday. She guessed the Saints weren't taking any chances with any of the team getting into any sort of trouble. Apparently he was starting at first base again after his performance yesterday. He'd dropped that little bit of news in the car, and Amelia had been surprised that the three other Castros hadn't exploded with pride.

"That wouldn't hold up in court," Em said, forking up eggs and bacon. She apparently wasn't suffering from the same nerves that had the rest of them picking at their food. Probably because she wasn't going to have to actually sit through the game. The Red Sox were still one up in the series, with the Saints' win last night. If they won today, the series was over. Whoever came up with the play-off system was a sadist.

"How are things at work, Milly?" Eddie asked.

"Busy," Amelia answered. "I've been running a big project to develop a new model for Australasian currencies. Hopefully it will be all wrapped up by the end of the month."

Across the table, Finn yawned ostentatiously as he always did when Amelia talked about economics. She balled up her napkin and threw it at him. "Sorry, did I use a word with too many syllables for you, jock boy?"

Finn grinned again. "No, your words are just boring."

"Finn, don't be rude," Mari said. "Amelia's work is just as important as yours."

"Yeah, she actually works for a living," Em added, grinning at her little brother. "Doesn't just swing a bat around."

"Ambulance chaser," Finn said.

"Muscle head," Em retorted.

"Enough," Eddie said. "We're meant to be having a nice family meal while we're all together."

Em and Finn rolled their eyes. "Yes, Dad." Amelia nearly laughed, torn between pleasure at being with all of them and a sudden wave of homesickness. She missed this. Missed silly family dinners and outings. Missed her mom, too.

Her mom, who wasn't going to be happy when she found out Amelia was involved with an athlete. Guilt twinged, and she forked up more bacon.

So why couldn't she just do the smart thing and tell Oliver that she wanted to end it?

Choose her family over a man who was still virtually a stranger.

Because she didn't want to.

That made her feel even more guilty. She put her fork down, even less hungry than she had been before.

Across the table, Mari was watching her, looking vaguely concerned. Crap. She picked up the fork again. Time to change the subject. Back to a topic Mari would find more interesting.

Like her son. She pointed her fork at Finn. "If I'm so boring, why don't you tell us something interesting, Mr. Baseball? Something that's not about the game tonight."

She expected him to refuse, but instead he leaned back in his chair and smirked at her. "Well, I just signed my first sponsorship deal last night."

"Holy crap!" Em said. Quickly followed by, "You didn't show me the contract."

"Because you're a criminal lawyer and I have an agent who does that shit for me," Finn said. "They wanted an answer fast."

"Who's they, honey?" Mari asked.

"Long Road Home. They make fitness trackers, GPS watches, that sort of thing. They're launching a new smart watch system."

Amelia knew the company; they'd been in the news with their gear for the last twelve months, and Wall Street rumors had them likely to take things public soon. "Impressive."

"Doing the photo shoot on Wednesday," Finn said. "Should be fun. The campaign rolls out during the World Series. They're using a few up-and-coming younger players."

Made sense. A small company didn't have the same cash to throw around on promotion as the big players. Getting younger guys who didn't already earn huge MLB salaries and sponsorship dollars was good business.

"Well, just make sure you don't party too hard when you win," Em said, grinning at her brother. "Going to take a lot of beauty sleep to make your ugly face photogenic."

He was going to start a movement to get baseball played during the day again. Too many damned night games. He understood the realities of television rights and advertising dollars, but that didn't make it any easier when he was forced to wait all through Sunday before he could go see Amelia again.

The day had dragged on forever. His impatience had driven him to summon his driver earlier than they'd arranged, and now he'd arrived way too early at Deacon Field. He'd been aiming for a time when there was the least chance of him running into any press. He'd so far steadfastly refused to speak to a single reporter. The Saints had issued a very bland statement about the fact he had been placed on the sixty-day disabled list with a hand injury and that was all the media were getting until he had a better idea what was going on. Some of them had gotten hold of the story that he'd been in a car accident, but with the other driver clearly at fault, there wasn't much juicy scandal in that side of the story. He wasn't going to feed the beast by offering himself up. He'd even hired a different car service to bring him today. Some of the paps and the sports media kept tabs on that sort of stuff.

But in timing his entrance, he'd forgotten one thing. Being early enough to miss the press didn't mean he was early enough to avoid all the other players. Everyone would be inside the stadium already, going through all the pregame rituals. Psyching themselves up.

Or doing their jobs in the case of the staff who did things other than hit balls, making sure all the systems were up and running. Mal's security team would be doing final checks, combing over the stadium one last time, checking and double-checking. Deacon had gained a reputation for having the highest level of security in the league now, and even though there was bitching each game on social media from idiots who'd had booze or worse confiscated or been refused entry or ejected from the games, the majority of the fans were unfailingly supportive.

As was he. Except right now, when it meant that there were very few places he could go inside Deacon for the next few hours where he didn't risk someone spotting him. Which would then bring Maggie and probably Lucas and half the team coming to see him.

He'd sent his buddies on the team—hell, even the guys he wasn't super friendly with—emails before each of the last two games wishing them good luck. And he'd spoken to a few of the guys he was good friends with—Brett Tuckerson, Sam Basara and Hector Moreno—a few times on the phone since he'd gotten home. But he hadn't let anyone come to see him. He hadn't wanted to mess with their preparation for the games. Or at least that's what he'd told himself.

Now he was forced to concede that part of his reluctance might have been not wanting the guys to see him walking with a cane and sporting a hand that looked like he was wearing one of Darth Vader's cast-off gauntlets.

He didn't want the pity and the looks. Baseball players were a superstitious bunch. No one wanted to talk about injuries or the possibility of careers ending. And here he was, the carrion crow at the party so to speak. Unavoidable proof that shit happened.

Bad shit.

So no, he didn't want to go to the locker rooms before the game. Didn't want to put doubt into their minds. They were still one down. Tonight was make or break. No way was he going to jinx it for them.

Which meant he had to think of a way to get into Deacon and find somewhere to lay low. Until he could go up to the owners' box and watch the game while he pretended not to watch Amelia. Which was going to be hard. He'd spent far too long thinking about her kisses. About the other things he wanted to do to her.

It was killing him.

Having to pretend not to know her for a second game was going to make things worse. He wasn't used to not being able to just go after whatever he wanted. He wanted Amelia. That's why he'd given her the key.

But no. Better not to think about the key. Or how he may have freaked her out.

Better to figure out how to keep his poker face in place for another six hours or so.

Only the knowledge that her friend was no longer staying with her and that she was all his after the game tonight was making it bearable. But bearable wasn't the same as fun.

He wanted to kiss her again. Badly. Wanted to touch her. To take her clothes off, and take her into his bed.

He glanced at his watch. Hours to go before any of that was possible. Unless . . . he had a sudden thought about where he might be able to hide himself away for a few hours. And where, if he played his cards right, he might get a chance to shorten some of that time before he got to be alone with Amelia again.

Chapter Nine

Amelia stepped out of the Castros' rental car and stared up at the stark walls of Deacon Field. No one would call it the prettiest baseball field in the world. Particularly not with its odd office tower with the slanted roof inset with glass supposed to resemble a saint's halo. Supposed to. If you squinted. A lot.

It looked innocuous, all that concrete and glass and steel. But inside that stadium a lot of people's hopes and dreams could be dashed tonight. Including Finn's.

Yes, there would be another season next year. But that would be little comfort to all the Saints players and fans if they lost this game.

She glanced at Eddie, who'd been unusually quiet on the drive from Staten Island. The fact that he'd agreed to let Amelia drive instead of doing it himself spoke volumes about how nervous he was.

Mari tucked her arm through her husband's. They had seats in the owners' box again. Amelia hoped that was an indication that the Saints' owners were pleased with Finn's performance.

Was it ungrateful to wish she could watch the game

from the stands with all the fans rather than sit in that pressure cooker of a room all over again? Because she did. The thought of being in the box again—let alone the thought that Oliver might be there—was ratcheting up her nerves by a factor of about a thousand.

She smoothed her hands down the sides of her coat. Two baseball games in a row was pushing her limit of noncasual Saints' colors in her wardrobe. With her hair and pale skin, white wasn't the most flattering of shades, and she usually preferred more slaty hues of blue rather than the Saints' royal blue. But she'd unearthed a bright-blue skirt she'd bought on a whim during the summer and teamed it with a black blazer and a white top then added jewelry for gold and silver.

As she clicked the fob on the car keys to lock the doors, her phone started to vibrate in the depths of her purse. Nerves turned to a more pleasurable anticipation. There was only one person who could be calling. Em was back in Chicago and Amelia had already banned her from texting until the game started after receiving at least fifty nervous messages from Em since her flight home had landed.

It had to be Oliver. A glance at the screen confirmed her suspicions, but she wasn't going to talk to him with Mari and Eddie as an audience. She hit the DECLINE button. "Let's go," she said to the Castros, and they headed for the stadium entrance. She'd barely walked twenty feet before the vibrations started again. Damn it. He wasn't going to give up.

"Hey, I think I left my glasses in the car," she said to the Castros. "You two go on ahead. I'll catch you up."

Eddie nodded briskly and set off again, his strides quick, shoulders set, like he was marching into battle. Amelia watched them for a moment then walked back to the car and opened the door in case the Castros looked back. Then she pulled out her phone just as it stopped vibrating.

Damn. Now she'd missed him

Or not.

Are you here yet? popped up in a message on her home screen.

Just arrived.

Where are you?

The guest parking lot.

What about Finn's parents?

They've gone on ahead.

Good. Don't go to the owners' box. Go inside and find Door Six.

What's at Door Six?

Don't spoil my surprise, Amelia. See you soon.

She glanced at her watch. They were early. It was only just six thirty. She had time. The Castros wouldn't miss her immediately. They'd managed to meet a few of the other parents of various players during their time in the box and after the game yesterday. So they'd have people to talk to.

Door Six was easy enough to find. As she approached it, a service door in the wall of the curving corridor opened and Oliver, wearing a cap and dark glasses, stuck his head out.

"In here," he said, holding out a hand.

She took it and let him pull her through the doorway. Which left her standing in a stark concrete stairwell with another narrow corridor running in either direction.

"Why, Mr. Shields, you take me to all the nicest places," she said. But she couldn't help smiling at the sight of him as he took off his sunglasses and tucked them into a pocket of his Saints jacket. He wore dark jeans and a white shirt open at the collar and looked damned delicious despite the fact that his right hand in its splint was still supported by a sling.

"C'mon," he said. He took her right hand with his left and started down the corridor.

"Where are we going?" she asked after they'd walked for a minute or so.

He just grinned down at her and then pulled open another door. Which opened not onto one of the access corridors that the public used around the stadium but to what looked like an office block foyer. With an elevator in front of them.

Oliver led the way to the elevator and then hit a button for the fourth floor.

When the doors slid open, they stepped out onto a seemingly deserted floor.

"Where are we?" she asked again.

"Saints' headquarters," he said. "Which is currently deserted because everyone is either downstairs with the team or up in the box or doing their jobs around the stadium. Which means we can have a couple of minutes in private."

He opened a door in the hallway and tugged her through again. Into some sort of office. One that didn't look like anyone was currently using it. The desk was bare apart from a computer monitor that wasn't plugged in.

Oliver limped over, turned, and rested his weight on the desk, slipping off the glasses and cap. His hair, freed from the hat, curled around his face and he pushed it back impatiently as he hit her with a smile that made her knees weaken. "Why don't you come over here and say hello, Amelia?" He slipped his right hand out of the sling while he beckoned her with his left.

That was definitely an invitation she couldn't refuse. No matter who might be waiting for her upstairs. She went to him, let him pull her close.

For a moment they just looked at each other. She could see her reflection in his pupils, a tiny version of herself, her cheeks pink, her chest rising and falling. "Hello," she managed.

"Don't take this the wrong way," he said. "But if you're freaking out about the key, can we ignore that fact for a minute or two so I can kiss you?"

Her mouth curved upward. "I think I'm on board with that plan."

"Good," he said fervently and leaned in to kiss her.

She thought she'd be prepared for it this time. For the blinding rush of having his mouth on hers. But once again it took her by surprise.

The way the feel of his lips on hers made her breathless in seconds, made her clutch his shoulders and open her mouth to him. Made her step closer, wanting to be as near to him as she could be, given where they were and the chance they could still be interrupted. Oliver's mouth opened and she met the demands of his kiss without hesitating. He tasted like all the good things she'd never known she wanted.

A taste she wasn't sure she could get enough of.

His good hand slid down her back, cupped her butt, and pulled her closer still so that they were chest-to-chest. She wanted more of his touch. The weight of his hand burned into her through her skirt, but it wasn't enough. Her nipples were aching and she pressed closer to him, rubbing herself against him.

Oliver groaned against her mouth. "Are you trying to kill me?"

"Kill you, no," she said. "Lead you astray, maybe."

That made him laugh and he pulled his head back. Then he leaned forward so they were resting forehead-to-forehead. Both of them were breathing too fast.

"As much as I would love to let you have your wicked

way with me, and as much as I can't believe I'm saying this again, I think we need to stop. Again."

He was right. She knew he was right.

She *hated* that he was right.

"I thought baseball players were all meant to be easy," she muttered, stepping away from him. If they had to stop, then she couldn't be touching him anymore. Because touching him and not going a hell of a lot further than kisses would kill her. She straightened.

"Believe me, this is purely a timing issue. Not a lack-of-enthusiasm issue." His head tilted as he put his hand back in the sling, still breathing deeply. "You do believe me, don't you?" He stood. She could see he was hard even through the denim.

She grinned and nodded at his groin. "There is evidence in your favor."

He looked down ruefully. "Trust me, right now, this doesn't feel like it's working in my favor."

"Hmmm." She tried not to laugh. Her lady parts were all protesting the abrupt stop to all that good kissing pretty loudly. It was nice to know she wasn't suffering alone. "I think perhaps how that particular part of your anatomy feels isn't the safest topic of conversation right now." She let her gaze travel down again, let her grin widen.

He groaned again. "Maybe this wasn't such a good idea. But I didn't want to wait any longer to see you."

"No, it was a good idea. I'm in favor of your ideas. But like you said, our timing sucks. So, I'd better go. The Castros are going to think I've been kidnapped by rabid Red Sox fans or something."

"And the key?"

She froze. Damn. She'd forgotten about the key. "You said I shouldn't freak out about the key." It was safe in the inner pocket of her purse, where she'd been sure she could feel it glowing at her all day, like a little miniature radioactive puzzle to be solved. Or about to blow her life up.

He nodded. "No freaking out. I just thought, with this"—he held up his hand—"that it might be just as easy for you to be able to let yourself in."

It made sense. But it still her made her nervous. "Can I ask you something?"

"Yes?"

"How many other girls have you given a key to?"

"None," he said.

And now the nerves were back. With reinforcements. "You've never lived with someone?"

He shook his head.

That she hadn't expected. "Never had a serious enough relationship to want someone to have a key?" She'd never lived with anybody, but Oliver was older than her. Not to mention hot, rich, and kind of sweet. How was it he hadn't ever gotten that serious with any one?

"There have been a couple of girls over the years. But somehow we never quite go to that point. I'm on the road so much, it always seemed easier to turn up on their doorsteps when I was home. Or get them to come see me wherever I was." He was watching her, expression wary. "How about you?"

"Me?" She shook her head. "No. There was a guy for a few years in college. But no, I've never lived with anyone."

"If it freaks you out, you can give it back," he said.

"Do you want me to give it back?"

He shook his head. "Not unless you want to. Like I said, it's practical. My hand is going to be out of action for a while."

"Does this mean you want me to come over often?"

"I think we just established I want you whenever I can have you, Amelia," he said.

"Wanting me for now and keys are two different things. Keys imply . . . longevity."

"All I know is that I have no intention of letting you out of my bed anytime soon, should you choose to climb into it." His eyes looked very dark suddenly. "Unless you're not planning to?"

She hadn't planned any of this. Everything seemed to be moving at a million miles an hour, and she wanted to find a way to stand still and catch her breath. But the weird thing was, when she pictured herself doing just that, she was picturing Oliver standing beside her. She took a breath, tried to reach for that stillness. But found only the need for him. So, no, she wasn't going to lie and pretend she didn't want him. She shook her head. "I think we can safely say it's been on my mind. So I'll keep the key."

His smile made her heart turn over.

"And you'll use it tonight?"

"Yes."

One little word shouldn't feel so big but it did. Huge. But, looking at Oliver, huge wasn't scary.

"Good," he said. "Let's go watch the ball game."

Six hours later, her heart was beating almost as fast as the elevator was shooting upward toward Oliver's floor. Which was dumb. Dumb to be nervous.

Just Oliver. Who kissed like a god. Who looked like a god. Who wanted her.

These were all good things. So what was there to be nervous about?

It sounded stupid even in her head.

For the hundredth time that day she slipped her hand

into the side pocket of her purse and felt for the key. Still there.

Just a key.

The key to Oliver's apartment.

Just a key. One any injured friend might have given her so she could let herself in. After all, she had one to Finn's apartment.

No biggie.

Except if she used this one then she was stepping over the threshold to more than just his apartment. No denying that. One small step for woman, one giant step into what could only be classified as a suicidal impulse in terms of romantic choices.

Ollie was an athlete. Gorgeous. Focused. Obsessed with his sport. Just like all those guys she'd watched play their hearts out tonight. And sure, right now he'd turned that focus onto her. But what happened when he could play again? Where did she fit then?

Would she move down his priority list? Or off it all together?

He was an athlete. His game was his life.

And he was perfectly able—and likely—to smash her heart into approximately a billion pieces.

A smart woman would have returned the key and sent one last gummy bear care package before running for the hills.

But apparently she wasn't being smart these days. Not since he'd kissed her. Not since he'd asked her to come here tonight.

The elevator came to a smooth halt and the doors slid open with a whispered whoosh. The key bit into her palm as she approached the apartment door.

She made herself relax her grip—and the key slipped through her fingers and hit one of the black tiles with a metallic clink that seemed very loud in the silence.

For a moment she stared down at it, tempted to take it as a bad omen, an excuse to turn tail and head straight back into the elevator and flee.

A smart woman would do just that.

She bent, picked up the key, straightened, and then unlocked the door.

The apartment was quiet. No music or sounds of TV gave her any hint where Oliver might be.

Maybe he wasn't back from Staten Island yet. The Saints had been celebrating their second win. They'd brought the series back to two all. So it would all be decided in the final game. Apparently that meant a little celebrating even if they did have another game to play. Oliver had vanished from the owners' box after the game ended. She'd assumed he'd gone down to the locker room to be with his friends. But by the time she and the Castros had found Finn in the throng of players, supporters, families, and press, Oliver wasn't anywhere to be seen.

But there'd been a single text on her phone saying *Don't forget. Use the key.* So she'd come. Let herself in. All she needed now was the man himself.

She hesitated, looked past the entryway. She could try the living room or the kitchen. She wasn't going to try his bedroom.

No way, no how.

She slipped off her coat and hung it on the coatrack where Ollie's leather Saints jacket hung, looking vaguely neglected. She smoothed a hand over the sleeve and caught a drift of his aftershave.

Which made her heart beat fast all over again.

So. Choose one and stop standing in the hall like a dweeb. It was just Oliver. Hardly bearding a monster in his den. Just a partly wounded baseball player.

Or perhaps a very wounded one, she amended as she

pushed open the door to the living room and saw Oliver lying on the long leather sofa, staring up at the ceiling, his bandaged hand resting on his chest. His face, unguarded for a moment, looked almost . . . grief-stricken.

He looked up as she closed the door behind her, the sadness vanishing in an instant. "You're late."

"I didn't think we'd set a time," she said. "The traffic back was awful and I had to take the Castros to their hotel." Her tone was crankier than she intended. Maybe it had been the wrong decision. If he was upset about not playing this might not be the ideal moment.

"I'm not mad," he said as he sat up. "Just . . . impatient."

"Impatient is good," she said. Impatient for her, she could live with. If that was all there was behind it. She wasn't so sure it was.

"Are you happy about the win?" she asked.

He scrubbed his good hand over his face. "I'm happy for them. I'm less happy for me." Dark eyes studied her. "Is that want you want to hear?"

"Just seeing where we are."

"Where we are right now involves me wishing there could be less talking and more getting naked with you." One dark eyebrow arched at her. "I want you, Amelia. That's all that matters right now."

She bent down, eased her shoes off, trying to pretend her pulse wasn't pounding. "How much is this you wanting me versus you wanting a distraction?"

"You want a percentage?"

She shrugged. "Humor me."

"I met you before I needed a distraction, remember? If that night at the party had gone differently, then this moment would have arrived a lot faster."

"It's been one whole week. I think that's pretty fast. So . . . percentage?" She knew it was kind of dumb to ask. She doubted she was going to leave no matter what he said. At this stage, she wanted to know what sex with him would be like. To give herself that moment even if turned out to be a dumb decision. To let the beautiful man take her clothes off and make her come her brains out.

She might pay in the morning. She was willing to pay.

But it might be easier to know what the chances of paying were from the outset.

The silence stretched. She held her breath.

Then "Eighty twenty," he said. "Happy?"

"It's honest. So, yes. I can live with that."

"Honest is good. Come here, Amelia."

She walked slowly. There was something about her having him at her mercy that suddenly caught at her imagination. After all, it wasn't as though he could run away. He couldn't even run after her if she ran away. And she doubted he could sweep off her feet right now.

That was okay. She looked forward to the day the pirate side of him was let loose, but right now she was the one who got to do the plundering. She'd pulled her hair up roughly for the drive back from Staten Island but now she tugged at it and let it fall down.

"So how do you see this working?" she said. She waved at the sofa. "There isn't really that much room on your sofa."

She stopped moving when her knees touched his knees.

"We did okay the other night," he said.

"Yes, but that was just playing around."

"I'm good with playing around for a little while." His good hand reached out, caught her wrist, pulled her closer. She let herself be coaxed, hitching up her skirt so she could settle on his lap.

"So you like playing games?" she asked.

"That depends what you had in mind. I'm not in the mood for Words with Friends."

"Word games weren't what I had in mind."

She bent and kissed him, cradling his face in her hands. Sheer pleasure washed over her from the simple act of putting her mouth to his.

"Something simpler?" he said when she pulled back.

She nodded, words escaping her.

He laughed, and the sound was a low rumble of wicked in the darkness. "How about you show me yours and I'll show you mine?"

"I can do that." She peeled off her jacket and discarded it. Then studied him. He had a shirt on. Tricky to remove with one hand. So she should be helpful. She leaned closer again, started undoing the buttons, pushing back the cotton as she went, baring skin to her gaze. Very nice skin. Dusted with dark hair. Smooth. Hot.

"I see you know how to play this game," he said.

She tugged the shirt away from his jeans. "I'm getting the hang of it."

"You might have to play both sides." He held up his bandaged hand. "I'm not sure I can return the favor tonight."

"Oliver Shields, are you telling me you haven't mastered the art of undressing a woman one-handed?"

She leaned back, ran a finger down the line of buttons that held her shirt together. Flicked the top one open with her left hand. "See, easy." She arched her back a little, hoping he enjoyed the view. "You try."

Long fingers splayed across the vee of skin she'd already bared. She wondered if he could feel how fast her heart was beating.

His hand slid over the curve of her breast, thumb dragging over the peak of her nipple before his fingers grasped the next button and undid it with a quick twist of his fingers.

She laughed. "I think you've done that before."

"Maybe I'm just a fast learner." He undid another button, then another. Soon enough her shirt was open like his.

She'd worn her sexiest bra, a bit of deep-red silk-and-lace nothingness she'd bought in a fit of whimsy. Apparently whimsy was paying off. The look on Oliver's face as he took in the bra was heated.

She decided to take care of the buttons on the cuffs herself so she could get rid of her shirt altogether.

He made a noise of approval. And cupped her breast again. Which meant it was her turn to make incoherent noises as his fingers set to work. Maybe it was just as well the man didn't have two good hands right now. She might not have survived double the rush of sensation.

"Good?" he asked and she nodded, wordless again.

"Let's go for better than good," he said and this time it was his mouth on her, tongue dampening the lace so the fabric dragged over sensitive skin, the texture enough to make her squirm in his lap. She put her hands on his shoulders and braced herself so he could do what he wanted. Apparently he still felt impatient because in the next second he proved that he definitely knew how to take off a bra one-handed.

His mouth on bare flesh felt even better.

He played with her for a long time. Until she was breathless, pushing herself against him to try and ease the need.

"I think it might be time to relocate," he said.

It took a few seconds to get her brain to function. "Does relocation involve a bed?"

"A big one."

"Good plan." She wriggled off him. Then held out her hand. His fingers gripped hers and he stood.

"Do you need the stick?"

"I can manage. It's only about twenty feet down the hallway."

Twenty feet took longer than she thought. Because he kept stopping to kiss her. Long, drugging kisses. She would have been happy to stop where they were and let him take her on the floor, but the kisses were too good to interrupt him with suggestions. Eventually he pushed open a door and pulled her through into his bedroom.

Big room. Big bed. Huge. And high. Well, he was a tall guy. And a big bed just left more scope for . . . experimenting. She pushed him toward the bed. "Sit down. I want to unwrap you."

"Your wish is my command." He sat. Then stuck out his foot. "Better start with the boot if you want to get into my pants."

"You don't have to keep it on?"

"It's just a sprain. I might not be up to the more exotic parts of the Kama Sutra tonight, but we can lose the boot."

"I don't need the Kama Sutra." She undid straps and eased the boot off his foot. Then dispensed with his other shoe. She slid her hands up strong denim-clad thighs. Gripped his waistband.

"I don't need the Kama Sutra, either," Ollie said. "Just you. Come back here, Amelia."

That was an invitation she wasn't about to refuse. She stood. Shed her skirt and stockings. Time enough for more exotic games later. When Oliver was better. But now all she wanted was him. The touch and feel of him. Wanted it so badly, she had to clench her hands not to just throw herself on the bed next to him.

Oliver had lost his jeans and the shirt. The sight of him wearing only black boxer briefs and a smile was enough to make any woman lose her mind.

God. She'd forgotten this. Forgotten the glory of a supremely honed male body. Wall Street guys worked out and ran and did all the right things, but she'd never slept with a guy with a body like this.

Oliver was all long, powerful muscles. He looked lean in his clothes but she was realizing that was deceptive. Somehow his height had disguised the power in those thighs and arms. The strength under his skin. The fact that his body had been honed to perfection with sweat and work and skill.

All lying there waiting for her.

"I thought you were coming over here?" he said.

"I lost my train of thought," she said. "You shouldn't just spring that"—she waved her hand at him—"on a girl."

He laughed. "I could say the same about the underwear you're wearing. Come over here and let me appreciate it some more."

She shook her head. "Nope."

"No? You changing your mind here, Amelia?"

God no. "Oliver, wild horses aren't going to drag me from this bedroom. But I thought if I did this, it might make things easier." She shucked off her bra, then her underwear. Her fingers trembled as she pushed the silk down her legs. Unlike Oliver, her body wasn't perfect. She had curves. Wobbly bits.

But as she straightened, the look on his face made her worries disappear.

"God, your skin," he said. "I vote for you to always be naked in the moonlight."

The low thrum in his voice made it hard to breathe. "Might make it hard to get much done," she managed.

"Getting stuff done is overrated. Now please come here and let me touch you."

"What was it you said? Your wish is my command?"

She moved back to the bed. Oliver lifted his hips and pulled off his boxers. Then she was speechless all over again. He'd been impressive before. Fully naked he was kind of astonishing.

She crawled onto the bed as he moved backward and somehow they were kissing again and his hand skimmed over her hip, dipped between her legs. God. Yes.

She hooked her leg over his hip, pressing closer.

"Good?" he asked.

She nodded. Kissed him again. Good hands. The man had very good hands. Or hand. God. She couldn't think. It was all about the feel of his fingers sliding over her, teasing her. Making her mindless. Making her want.

"You feel good, Amelia," he said. "So good."

"You're not so bad yourself." She gasped as his fingers slid inside again, hitting just the right spot. "God. Do that again."

"What? This?" He repeated the motion and she moaned. "If you keep making that noise I'll do whatever you want."

"What I want is you," she said with an effort. His hand slid free.

"Whatever you want." He rolled away, came back with a condom. Held it out to her. "Not sure I can do this one-handed."

"I got it. Lie back." Now that she thought about it, there might be benefits to his injury. Like him letting her take the lead. She slid her hand over his cock, and he shuddered. So she did it again.

God. She loved the feel of him. Hot smooth skin over all that hardness. All that waiting for her. She dealt with the condom, and then swung her leg over his hips to straddle him.

His eyes locked onto hers. "Whatever you want," he repeated.

She bent so they could kiss again. She was never going to get tired of kissing him. But the feel of his hardness between her legs was irresistible and she straightened again. Lifted her hips and fitted herself over him. His hand gripped her hip fiercely and she froze, worried for a moment, but then he pushed into her, pulling her down at the same time, and any thought but the feel of him fled from her head.

She put her hands on his chest and moved with him. Rising and falling. So good. He was strong and hard and sure beneath her, his hand holding her hips, keeping her where he wanted her. Where she wanted to be. She'd thought it might be slow and sweet with him, that he might be cautious given his injuries, but he drove them faster and harder, no letting up, not letting her lose the building wave of pleasure rolling through her, not letting her move her eyes from his, falling into those dark eyes as she melted around his body and finally came, shouting his name.

Chapter Ten

She nestled against him, breathing in the smell of sex and fresh salt-sweat and Oliver. A tantalizing combination. Even now, boneless and sated, it made her want more.

"I think I just found my incentive to do all my hand therapy," he said, half laughing. "Because I want to make you feel as good as you just made me feel."

"Trust me, I feel pretty damned good." She felt the aftershocks of him in her body, satisfaction singing through her. There was maybe a little hunger still building there beneath the immediate post-orgasm glow, but she had no doubt they'd take care of that.

"Trust me, I'll make you feel even better with two hands."

"Promises, promises," she said. The shiver that ran through her may have made her teasing tone less believable.

"Satisfaction one hundred percent guaranteed."

"I'm going to hold you to that," she said. Her fingers traced circles on his chest, started to drift lower.

Oliver made a low noise. "Hold that thought just a few

more minutes." His arm tightened around her as he shifted on the bed.

She stopped her circling. "Do you feel all right? That didn't hurt your ankle or anything?"

"I'm fine. Just need a few minutes for recovery."

He had just had surgery a week ago. He was doing pretty damned well as far as she was concerned, and she was prepared to wait for her next fix.

"Okay then," she said. "So. Awkward post-sex small talk?"

"Why awkward?"

"I don't know. Isn't that what it's supposed to be?'

He laughed again, the sound vibrating through his chest. Then kissed the top of her head. "I don't feel awkward. Do you?"

She shook her head. "Weirdly, no."

"What's weird about it?"

"Well, we're kind of doing this backward," she said. "We haven't actually spent that much time together. We've probably spent more time playing Words with Friends than we have face-to-face."

"You want to do the getting-to-know-you thing? Now? Isn't that a little late?"

"Did you have something else planned?" she said. "You're not going to fall asleep on me, are you?'

"Not a chance," he said. "All right. Getting to know you it is. So, Ms. Graham what's your favorite ice cream flavor?"

"Chocolate chip cookie dough," she said promptly. "You?"

"Actually, lemon gelato."

"Gelato isn't the same thing."

"Okay. Then pistachio."

"Green, huh? I've never been convinced ice cream should be green."

"I'm quite fond of green," he said. "After all, it looks good on redheads." He laughed. "Now I kind of want to smear some on you."

She was definitely in favor of that plan. But not right this second. "Technically I'm a strawberry blonde," she said. "Indecisive hair."

"Gorgeous, not indecisive," he corrected. "Okay. Next question. Favorite movie."

"*Bull Durham*," she said without thinking.

His sudden shout of laughter almost deafened her. "Why, Amelia, don't tell me you're a secret baseball groupie."

"It's the Kevin Costner factor. And that speech he makes."

"The one about long slow wet kisses?"

"Yeah." She went silent for a moment, thinking of Oliver's kisses.

"I don't mind that one myself. But I'm not accepting your Costner explanation."

"You are entitled to your own delusions," she said. "What's your favorite movie?"

"*Almost Famous*."

She giggled. "By your theory that makes you a wannabe groupie."

"No, I think it's the rock-star thing."

"Like being the center of attention, do you?"

"Depends whose attention it is. Next question."

"Favorite food."

"New York cheesecake. Junior's."

"Hey, mine too."

"I take that as a good sign. Hmmm. Okay, how about, What would you do if money was no object?"

"That's easy. Travel. Jump on a plane and see the world."

"Really?"

She tilted her head back to look at him. "Yes. I've always wanted to travel. Ever since I was little. I always used to get library books about other places. And drove my mom up the wall making her watch all the National Geographic specials."

"Have you been to some of those places already?"

"No. We never had money for big holidays. And I was too busy keeping my scholarships at college."

"But you work on Wall Street. You haven't treated yourself to some exotic location vacations?"

"No. Not yet."

"Any particular reason?"

"I wanted to help my mom buy an apartment so she could retire. She finally bought one at the start of the year."

His arm tightened around her. "You're good people, Amelia."

"How about you? Have you gotten to go anywhere exciting?"

"Most of the fifty states. Canada. I did once go to Paris for a week."

"Paris." She sighed enviously. "Sounds wonderful."

"I liked the city," he said. "But it wasn't the greatest week of my life."

"Why not?"

"Turns out the girl I took with me was more interested in the clothes my credit card could buy her in all the designer stores than in the joys of Paris. Or me, I guess."

"Ugh."

"It's okay. I wasn't madly in love."

"Where else have you been?"

"I try to go somewhere warm in the off-season," he said. "I've been to Mexico a few times, the Bahamas. Hawaii. Fiji once. But honestly, I travel so much all season, it's nice just to stay home."

She could see how that might be. "Home is nice, too." Though right now, she was trying not to feel envious. Fiji. The Bahamas. She wanted sand under her toes and unfamiliar smells and tastes and sounds. Wanted to know how it felt being somewhere so different.

"Do you miss Chicago?" Oliver asked.

"I miss my mom. Em and the Castros, of course. But I love it here. I mean, if you're going to stay in one city for a while, then New York kind of has everything, right?"

"Yeah. I'm fond of it."

"Where did you grow up?"

"New Jersey," he said. "It was nice. I moved into the city when I got drafted by the Saints. No. That's a lie. I lived on Staten Island for a couple of years. But as soon as I turned twenty-one, I moved to Manhattan."

"You don't mind the commute back to Staten Island?"

"I like the ferry," he said. "The team has apartments where we can stay on days when we don't want to travel after training. And like I said, we're out on the road so much, most of the time my commute is jump on a bus from the hotel and go to a stadium. Then take another bus back to the airport."

"Your frequent flier miles must be pretty good. I have envy."

"Yeah, we rack up plenty of time in the air. It's not as glamorous as it sounds. Travel like that is a lot different from traveling for fun."

"Well, eventually you'll be able to put them all to good use."

"Let's hope not for a few more years." He lifted his bandaged hand, studied it for a moment.

"Your hand is going to be fine." She pressed her lips to his chest. Felt him shiver and then shift restlessly.

"I hope you're right," he said. "But in the meantime, how about you kiss me and make me feel better?"

She smiled at him, then turned and draped a leg over his hip. "I can do that."

It was way too early when her phone started chiming softly. Beside her Oliver stirred on the mattress, opening one eye.

"Someone calling?"

"My alarm. I have to go to work." She turned the alarm off, rolled back to him. "Go back to sleep. No reason for both of us to suffer."

"What time is it?"

"Five thirty?"

"Five thirty?" he groaned. "You're not a morning person, are you?"

"No. But I have to go home and change and then get to work." It was a while since she had done the sneaking-home-before-daylight thing. She should've planned better. But it would've been hard to cart an overnight bag to the Saints game last night without having to explain to the Castros what the hell she was doing with it. She kissed him fast, then climbed out of bed before she could change her mind and succumb to the temptation to stay right there with him.

Because Oliver's bed was definitely her new favorite place. "Go back to sleep," she said again as she picked her skirt and underwear up off the floor.

Cuddling the clothes to her chest, she slipped out of the room, heading for the living room and the rest of her stuff, intending to leave him in peace.

But as she was wriggling into her skirt, Oliver appeared in the doorway, hair sleep-tousled, stubble darkening his jaw. He'd pulled on a T-shirt and boxer briefs and the sight of him silhouetted in the light from the windows melted her resolve all over again.

Damn.

No. She had to go to work. She had a project to finish.

The lights clicked on and she blinked. Then she started giggling as she saw what was written on his shirt. "Kiss a Saint and go to heaven?" she said. "Really?"

He looked down at his T-shirt. "The Angels gave them to all the guys in the team last Christmas." He looked back up, waggled his eyebrows. "Wanna go to heaven?"

She shook her head, sat down on the nearest chair so she could pull on her shoes. "I'm pretty sure corrupting Saints doesn't get you into heaven."

"Depends on your definition of heaven," he said. "I, for one, am all for corruption. Of the naked kind." His voice was still low and sleepy. Made for tangled sheets and sex.

Just as well she was sitting down. "Well, your fall from grace is going to have to wait a bit longer. Some of us have to go out and earn a living." She remembered their sleepy conversation earlier. She'd never wished more fervently that money truly was no object. Because then she could ignore the world outside this apartment and drag Oliver back to bed.

But sadly, there were bills. And projects. And demanding bosses.

"You won't even let me make you coffee?" he asked. "What are you, some sort of love-'em-and-leave-'em femme fatale?"

"Not fatal. But today, yes to leaving," She stood. Checked her purse. Phone. Wallet. Keys. Both hers and the one he'd given her. "But I'm not leaving forever." She paused. "Are you going to go to Boston for the last game?"

He shrugged. "I hadn't decided. I'll see what Lucas thinks. I'm meant to start hand therapy this week. You're not going?"

She shook her head. "Too hard to get back for work. Why can't all baseball be in New York?"

"If we get through this game, the championship series will be. The Yankees cleaned up the Twins."

"Convenient." It would be if the Saints actually managed to take out this final game to win the series. Though then coming up against the Yankees who'd dominated all season had to be a daunting prospect.

"I think so. It would be nice not to travel six months of the year every year."

Did he really mean that? And what happened if he did travel half the year? How did that work in a relationship? Some of her post-sex glow of happiness dimmed. She needed time to think. To process. Without him being there, fogging her brain with that body and those kisses. "I really have to go."

"Not even a kiss good-bye?"

Oh so tempting. But she had a fairly good idea about what would happen if she walked over there and let him touch her again. "I kissed you before I got out of bed. That is just going to have to tide you over until tonight."

"Ms. Graham, there's someone in reception asking for you."

"There is?" Amelia frowned at the voice coming from her speakerphone. She didn't get visitors at work. It was five p.m. The Castros should be safely in Boston by now, if not already at Fenway Park itself.

"Yes. A man. Said his name was Mr. Oliver."

Amelia nearly dropped the phone. The receptionist sounded calm. So either she wasn't a baseball fan or she hadn't yet realized who Oliver was. In other words, no time to waste if she didn't want the Pullman grapevine to be full of the news that she was dating a baseball player in about five minutes. "Okay, I'll be right down." Her pulse started to race as she hung up the phone and grabbed her security pass. Oliver was here? She doubted anyone else using 'Mr. Oliver' as an alias would be looking for her and she didn't know anyone whose actual last name was Oliver. Other than John Oliver, the comedian. Unlikely that he'd suddenly decided to look up an economist he'd never met.

A rummage through her purse resulted in hastily applied lip gloss and a spritz of perfume.

Oliver here.

She hadn't expected that. But she wasn't going to find out what he wanted standing in her office. She practically jogged to reception.

In the pale wood and gleaming glass lobby, Oliver stood out. He wore a suit jacket and dark jeans, metal-framed sunglasses hiding his eyes. He looked much as you might have thought a pirate would standing in the middle of a ballroom. Dark. Sexy. Unmissable. Not even the walking stick and sling could ruin that. In fact, it might have enhanced the effect.

Elsa and Reiko who staffed the reception desk were looking at him much the way a hormonal woman might stare at a big box of cupcakes. It was clear they thought he was edible. But had they figured out who he was yet?

Amelia nodded to them as she passed them, trying to walk as though it were nothing new for her to be meeting a mysterious hot guy at work.

"Hello," she said, taking his arm as she reached him. "What are you doing here?" She tried to steer him back toward the elevator, but she might as well have tried to move one of the granite sculptures that sat in the downstairs lobby.

Oliver smiled as she tugged on his arm. He didn't re-move his glasses. She wasn't sure they did all that much to hide his identity. The back of her neck was tingling. Reiko and Elsa were watching them, she knew it. Watching would lead to speculating unless she got rid of him.

"I decided to go to Boston," he said. "I thought you might want to come."

"Oliver, it's five already. It will take four hours to drive to Boston. Maybe more."

"Who said anything about driving?"

"Flying isn't going to be that much faster."

"It is if you have a helicopter."

She blinked. "You're going by helicopter? Isn't that expensive?"

"Less when you know someone who owns a helicop-ter charter."

"Right. Lucas's wife. She's a pilot." After a day of try-ing to decipher IT-speak and wade through data, any career but economist sounded good. "Isn't she in Boston already?"

"Yes. But she's not the only pilot in the firm. So. What do you say? We can be at the heliport in fifteen minutes."

She couldn't remember the last time she'd left work so early. If ever. The mental list of everything she still needed to do today was long. Very long. But this was the final game in the series. A big moment for Finn. One she would love to witness.

Oliver Shields wanted to fly her to Boston in a heli-copter so she could see Finn play. It would be downright rude to say no to anyone making that offer. Coming from Oliver it was irresistible.

"I think this is what you call an offer that I can't re-fuse," she said. "I need to grab my stuff from my office. Go wait downstairs. You kind of stick out here."

"You worried about the office grapevine?"

She gave him a little push. "Just go. I'll be five minutes. Maybe ten." She needed to make sure there wasn't anything urgent she had left undone. Sneaking off early once wasn't going to be an issue—she hoped—if she'd crossed her *t*'s and dotted her *i*'s for the day.

Oliver turned and she didn't wait to watch him go. Instead she made a beeline for her office, ignoring the girls in reception as they turned in their chairs to watch her.

It didn't take long to gather up all her stuff. Then she sat to give her email one final scan. There was a reply from the project team on one of her queries, and she forwarded it to the IT guys. Then she skimmed through the other four emails that had popped up since she'd gone to see who was in reception. Two internal memos. One calendar invite for a staff meeting that she accepted without reading. The last email was unexpected. A message from Leon Tang, who worked in the Hong Kong office. She'd pinged him earlier in the day to see if he'd heard anything about any transfer positions opening up but hadn't expected a reply so quickly.

Nothing concrete. But rumors of a big project floating around. So far anyone who might know anything is very tight-lipped. Will keep an ear out.

Well. That wasn't what she'd hoped for. She typed a quick thank-you. Rumors. Nothing concrete. But a suggestion that maybe Daniel wasn't just randomly dropping by her office.

As though just thinking his name could summon him, she looked up to see Daniel standing in her doorway.

"Was that Oliver Shields in reception?"

How the hell did he know that? She hadn't seen Daniel when she'd been talking to Oliver. Then again, she'd been facing the outer doors. He could have walked past behind her. Damn. "Um, yes," she said.

"I thought he'd be in Boston." He lifted his eyebrows at her.

She blinked. "I thought you didn't follow baseball?"

"Hard to miss at the moment with two New York teams in the—what do you call them?"

"The divisional series," she said.

"Yes. That's it. We had a leadership team meeting this morning and it seemed to be a topic of interest. So was it Shields? He's the one who got injured, isn't he?"

"Yes."

"A friend?"

"Yes. I told you I knew someone who played for the Saints?"

Daniel nodded.

"Well, I've met other players because of that."

"That still doesn't explain why he isn't in Boston."

"He's headed there now. He came to see if I wanted a lift. He knew I was working today and couldn't get to Boston to see Finn—that's my friend—play."

Cool gray eyes studied her. She couldn't help feeling that she was facing a test. One she was fairly sure had a right answer. But that right answer involved staying here tonight and working late. Which she wasn't going to do unless Daniel flat-out ordered her to. "What did you tell him?"

Now or never. She took a deep breath. Daniel was just her boss. Not a monster. "I told him, 'Yes, please.'" She hit the mouse to close down her email, stood, and then nodded at her purse at the desk. "So I really need to get going. Unless there was something urgent you needed?"

For a moment she thought he was going to say yes. To assert authority, or to mess with her, or because he did actually have something urgent for her to do. But as she held her breath, he stepped back from the door. "Sounds like a good offer. Never wise to pass one of those up."

What the hell did that mean? She had no idea and no time to try and figure it out. "I agree," she said. "I'll see you tomorrow morning." There. At least he knew that she wasn't planning on playing hooky for more than one night. But she wasn't sure what he thought as she walked past him to leave. She was, however, sure that she could feel the weight of his gaze all the way down the corridor as she headed to reception and Boston.

Oliver watched Amelia staring down at the darkening scenery beneath them and shifted in his seat, trying to ease his ankle. The delighted smile on her face was worth the pain. And the pilot—Deena—was keeping things smooth, which was keeping the discomfort to a minimum. But climbing into the helicopter had been harder than he'd expected. With only one arm to pull himself up and in, he'd had to put more weight than he'd anticipated on his bad ankle. It had hurt. And now it was sending angry twinges up his calf every time the chopper's movement jostled it too hard. Getting out was likely to be even crappier. But he was going to grit his teeth and bear the pain. And the lecture he was going to get from Lucas if he found out how they'd gotten to Boston. Maybe he should have used a different charter firm.

But Charles Air was reliable and, thankfully, had had an available chopper at short notice.

So he was going to the game.

Going to see if his team could win their way through to the championship series. Without him.

It was still a hard pill to swallow.

But swallow it he would. He still had a bone to pick with Castro but for now, he didn't want to rock the boat. And he definitely didn't want to upset Amelia. Amelia who was the one good thing to come out of this whole screwed-up situation. Amelia who'd given herself without hesitation last night and made him feel good in a way he wasn't sure he'd ever felt before.

Amelia who wasn't afraid to lay her cards on the table. Or to play all-out once she had.

Amelia who tasted like heaven.

He twitched his injured hand irritably. He'd never resented the bandage more than he had last night when he could have been touching her with both hands. Using just one had been a new kind of torture as well as an exercise in logistics. But it had worked. He'd gotten to watch her face as she'd come while he was buried deep inside her.

Now he was getting to see her smile as he took her to see her baby brother. He was starting to realize that even though she called Finn a de facto little brother, the reality was that the Castros truly were part of her family. That had been clear from the way she'd lit up when they were around. He'd watched them at the two games at Deacon Field, she and Finn's parents and Finn's sister, watching the game, cheering wildly as a unit, sharing little reassuring looks and touches during the tense moments.

If it hadn't been clear from Amelia's red hair that she wasn't related to the three dark-haired Castros—four if you counted Finn—then it would have been easy to conclude that Em was Amelia's sister rather than her best friend.

She'd said her dad had left. That her mom had gotten sick. Clearly the Castros had stepped in to fill the gap. But he knew he still didn't have the full story. She sounded proud of her mom when she talked about her, but there was worry there, too. Things obviously hadn't been easy.

Despite that, Amelia's mom—damn, he needed to find out her name—had clearly done a good job. Amelia had obviously had an excellent education and been bright enough to win scholarships to college, but he wondered how much time with her daughter—and maybe her own health—her mother had had to sacrifice.

Family issues. He knew about those. His own family was mercifully close—too close sometimes—but he'd watched Maggie and her dad over the years. They'd been a unit, but Tom Jameson had been an overly busy dad. He sometimes wondered if Maggie had developed her love of baseball as a defense mechanism, a little girl's instinct for how to get some time with Daddy honed to a sharp focus. He didn't doubt she loved the game now— but would she have been so baseball-crazy if her mom hadn't died? Or if Tom had remarried while Maggie was young enough to benefit?

Not that it mattered now. He shook himself and looked out the window. He could see the glow of skyscrapers in the distance; they were closing in on Boston itself. Not much longer.

His stomach rolled suddenly.

God. What if they won?

Or what if they lost?

He didn't know which would be worse.

Watching the Saints play the last few days had been hard. But knowing they were out of the running to go any further would be bad, too.

They'd worked bloody hard all year. Dan Ellis had worked them liked dogs in spring training and hadn't let up during the season. Oliver had been in the best shape of his life before the accident. Confident that he'd play for years yet.

Now he wasn't playing at all. Didn't know if he would ever play again.

The wound in his hand ached and itched, which was a combination he could do without. He couldn't scratch it. Couldn't risk popping stitches or doing something else that might affect his recovery. He had his first appointment with the hand therapist on Wednesday, and the thought of that made him almost as nervous as the thought of Fenway Park and the game that was about to happen.

Not that he could do a damn thing about how either event worked out. He could cheer his team tonight and he could do his therapy and everything the doctors told him to do, and everything could still go to hell.

Amelia had asked him what he wanted to do after baseball. He hadn't been lying when he'd said he had no idea.

Ex-players became coaches or scouts or media personalities or invested their money in businesses completely unrelated to sports.

None of those options sounded appealing.

Who was he without baseball?

Judging by the last week, someone who was easily bored. Amelia was saving his sanity, that much he knew.

He turned back to her.

"We're almost there," he said over the headset. "Have you been to Boston before?"

"Once," she said. "I've never been to Fenway, though. The timing never worked out this year when you guys were playing there."

"It's a very cool place." He loved the older parks. Deacon wasn't in the league of Fenway or Wrigley Field—it had had an ugly refurbishment in the seventies that had taken the charm out of it. It had a past, the Saints had been around a long time, but there was something about stepping onto the field at one of the truly iconic ballparks. A feeling of the history of all the guys who'd stood where he was standing. Hearing the crowd roar and smelling the unique grass-dirt-sweat-hot-dog-people-age smell of baseball. Knowing that you were about to go into battle with your closest friends. All for the love of a bat and a ball.

Crazy.

Much like flying here tonight was. Or the way he felt about the woman flying with him. But honestly, if that was crazy, then he was just going to be crazy. And hope it might carry him through.

Chapter Eleven

Because they missed the start of the game and because she had no idea where she was going at Fenway Park, she stuck close to Oliver as they made their way through the last of the stragglers arriving at the box that had been assigned to the Saints' owners and their guests.

When she reached the outer door, she hesitated.

"You want to go in alone?' Oliver said.

"Is that weird?" she said. "Finn's parents will be here."

He shrugged. "It's up to you."

"It might be better."

"How are you going to explain how you got here?" he asked.

"I was kind of hoping they'd be too distracted by the game. But I can say I got a last-minute flight. Tell them I was on standby or something so I didn't want to get their hopes up."

"That works," he said. He glanced around the corridor then bent to kiss her.

"It won't work if you keep doing that," she said somewhat breathlessly when he stopped.

"Tempting," he said. "But I believe there's a ball game

on. So you go on and I'll wait out here a couple of minutes."

"Maybe you should go first. After all, it's your team."

"We've only missed twenty minutes. And according
to the wisdom of Google and ESPN, nothing drastic has
happened yet. Go on in. If you can't find me after the
game, get a cab to the heliport. I'll meet you there."

"Don't go without me."

"Wouldn't dream of it," he said, then opened the door
for her.

She tried to duck into the box discreetly but even as
she scanned the crowd from the back of the room, she
saw Maggie Winters's dark head twist toward her, saw
her smile a welcome, touch Alex's arm, and whisper
something in his ear before leaving her seat and coming
over to say hi.

"Amelia. Hello," Maggie said. "Finn didn't tell me you
were coming."

"I wasn't sure if I could make it," Amelia said. "Last-
minute standby came through. So I thought I'd take my
chances up here."

"I'm sure we can squeeze you in," Maggie said.
"Mr. and Mrs. Castro are sitting down front. I'm not sure
there's a spare seat next to them at the moment. Maybe
during one of the breaks." She craned her neck, peering
around the room. "Ah, look. Perfect. There's a chair next
to Raina and Sara."

Before Amelia could protest, Maggie was steering her
over to sit with the other two owners' wives. Sara, whom
Amelia had spoken to a couple of times now, smiled at
her. And Raina, after Maggie made a soft-voiced introduc-
tion, grinned too. She was tiny, but her shock of vivid red
hair suggested she wasn't a shrinking violet. Her lipstick matched her hair. As did the soles of her very nice
black boots.

Louboutins. Damn. Apparently marrying a baseball team owner came with good shoe perks.

"Welcome to the madhouse," Raina said when Amelia had seated herself.

If it was a madhouse, it was a very tense one. Everyone—apart from Sara and Raina—seemed to be gazing down at the field as though sheer force of will could manufacture a win.

"Don't call it that," Sara said. "You'll scare Amelia off."

"Well, it is a madhouse," Raina protested. "I run a nightclub. I know crazy when I see it. The tension's so thick in here, you'd need a chain saw to hack through it."

"They're allowed to be nervous. This is a big deal," Sara said. She turned to Amelia. "She doesn't like to tell anyone but Raina's a Yankees fan at heart."

"You don't go for the Saints?" Amelia said.

Raina shrugged. "Sure, as long as they're not playing my Yankees. Though I might have to pretend if the Saints win tonight. I'm not sure Mal's nerves will see the funny side of his wife barracking for the opposition in a championship series." She nodded at the big dark-haired man who sat next to Alex. "As it is I was tempted to slip Valium into his coffee earlier."

Sara giggled. "I found other ways to distract Lucas."

The two of them grinned at each other. "At least baseball season is almost over," Sara said. "Then we get to see them a bit more."

Raina rolled her eyes. "You hope." She leaned into Amelia. "If you think being a Yankees fan is bad, then Sara will shock you. She barely knew a home run from a foul ball when she met Lucas." She eyed Amelia a moment. "Wait, who's your team?"

"Well, the Saints now that Finn is playing for them," Amelia said loyally.

"Sure," Raina said. "But who was it before then?"

Amelia grimaced apologetically. "I grew up in Chicago."

"Oh God," Raina said. "Tell me you at least have the sense to support the White Sox."

"Um, go Cubs?" Amelia managed.

Raina patted her arm sympathetically. "Ouch. That's almost as bad as being a Saints fan. No one will hold that against you. Mock you mercilessly, maybe, but not hold it against you." She grinned again and picked up the glass by her hand. She took a sip then glanced up at the nearest TV screen. "God, I hate watching games from up here."

"She'd rather be down on the field with her cheerleaders," Sara said.

"Dance troupe," Raina corrected. "And no, actually I just like being down in the bleachers. But that isn't the done thing." She wrinkled her nose. "You lose all the atmosphere up here."

"It seems pretty nice to me," Amelia said as a suit-clad waiter appeared and offered her a tray with a glass of champagne.

"The booze is better, can't argue with that." Raina said. Then she turned and smiled over Amelia's shoulder. "Oh look. Oliver's here."

"He is?" Sara twisted. "When did he get here?"

Raina's green eyes moved back to Amelia's face. "You can ask him later," she said. "No reason any of us would know." One perfectly groomed eyebrow arched slightly at Amelia. She willed herself not to blush.

Damn it. She and Oliver had been playing it very cool. But had Maggie jumped to a conclusion about them? Worse, had she shared her suspicions with Raina and Sara?

"If he came in a chopper, Lucas is going to be upset,"

Sara said. "Not the easiest things to climb into with a bad ankle and one hand. He can't afford another injury."

Amelia almost winced, avoiding it only with an effort. She didn't turn to look at Oliver like Raina and Sara were, pretending instead to be fascinated by the action on the TV screen. Here at the very back of the box, it offered a better view than the glass at the front.

"I'm sure Oliver can take care of himself," Raina said, "He's a smart guy. Knows what he wants."

Amelia ignored that comment. Which she was pretty sure was directed at her. Fortunately before Raina could dig any deeper, there was a roar from the crowd and all three of them turned back to see what was happening on the screen. Which showed a Red Sox player scooting around second base and sprinting for third. The camera flashed on Finn's scowling face for a second before switching to the Saints' outfield, scrambling for the ball. But by the time they got it together, the Sox batter was home.

"Fuck," Raina said savagely. She leaned forward. "C'mon, guys."

"Not quite as unconcerned as she pretends," Sara said. But she, too, had suddenly focused on the game. Amelia looked and saw Eddie and Mari holding hands as they stared out at the field. Mari's knuckles were white. Amelia pictured Finn's face—full of fury—again and winced.

"C'mon, little brother," she said under her breath. "Do not mess this up."

By the end of the sixth inning, Oliver was starting to wish that he hadn't taken such a strong stance against narcotics. Because a painkiller or two might dull the pain of watching this game. The Saints were fighting hard but they were starting to crack. Finn had already fumbled a couple of easy catches, letting Sox players slide to safety under his nose. He wasn't the only one screwing up, but his mistakes were the hardest to watch. Because it should be Oliver himself out there, stopping those Sox bastards in their tracks not letting them score runs. Helping his team goddamned win.

His left hand curled into a fist and he forced himself to relax it for what had to be the twentieth time since he'd arrived. Between ignoring Amelia and wishing he could ignore the game itself, he was starting to wish he could drink something stronger than the soda he was sticking to.

Surely one drink couldn't hurt? He wasn't taking anything that shouldn't be mixed with alcohol anymore. Everyone else in the goddamned room had a drink in their hands. Even Amelia, who'd moved from sitting next to Raina and Sara—which had made him distinctly nervous, because every time he'd dared to casually glance in that direction he'd found himself staring into Raina's amused green eyes.

Amused Raina never boded well.

He'd just about decided to grab the next waiter who passed when he noticed Alex and Lucas making their way through the crowd to the back of the box. Mal was two steps behind them.

All three of them were stony-faced. Alex stopped when he reached Oliver.

"Problem?" Ollie asked.

"Can we talk to you outside?"

"Sure." Half the people in the room were looking at the four of them with various degrees of concern on their faces. Wondering if there was more bad news about to unfold. Better to take whatever this was outside. He waved the three of them ahead of him and then followed at his slower pace, ankle throbbing.

When he closed the door to the box and turned to face them, Lucas was looking at him with his doctor face on.

Damn it. He'd been hoping to avoid Lucas.

"Ankle bothering you?" Lucas asked.

"No more than it has been," Oliver lied.

"Sara told me you chartered a chopper. Not your smartest choice for transportation right now."

Damn. Ratted out. He should have figured Sara would tell Lucas. But he'd assumed she was safe in Boston already when he'd made his last-minute booking and wouldn't find out until after the game. "I think you have bigger things to worry about just now than my injuries."

Lucas scowled. "If you weren't injured then you'd be out there and I might have less to worry about."

Oliver bristled. "Thanks for the reminder. Can I remind you that I'm not actually the one who screwed up my hand? That it's actually the guy who's down there on the field currently forgetting how to catch a damned baseball at first base who caused all this?"

Alex held up a hand. "I think the Hummer driver also had something to do with it."

"I was only in the path of the fucking Hummer driver because of Castro." Oliver stopped. Paused. Took a breath. "Sorry."

"I'd be pissed off in your position, too," Alex said, tugging at the Saints tie around his neck. "So rant all you want. But right now I need you to suck it up and do me a favor."

This wasn't going to be good. "What?"

"Dan called up. Wants to know if you'll talk to Finn. Give him the lowdown on some of the Red Sox players. Tell him—"

"How to do his fucking job? Alex, Castro is the last guy in the world who wants my advice. He's not going to want to listen to me."

"Then he's going to have to suck it up, too," Alex said calmly.

"You really think that me talking to him is going to steady his head?"

"It had better. Otherwise we'll have to bench him."

"You won't hear an argument from me." Maybe that was unfair of him, but Castro hadn't done anything to earn his loyalty. "Pull him. Put Leeroy on first."

"Leeroy's nursing a bruised finger. We need him to get some runs on the board right now, so no, not risking him at first base. Finn needs to get it together," Lucas said.

"Finn can hit."

"Yeah, but he's a better first baseman," Mal said.

"Not today he isn't," Ollie pointed out.

"Which is why we need to try this. If this wasn't Castro, you'd be happy to help, right?" Mal said.

Oliver swore under his breath. "Right. And I'm willing to help now. I just don't think it's going to have the effect you think it will."

Alex shrugged. "He can't get much worse if you piss him off. So if Dan thinks it's worth a try, then it's worth a try."

This was for his team, Oliver reminded himself. For the Saints, not Castro. Even if it annoyed the crap out of him. "Fine. As long as whatever happens is on your head," he said to Alex. "Get Dan to put a headset on the kid and I'll talk to him."

A buzz of voices ran through the box when Oliver and the terrible trio—as Raina had called them earlier—came back inside at the start of the next inning. Amelia risked a glance over her shoulder. Oliver looked grim, and the expressions on the faces of Alex, Lucas, and Mal weren't much happier.

But Oliver's face softened slightly when she caught his eye. She flashed him a quick smile before turning back to the windows. The Red Sox players had taken their positions around the field. Amelia's stomach tightened. The Saints were currently four runs down. They needed to get things moving if they were going to have any hope of working their way back to victory.

She wanted them to win. For Finn. For everyone else in the room.

But sitting here watching was torture.

It would be easier if she could hold Oliver's hand, but no. That wasn't going to happen. She gritted her teeth and settled in to watch.

For a time, it seemed like the Saints were recovering. They narrowed the gap to two runs before the second half of the seventh. But when Finn fumbled an early catch and let the batter get by him, everything fell apart.

By the time "Sweet Caroline" boomed over the PA system just before the bottom of the eighth, it was clear that the Sox had the game sewn up. The mood in the box turned somber. The start of the ninth inning was like a funeral.

Unable to watch, Amelia excused herself and headed to the ladies' room. When she found it deserted she used the temporary solitude to text Oliver.

Sorry. Are you okay?

The reply pinged back faster than she expected. *Yes.*

Really?

It's our best result since I started playing.

Doesn't mean you can't feel crappy right now.

I'll be fine once we get out of here.

She winced. If it wasn't for her wanting to keep things on the down-low, she could be standing next to him. *Sorry.*

You can make it up to me later.

That made her grin. He couldn't be too pissed if he was thinking about sex. Or could he? Men were strange creatures sometimes.

Can't wait. She hit SEND and put her phone away.

She'd probably dragged out her absence as long as possible. Time to go back in and commiserate. God. She had no idea what to say to Finn. He wasn't going to take this well. Not that it was his fault. He wasn't the only Saints player who'd made mistakes tonight. But she knew Finn. He'd blame himself.

When the game—and the torture of knowing what was coming—finally ended, Amelia sat with the Castros for a few minutes. The three Saints owners, Maggie, and Oliver had all vanished down to the locker rooms, leaving Raina and Sara to deal with the guests in the box. Eddie Castro refused the offer of another drink, seemingly lost in thought as he stared out the window of the box, watching the crowd start to disperse. Or at least, the Saints fans were leaving. The Red Sox fans were going nuts.

"Are you going back to New York tonight?" Mari asked Amelia, obviously desperate to talk about anything other than the game.

"Yes. I have to work tomorrow." Daniel hadn't seemed too upset with the fact she'd taken off for Boston but she didn't think his tolerance would continue if she failed to show up to work in the morning.

"You work too hard," Mari said.

"Says the woman who still refuses to retire," Amelia said.

"Teaching English to adults isn't the same thing," Mari said. "Three days a week and I'm home by four."

"I know," Amelia said. "But they don't let economists go home by four. At least not on Wall Street."

"You should teach," Mari said. "Become a professor or something."

Amelia wrinkled her nose. "I've thought about it. Maybe one day. But academia is hardly a secure job. I'd need a PhD, too."

"*Mija*, nowhere is a secure job anymore. There's more to life than money. It worries me seeing you and Em working so hard. No men. No children."

"We're hardly on the shelf. People have kids later these days." It was an old argument. "Don't worry, I'm sure Em and Finn will provide you with plenty of beautiful grandbabies eventually."

"Hmmph. I don't want to be too old to enjoy them. Besides, your mom deserves beautiful grandbabies, too."

"Right now, I think she's just enjoying not working," Amelia said.

"You're a good girl," Mari said. "But you don't know how a mom feels about these things."

"Well, I'd need a husband before I got to the babies part." She'd seen what being a single mom was like. She'd made up her mind a long time ago that if she ever had kids, it wouldn't be alone.

"New York is full of men. Look where you are. Surrounded by men. Men who earn good money. And who look good in tight pants."

That made her laugh. Which earned her a dirty look from one of the guys standing near them in the box. But she was not about to chat about the possible benefits of dating a baseball player with Mari. She'd screw up and let something slip and then where would things be? Luckily she was saved from any further conversation in this direction by Sara, who came over to tell them that friends and family could go down and see the team now.

"Do you have time to come and see Finn?" Mari said. "What time is your flight?"

"I have time," Amelia said, avoiding the question. She gathered her things and the Castros'. Eddie was still very quiet. God. What was she going to say to Finn? *Better luck next time*? Seemed a bit harsh even if it was highly likely that Finn was going to get another chance to play in a divisional series. He was still young.

Unlike Oliver. Who might not get another shot if his hand didn't heal.

Well, him at least she could make feel better. Once they were safely away from Fenway.

But first, Finn.

By the time they reached the locker rooms, weaving their way through what seemed like hundreds of people—including press and photographers—her stomach was in knots all over again.

"Let's wait a few minutes," Amelia said. "Just until things get a bit less crazy."

Eddie looked at the crowds and nodded, and they moved back to stand against the wall. After a minute or so, Maggie emerged from the locker room and began directing the press away. It was surprising how much less crowded the corridor felt without a gaggle of cameras and people wielding microphones on poles.

As she came back, Maggie caught Amelia's eye and mouthed something she thought might be *five minutes* before disappearing back inside.

Sara, who'd come hurrying down the corridor shortly before Maggie reappeared, looked apologetic. "Sorry, they must have decided to keep the guys together a little bit longer. I'm sure it won't be long."

"It's not a problem," Amelia said. She glanced at her watch. It was after eleven. Ollie had said to meet at the heliport. Presumably the chopper would wait for them but she wanted to get away. It was going to be late by the time they got back to Manhattan. She couldn't see Oliver anywhere outside the locker rooms. He must still be inside with the team, right?

Surely he would have texted if he'd actually left Fenway?

He wouldn't leave her stranded in Boston. That was ridiculous. She shoved the thought away, trying to focus on being calm.

"Sorry, this is one of the annoying parts," Sara said. "It's not usually this bad after a game. It's just because it's the—"

"Division series. I know," Amelia said.

They weren't the only families waiting to talk to players. There were quite a few women standing nearby, some glamorous and alone, some glamorous and with kids. Plus a few older men, women, and couples who were obviously parents like the Castros. Their stoic expressions made it obvious that they were feeling just as bad about the loss.

No one talked much. Everyone watched the locker room door.

Which finally opened.

The first person who Amelia bumped into—literally—when she walked into the room, trying to see Finn, was Oliver. He caught her with his left hand, steadying her. She stared up at him, trying to see if there were any clues to how he was feeling on his face.

But if he was upset, he was giving nothing away. Though maybe the lack of his usual welcoming smile was proof enough. "Sorry," she managed.

"It's okay," he said.

"Amelia? Are you going to introduce us?" Mari said, stepping up beside them. She gave Oliver an unsubtle once-over then turned to Amelia, curiosity clear in her eyes.

"Um, this is Oliver Shields. He's one of the Saints players," Amelia said. "Oliver, this is Mari Castro, Finn's *mom*. And that's Eddie, his dad, behind her."

"What position do you—" Mari broke off, clearly

noticing the sling for the first time. "Oh, you're injured? What happened?"

Amelia froze. Oh God. Finn hadn't told his parents who had been in the accident with him?

"Just a bit of a sprain," Oliver said. "You must be proud of Finn. He played well tonight."

She'd never wanted to kiss him so much in her life. He'd have had every right to tell Mari exactly how he'd been injured. But no, not this man. She smiled at him, trying to keep her expression to polite rather than enchanted.

"Did you hit your head when you hurt your hand? No one played well tonight," Eddie muttered. "But it's nice of you to say so." He looked past Oliver, clearly still searching for Finn.

"How do you know Milly, Oliver?" Mari said, nudging her husband with an elbow.

"We met briefly at a party the other week," Oliver said.

Yikes, the conversation was definitely straying back into dangerous territory.

She tried desperately to think of something to say to change the subject. But her brain had gone blank. Until Finn appeared behind Oliver, face like thunder. "There's Finn," she said, feeling like an idiot.

Oliver turned. "Castro," he said pleasantly.

"Shields." Finn's reply was curt. "Always showing up, aren't you?"

"It's my team, too," Oliver said. His tone was mild but Amelia could see the chill building in his eyes.

"Finn, we were looking for you," Amelia said, putting her hand on Mari's arm. "I don't have much time before I have to get back to New York."

Finn's expression darkened at that, shoulders hunching. "I thought you weren't coming. How did you get here?"

"Flew," she said. "All the way to Boston to see you play. I—I'm sorry, you lost."

"You don't say," Finn snapped.

"Finn!" Mari said. "Be nice. You can be upset about the game but don't be rude to Milly. It's not her fault."

Finn spun on his heel and walked away and for a moment Amelia forgot how to breathe. Like he'd slapped her or something. But no. Mari was right. This was not her fault and he could take it out on someone else.

"Maybe I should just go," she said, not looking at Mari. "It might be better if it's just the two of you."

"Ignore him, *mija*," Eddie said. "But yes, you get going. Don't miss your flight. Finn will be all right."

She didn't know if she believed him, but she wasn't going to argue. She could try again with Finn when he had calmed down. So time for an exit. She kissed Mari and Eddie and sent one last look at Oliver before heading for the door.

Chapter Twelve

Oliver was quiet all the way back to New York. He answered if she spoke to him. Distractedly. Mind obviously back in Boston. After the first few attempts to draw him out, she decided to leave him alone with his thoughts and just watched the glittering lights and dark patches between towns slip by under their flight path, trying not to think about Finn.

About him snarling and then walking away like that.

Like she was to blame.

Which was ridiculous. He needed to learn how to cope with losing better.

She chewed her lip. Maybe she should have come clean about Oliver. Let Finn be mad straightaway. Instead of adding to his frustrations.

But no. Finn's moods were his responsibility. Not hers.

Hopefully he'd be fine after a day or so to get the shock of the loss out of his system. He had his parents there. He didn't need her as well.

She'd call him tomorrow. Maybe. Or wait until Wednesday. Let him calm down. Send him a good-luck text before his photo shoot.

The flight was uneventful and as they stepped out of the heliport and into a waiting town car, she decided she could get used to helicopters. Much less hassle than airports.

To her surprise, Oliver gave the driver her address.

"You don't want to go to your place?" she asked.

He shook his head. "You have to be at work in the morning. This will get you a bit more sleep. I've already stolen half your night."

That was true. She was tired, both from a long day and the slow coming-down from the adrenaline before the game. But she wasn't ready to sleep just yet. Not until she knew he really was okay. "Will you stay with me?"

That brought a smile to his face. "Nothing I'd like more."

She wrapped her hand around his, rested her head on his shoulder, and they sat in silence for the rest of the journey. She was halfway to falling asleep when the car came to a stop. Oliver nudged her and she shook herself awake, wondering how they'd gotten through the city so fast. Then realized it was nearly two a.m.

"Bedtime," Oliver said gently and slid out of the car before helping her. "Which way?" he asked as the car drove away.

Right. He hadn't actually been to her apartment yet. That woke her up. For one thing, she had vague memories of failing to do anything sensible like make her bed or buy groceries in the last week or so.

Well, screw it. He was going to have to take it or leave it.

When they reached her apartment, she tried to scan the living room discreetly.

"Do you want me to stand here with my eyes shut while you run around and tidy up?" He grinned at her.

Busted. "Are you saying you think my apartment is a mess?" she asked, mock-indignant. Well, mostly mock.

"It looks fine to me. But I did kind of spring this on you. And you girls can be weird about that stuff."

"Says the guy with a housekeeper."

"Guilty," he said. "I hate cleaning. Lila stops me from living in squalor. Or starving."

She sighed, envious. "I need a Lila." Then she frowned up at him. "Are you saying you don't know how to cook?"

He looked around the room. "I can cook. And I can run a washing machine and a vacuum cleaner. It's easier not to during the season. Saves time. Besides which, I can afford not to. But if this is your idea of a mess then I'm not so sure about you needing a cleaner."

"Maybe not. But it would be nice. Now, are you hungry? Thirsty? Sleepy?"

He eyed her, and that grin reappeared. "Not sleepy."

She could feel her brain melting as he watched her. Honestly, the man should come with a health warning. "We could play Words with Friends."

He shook his head. "Not in the mood for that right now."

"I don't think I own any other games," she said, trying not to grin back at him.

"I had a different sort of activity in mind."

"Is that so?"

"Yes. I think you'll like it," he said, wiggling his eyebrows. "It starts with ladies' choice."

Her choice? Was it suddenly hot in her apartment? She glanced down at his foot and then at his hand. "Ladies' choice?" That brought all sorts of idea to mind. "Are you allowed to get that wet?" she asked.

"My hand?"

"Yes?"

He nodded. "The splint is plastic and the bandage comes off. The dressing is waterproof. So if you can re-bandage me, then yes, it can handle a little water."

"In that case, I don't know about you, but I'm feeling a little grimy after all that travel. Want to scrub my back?"

"That's a yes," he said. He glanced around as he started to lift the strap of the sling over his head. "Where's the bathroom?"

"This way." She stepped out of her shoes and led the way. The bathroom had its very own radiator, so it wasn't cold. Not that it was possible for her to feel cold with Oliver looking at her the way he currently was.

She shrugged out of her jacket and turned on the shower. Her apartment wasn't anywhere as big as Oliver's but the bathroom was big enough for two people and the shower wasn't over the bath. It should be easy enough for Oliver to step into.

Fingers moving down her shirt, she opened the buttons and let it join the jacket on the floor.

"Amelia, you're spoiling all my fun."

"Oh, you'll get your fun," she said, smiling as she shimmied out of her skirt then her stockings. At least she'd worn a decent bra and underwear under her suit. Not her sexiest but lacy and pretty. Judging by Oliver's expression he approved. But he stayed where he was, half resting against the vanity just watching her. She lit the candles she had in the little niche in the tile at the end of her bath, straightened as the flames flared to life and then flicked off the light switch.

The candles gave just enough light. Enough to stop either of them from killing themselves in the darkness, but not enough to ruin the intimacy wrapping around them.

Oliver sucked in a breath as she turned back to him, and her pulse started to pound.

He was very still. Only the movement of his chest up and down with each breath showed him to be a real live man rather than a figment of her overheated imagination.

She still wasn't used to the fact that she could do this. Could walk over there and touch him. Take off his clothes. Put her hands on his body. That he wanted her to. It was dizzying and she was glad of the candlelight, hoping it hid the flush on her face. Oliver's skin had turned a deeper golden shade in the light, almost the color of the palest part of a flame itself.

Tempting her to move to the light.

Tempting her to embrace the heat.

Tempting her to burn.

She was so giving in to temptation.

She moved in, stopping when she was just out of reach. Gave herself another moment to take him in. Then she looked up at him and smiled.

"Amelia?" he said, the sound more breath than voice.

"Sssh. Ladies' choice, remember? Stand there and let me do what I want."

"Oh, I'm not moving. Not even if the building catches on fire."

She moved closer, put her palm flat on his chest. Felt how warm the cotton of his shirt was, heated by his skin underneath. Felt the vibration of his heartbeat beneath her touch. A little too fast. She did that to him.

Her.

Plain old Amelia Graham.

She made Oliver Shields's heart race.

The knowledge made her own heart race, blood rushing through her like hot wine, making her dizzy. Making her want. She wanted to put her hands on him. More than her hands.

His buttons were faster to open than hers had been. And she knew how his cuff links worked. Sliding the shirt off him had to go a little more slowly because of his right hand, but it still didn't take long.

Naked from the waist up, he looked even more like a fantasy. Like every ridiculous male-model pose come to life. Only on him it wasn't ridiculous. On him, it was delicious.

Tantalizing.

Appetizing.

He hadn't worn a belt and hell, she didn't need him fully undressed for this part anyway.

She let her hands slide down his chest, down his abdomen, tracing the muscles like the contours of a map. Resting them for a moment on the vee of muscle that arrowed down from each hip like a signpost. She had no idea what that muscle was called, but it had always been one of her favorite parts of male anatomy.

Part of the temptation of the jocks she'd been attracted to but never let herself date.

If that made her shallow, then screw it. Tonight she was going to be shallow. Tonight she would have her way with him. Hopefully he would return the favor.

Her hands drifted to the button at his waistband. His muscles tensed beneath her hand, but apart from that she wasn't sure he was moving. If he was breathing.

Until she flicked open the button and dragged her fingers down the hard length of cock imprisoned by his straining boxer briefs. That drew a groan from him that made her toes curl.

The sound was need, pure and simple. Male and raw. Hungry. For her.

"So impatient," she said. And repeated the movement. The second noise torn from his lips made the heat bloom so quickly between her own legs that she forgot about teasing him and just yanked the trousers down off his hips before shoving his briefs down to free him.

His erection sprang free. Hard. Eager.

Well, she was pretty eager, too.

She sank to her knees.

Oliver's breath was a rasp. She stared up at him, saw the wild black of his eyes burning down at her, then closed her hand around him and bent her head to taste him.

He was hot against her tongue. Hot and male, the first taste of him, only making her want more.

She pressed her thighs together, but that only intensified the ache.

So she focused on him. On the slide of his skin under her tongue. On the subtle curves and hollows of him. On learning the sensitive places that made him shiver when she licked or sucked or blew.

His hand came down in her hair, tangling in it, urging her closer. She didn't need the urging. She loved doing this. Loved having him in her power.

Loved the sounds and the shudders that ran through him and the way he grew harder and hotter against her lips with each passing second.

It had to almost hurt to be that hard, that ready. The way it almost hurt now that she wasn't lying with him inside her, easing the ache between her legs. Her nipples were rock-hard, the slight friction from the silk of her bra almost unbearable.

She didn't know how much longer she could take it, let alone him. But she wanted to make him come this way. Wanted to make him come apart. She added her hands to the game, one hand holding him to take the rest of him into her mouth, the other gripping his butt to make sure he stayed where she wanted. He arched into her, the movement rough now, but she didn't care.

Just kept going. Took the thrusts as deep as she could and urged him on until finally he shouted her name and she tasted salt as he came hard.

When his grip in her hair eased and he slumped back against the vanity, she rose, reached past him, and filled the glass she used for brushing her teeth with water.

"Amelia, you really need to warn a guy before you do that," he said.

She tilted her head. "You asking for a time-out?" She took a quick gulp of water.

His eyes narrowed. "No," he growled. "It's my turn." He held out his right hand, and she knew what he was asking. She tried to be careful as she removed the splint and unwound the bandage but her hands were shaking, the longing scorching her skin now that he was focused on her again.

The dressing on his hand crossed the width of his palm but hid the exact extent of his injury from her view.

Still, it was odd seeing both his hands free. She pressed a kiss to his fingertips then bent to loosen the walking boot and his shoe so he could step out of his pants.

"A little water won't hurt that," he said as she put her hand to the bandage on his ankle. "And it's my turn now."

"I thought anticipation was a good thing?" She slipped off her bra. Stripped out of her underwear. Took a little extra time with it just to see his expression go even more intent.

"Only within reasonable limits. And you blew past my reasonable limits when you put your mouth on me." He moved to the shower, turned the water on. Waited for it to warm then crooked his finger. "Ladies first."

"I thought it was ladies' choice?" But she wasn't a masochist so she went into the shower willingly, stepped through the cascading water—thankful for the excellent water pressure as always—and turned, moving back until her spine hit the tiles so there was room for him to follow her into the heat and steam.

"Are you sure shower sex is a good idea?" she said. "Slippery. Hard to balance."

In reply, he just grinned. Then unhooked the handheld shower attachment from its clip. "Oh, I think we can manage," he said. "I'm inventive."

She looked at the showerhead, gulped. She had, on occasion, gotten inventive with the showerhead herself. It had made her think fondly of whichever past inhabitant of the apartment had installed the sybaritic device. It made a nice change from fingers or her favorite vibrator. It got the job done but it had never made her knees wobble at the sight of it before. Oliver's fingers wrapped around the chrome, however, made her lose her breath. She braced a hand against the tile, unsure whether she was going to be able to stay upright. And here she'd thought that he was the one who needed to be cautious. Oliver moved closer then flicked the lever on the shower that changed it from the overhead stream to the handheld one.

"Like I said, my turn now." He kissed her then, doing nothing more with the water than letting it play over both of them while he took her mouth. Fierce kisses. Nothing gentle or cautious about them. Kisses designed for one thing. To make her hotter and wetter and needier than she already was.

He didn't touch her with his injured hand, which meant, with his good hand holding the shower, that he didn't touch her at all. And oh, she wanted to be touched. She arched herself against him, wanting friction. Wanting skin on skin. The hair on his chest scraped against her nipples. Good. Very good but not yet enough.

"Please," she said, writhing harder. "I want—"

He stepped back and she felt the spray change to a heavier stream of water. It moved across her body, making her flesh pulse and tingle everywhere it hit, as though it was his hand sliding across her. She closed her eyes, rested her head against the tile, sure the heat was going to consume her.

The water moved lower. "Open," he said.

She didn't think he meant her eyes. She wasn't sure she could have opened her eyes if she'd tried. But her body knew what it wanted and she moved her thighs farther apart.

"If only you could see how good you look right now," he said. "God, Amelia—"

"Please," she interrupted. "I need to come. Please."

He groaned and kissed her again. And then the water hit her between her legs. The hot rush of pressure against her clit made light pinwheels across her closed eyelids and she heard herself gasping. The pressure didn't move, didn't relent, didn't let her get away from the pleasure that rushed to answer it. Not even when she started to arch and tremble as the orgasm exploded through her. Oliver swallowed her cry of pleasure with his mouth. Moved the water away, let her tangle her arms around his neck to hold herself upright as the aftershocks moved through her, made her boneless.

When she finally lifted her head and blinked up at him, smiling like she was drunk, he grinned. "Very good, Amelia," he said. "Now, how do you feel about an encore?"

When they made it back to the bed, Oliver pulled her close to his chest and she snuggled up gratefully, the combination of a very long day and several mind-blowing orgasms making her very, very sleepy. The shower had chased away the tired ache of a long day but replaced it with a desire to melt into a happy puddle of oblivion for a while. She didn't want to think about the way-too-few hours between now and when her alarm was set to shriek.

There wasn't going to be enough coffee in the world to make tomorrow pleasant. She might as well enjoy this moment of pleasure while she could.

"Finn didn't look happy to see you talking to me," Oliver said, out of the blue.

She craned her neck back. "You know he's not a fan of yours."

"That feeling is mutual. Particularly after the way he talked to you tonight."

"He was pissed off about losing."

"I'm pissed off about losing," Oliver said. "I'm not taking it out on you."

Well, not in the same way as Finn had. If bathroom sex was Oliver's way of distracting himself, then she was on board.

"It's not quite the same, though, is it?" she asked. "I mean, tell me if I'm being dumb, but you didn't play tonight."

He stiffened underneath her. "Don't take this the wrong way, but that is dumb. I've played for the Saints for fifteen years. It doesn't matter if I'm on the field or not. They're like my—"

"Family?" she said softly.

"I guess," he said. "I mean, I have a great family of my own. I love them all to death but I never quite fit in with them."

What? She'd seen the pictures. He hadn't looked like the outsider kid in any of them. Her confusion must have shown on her face because Oliver shook his head.

"I don't mean they don't love me," he said. "Or that they were anything less than supportive. But people in my family are lawyers and doctors and engineers and business barons. Everyone is big on brains and using your mind to make a success of life. Whereas me, well, I fell in love with baseball the first time I picked up a ball and threw it. I need to move. Need to play. Need to use my body. I'm not stupid, I had early acceptance to colleges when Tom Jameson recruited me. But the thought of being cooped up at a desk all day . . . well, that's not me."

"You're an athlete," she said. She ran a hand down his chest, feeling the ridges of muscle that proved her words true. His body was finely tuned. Hard-earned. "I can understand that."

"Yeah, well, I'm not sure my family ever has. They love me and they're proud of me but I'm pretty sure there's a part of my mom and dad just counting down the days until I retire and get a real job."

"Even after all this time?"

He shrugged, which felt distinctly weird from her current position. "Families are strange. But it's okay. Because the Saints are my family, too. They understand the part of me that my own family doesn't. Understand what it means to love baseball. They get me." He hesitated. "Is that how it is with the Castros for you?"

She turned in his arms, propping herself up. "What do you mean?"

"You're obviously close. You told me what they did for you and your mom. And your mom isn't here tonight."

"My mom hates to fly," Amelia said. "I offered her a train ticket but I think she thought the series was going to be over quickly and it wasn't worth the time. She's not really into sports. She's never had much spare time, so she always made sure she did stuff she enjoyed when she wasn't doing stuff with me."

"She worked a lot?"

Amelia nodded. "It was just her. It probably would have made more sense for her to leave Chicago, move back to her hometown—she's from a little place down in southern Illinois. It would have been cheaper, for one thing."

"So why didn't she?"

"I never asked. If I had to guess, I'd say it was part stubbornness, part embarrassment that her marriage had failed. She always said the schools were better in Chicago. I'm not sure she fit in herself back home. She married my dad while she was still in college. Dropped out." *Because she was knocked up with me.* She didn't say that part.

"Tough woman to bring you up on her own," he said. "I'm glad you had the Castros."

"Me too."

His arm tightened around her. "We're going to have to tell Finn sooner or later, you know. Unless you're planning on just using me for sex for a few weeks and then breaking my heart."

She sucked in a breath. Breaking his heart? His tone was light, but something about his face made her think he'd just admitted something. Something maybe he didn't quite realize himself yet. "Not planning to, no," she said. "So yes, we can tell Finn. But maybe let's give him a few more days."

"You know, you don't have to tiptoe around his feelings. He's a big boy. I'm sure he can handle it. Eventually. And if he doesn't, screw it. You don't owe him your happiness."

She hesitated. "Maybe not. But his sister is my best friend. If there's a way to do this with minimal fallout, then I'd like to try that way first."

He tilted his head. "Why do I get the feeling you're not telling me everything? Finn was a flat-out dick to you tonight and yet you're cutting him slack. I have to confess, I really don't get it. You seem to spend a lot of time worrying about his feelings but does he worry about yours? What's Finn ever done for you?"

"He saved my mom's life," she said, the words tumbling out before she could stop them.

Oliver's eyes widened. "What?"

"He saved her life. My mom's cancer, well, it was bad. She had a lumpectomy at first. Chemo. They thought it was all fine. But then it came back. This time she had a double mastectomy. More chemo. It knocked her around. She seemed to be getting better. But about a year later, she was tired all the time, not feeling well. They thought the cancer was back but it was aplastic anemia—that's a blood thing where your body stops making enough new blood cells. In her case because of all the chemo. It did a number on her immune system. Lots of people recover from it but she wasn't getting any better, no matter what they tried. So they decided she needed a bone marrow transplant. We all got tested—Finn was too young so he couldn't, but no one was a match. She was on the registry for a donor but no match. The day Finn turned eighteen, he went to her doctor and got tested. And he was a match. So he donated. Missed a couple of his high school championship games to do it and everyone tried to talk him out of it because of that. But he insisted. And it worked. Finn saved her, Ollie. I can't ever repay that."

Oliver didn't say anything. He just watched her, an expression that wasn't quite a frown drawing his brows together. The silence started to make her nervous. "Say something."

His frown deepened. "I'm not sure what to say."

"Why? Because you can't imagine Finn being a good guy?"

"Maybe. He doesn't exactly play the white knight around me. But no, that's not it."

"Then what?"

"Not sure I know how to say it . . . I understand you must feel grateful to him—that's a hell of a thing Finn did—and I know the Castros have done a lot for you.

But have you ever thought that maybe you don't have to repay it? That they don't expect it. Or at the very least, you don't have to let gratitude outweigh the fact that you deserve to be happy. And treated well."

"The Castros treat me well."

"We're talking about Finn."

"Finn does, too," she said stubbornly. "Tonight wasn't a normal situation."

"If he keeps playing ball, at least in the majors, then being under this much stress will be normal. Are you going to let him get away with it if he keeps behaving this way?"

She bit her lip. "No." She sounded certain. But she couldn't help thinking that Ollie was right. That maybe she and the Castros had been cutting Finn too much slack for years. "No, I'm not going to let him get away with it. But right now, I don't see that adding fuel to the fire—right when he's dealing with losing a big game— is going to do any good. So can't we keep this between us just for a little while longer?" She put a hand on his cheek. "Please?"

He didn't look completely happy about the idea, but he nodded. "Okay. You have more to lose out of this than I do right now. So I'm willing to let you try things your way. But have you thought about what happens when we tell him. What if he really throws a fit? Whose side will the Castros take? Or Em?"

"They'll be okay," she said stubbornly. "We're family."

"I know," he said. "But sometimes, that kind of family, the found kind, sometimes you have to outgrow them."

"Are you going to outgrow the Saints?" she shot back.

He tensed. "I guess I might have to. When I retire. Depends what I decide I want to do."

"What do you want to do?" Maybe it was chicken to change the subject back to him, but she didn't want to think about Finn and the Castros. About what life might be like without her second family. About maybe losing Em. Because she wasn't going to let that happen.

Another shrug. "Still working on figuring that out."

Her eyes narrowed. "That's different from what you said last time I asked," she said. "Are you thinking about it? Retiring? Did the doctor say something about your hand?"

"Semantics, Amelia. No, the doctor hasn't said anything about my hand. In either direction. Which means I have thought about the subject occasionally this last week." His mouth went flat. "Not that I have any answers."

"You'll figure something out. You could always start by going back to school if you wanted. Try out some classes. See what catches your interest."

"Sweetheart, I think when I retire the first thing I will want to do is enjoy the novelty of doing nothing for a while. And staying in one place all year instead of less than half of it."

She couldn't really picture him doing nothing for very long. It was obvious that being out of action was already driving him a little bit crazy. "I'd travel," she said. "If I could do anything I wanted."

He nodded. Then yawned. "I think we had this discussion already, didn't we?" He peered over her shoulder. "Christ, it's after three. You should sleep."

"At this point I'm not sure that three hours of sleep is going to be any better than none."

His expression turned speculative. "Oh? Really? In that case, what exactly did you plan for the next three hours, Ms. Graham?"

"I was just going to count sheep," she said, batting her

eyelashes at him, fatigue vanishing as she watched the heat filling his eyes. "Unless you have a better idea."

He dragged her hand down from his chest. Placed it over his rapidly hardening cock. "You know what, I suddenly have several."

Chapter Thirteen

All things considered, she should be feeling much worse than she was. Sure, she was on her third cup of coffee for the morning, and she knew that she'd pay for the lack of sleep eventually. Still, she wasn't dragging her ass through the day like she usually would if she'd scored less than three hours of sleep.

No, instead she couldn't stop herself from grinning stupidly every five seconds. Apparently starting the day with shower sex with Oliver Shields did wonders for a girl's powers of recuperation. In which case, she was just going to have to keep having it. Think of all the things she could get done if she could get by on just a few hours of sleep a night, buoyed up by the powers of orgasms and completely satisfied hormones. She could damned well conquer the world.

The thought, crazy as it was, made her smile again. She finished her coffee and pitched the empty take-out cup toward the trash can in the corner of the room. It arced perfectly through the air, landing neatly with a gentle thud.

"And the crowd goes wild," she said loudly and then

forced herself to turn her attention back to the stack of work waiting for her.

Every so often as she worked, her attention strayed to her phone. She moved it out of reach on the farthest corner of her desk where she wouldn't be tempted to pick it up every five seconds to see if Oliver had texted her.

But it wasn't only Oliver she was thinking of. She'd had a very quick call from Mari just after she'd gotten to work. She'd wanted to ask about Finn but Mari hadn't let her get a word in edgewise as she launched a rapid-stream *Thank you and we're at the airport already and about to board and do you want me to take a message to your mother?*

She'd laughed and told Mari to give her mom a hug and take one for herself at the same time. But after she'd hung up, she'd wondered whether Mari was just being her usual live-life-at-sixty-miles-a-minute self or whether she hadn't wanted to give Amelia the chance to raise the subject of Finn.

No. She'd said she'd give him a day or so to cool off. And that she wasn't going to let him treat her like crap. So she should just stop worrying about him. She would call Em later, see what she'd heard from her parents, who would be back in Chicago by lunchtime. Knowing Mari, she'd be insisting Em come for dinner so she could be given the play-by-play of Finn's game. If she called after dinner, then she had the best chance of getting a report on Finn's mood.

At least there hadn't been any mention of Saints players in the papers today for any reason other than not making it to the championship series. The New York papers always seemed to favor the Yankees and Mets over the Saints—maybe because the Yankees and Mets didn't have the same less-than-stellar performance history that the Saints had had until Alex Winters and his friends had taken over. Today there was a certain degree of satisfaction that it was the Yankees who were going to take on Boston for a berth in the World Series.

Or so she'd gathered from the few minutes she'd spent trying to read the news on her phone and navigate Manhattan streets as she'd walked to work. She could've caught a cab but she'd been hoping that the walk would help wake her up.

So, no, leave Finn to himself. Unless he called her first. He should call her first. After all, he was the one who'd behaved badly.

Thinking about it killed some of her buzz. Her energy level started to fall and she looked at the trash can. She absolutely couldn't have another coffee until she had lunch or she'd dissolve her stomach. Plus probably turn herself into a jittery mess.

She had things to do. No jittering allowed.

There was, however, no rule against chocolate and she had an emergency stash of See's Candies in her desk drawer.

She pulled out the box and ate three in rapid succession. The sugar hitting her bloodstream perked her up and she turned her mind back to her email.

She was reading the latest status report from the IT guys about her model when the email notification pinged again.

The sender was Leon Tang. From Hong Kong.

Her heart started to thump. She fumbled the mouse and accidentally opened the wrong email in her eagerness. By the time she'd gotten to the right message, she was so nervous she had to read the short note twice to understand it.

Boss just said big new project being announced next week. Maybe Monday. Maybe Tuesday, Leon had written.

The word seems to be an acquisition. They've been sniffing around a few smaller banks here. Will keep you posted.

She sat back in her chair, heart still racing. An acquisition of another Hong Kong bank would definitely require some extra bodies on the ground in the Hong Kong office. The question was whether one of those people would be an economist.

And if Daniel would pick her to be that economist.

God. For a moment she let herself imagine it. The sprawl of Hong Kong, as she'd seen it on TV and in movies. So much life and bustle crowded into one small space. So very different from everything she knew. She saw herself standing in the middle of it. Living in another country.

Living her dream. A goofy grin spread over her face just at the thought.

And then she remembered Oliver.

It was late again when she got to Oliver's apartment that night—though not as late as usual. She'd made it to seven p.m. but then left, worried she might actually fall asleep in her office if she didn't. Daniel had left early for a client dinner with two of the other VPs. That meant he wasn't coming back.

She could have gone home, of course. Gone home and slept for eight or more undisturbed hours, but she wanted to see Oliver. Even though now, as she stepped out of the elevator, she was feeling unaccountably nervous. Leon hadn't heard anything more when she'd emailed him near the end of the day. So there was no need to tell Oliver anything yet, was there? That she might be leaving? At least for six months or so? She didn't even know if there was a project or if she might have a shot at a transfer.

No point causing trouble until she had to. Not when

they were both tired and he was still dealing with the Saints losing.

She'd tell him when she knew something.

Then they could figure out what it might mean.

After all, they'd been together less than two weeks. They weren't even public yet. If Oliver didn't want her to go, could she give up her dream for something so new? Should she even contemplate that possibility when she'd spent five years working for this?

She didn't know.

That made her nervous. Her stomach had been churning all day.

She let herself in and put her bags down in the hall, along with her coat, before heading into the living room where she could hear the sound of the TV.

Oliver had his foot propped up on the ottoman, an ice pack weighing down his ankle, a frown on his face as he stared at the TV. He looked up as she came through the doorway. "It's nearly eight," he said, sounding cranky.

"Which means I left work early. So why don't we try this again. Hi, Oliver, how was your day?" She paused, waited to see how he was going to respond. She spent enough time around masters of the universe to know that letting them get away with the shit they tried to pull was never a good idea. But she'd also learned that some of them didn't take kindly to being called on their shit. If he was that type, then he was going to find himself out of luck tonight. She was too tired. She could just go home again.

But to her relief, he smiled. "Hi, Amelia. How was your day in the towers of capitalism?"

"Full of long meetings and too much coffee. How about you?"

"You know, woke up. Hobbled to the couch. Did some

excitingly painful physical therapy. Hobbled back to the couch. A thrill a minute."

She nodded at the shiny black-and-silver exercise bike that was standing a few feet away from his sofa. "That's new. That must be a good sign, if they're letting you use a bike?"

"Not just yet. Another day or two. Even then I get to do a whole ten minutes a day." His scowl reappeared. "Ten minutes!" He sounded disgusted.

"Ten minutes is better than no minutes."

His fingers were tapping out a restless beat on the thigh of his sweatpants. Really loose, ratty faded gray sweatpants that had one leg chopped off above the knee shouldn't be hot.

But they were. He was. God. She was in trouble.

"Ten minutes sucks," he said.

Being limited to ten minutes of exercise a day sounded pretty good to her. Though she wasn't getting much exercise that wasn't walking to and from work lately. Too many late nights and early mornings. Her yoga teacher was going to give her the frowny face when she made it back to class.

"Do you want me to get you more ice?" she asked.

"No, I'm almost done." He fiddled with the ice pack then sat back. "The good news is I've been given the okay to lose the boot. Just have to keep the ankle strapped for another week and keep resting and icing it."

"Really?" He'd been limping by the end of yesterday. But she wasn't a physical therapist so maybe that was normal.

"Yes, really."

"That's great." She flopped down on the couch next to him, almost groaning with relief that the day was done and she could relax.

"Tired?"

"A little."

"Me too," he confessed.

She smiled at him. Then noticed that the bandage on his hand looked different, more of his fingers poking out. "Did your physical therapist change that?" She nodded toward the hand.

"I did two lots of excitingly painful physical therapy today. One with the physical therapist and then I went to the hand therapist."

"Different person?"

"Apparently it's a specialized field."

She waited but he didn't offer any further comment. Curiosity, however, got the better of her. "What did they say?"

He looked down at his hand, lips compressing briefly. "They said there's a long way to go."

"Well, that's something, isn't it? Sounds like they think you'll be fine."

He shrugged. "Good would be, *You'll be good as new in four months, Mr. Shields.*" He looked cranky again.

"I'm sure they were just being cautious. Doctors never want to give you the best-case scenario. Bodies aren't an exact science after all."

His expression didn't change.

"Did the therapist give you exercises to do?"

"Yes. I've done them. Following doctor's orders like a good patient. Not that moving a rubber ball with my fingertips is what I call exercise."

He sounded frustrated. She'd cabbed it uptown to Ollie's apartment. The most exercise she'd gotten today was walking between meetings or ducking downstairs to grab a coffee from the nearest cart, and she was fine with that. But Oliver was an athlete. Used to working out. To being able to do whatever he wanted with his body. To being in motion. He was probably one of those annoying people who got a runner's high.

Amelia put in her time at the gym and yoga but she'd never felt much more than sweaty and relieved it was over at the end of a session. She relied on chocolate for her endorphins. Still, if Oliver was missing his workouts, that could explain part of his bad mood.

"You're just cranky because you've got endorphin withdrawal or something," she said.

He looked skeptical. "Endorphin withdrawal?"

"You're used to exercising. Working off tension and stress physically. We just need to figure out another way for you to deal with stress until you can do that again."

Dark eyebrows shot skyward. "Are you about to tell me to take up meditation?"

"No," she said. "But you need something to make you happy."

"Interesting theory, Amelia. And now that I think of it, I know something that would produce plenty of endorphins." A wicked grin spread across his face, and heat rushed into hers.

"I—" she began.

"You brought up the subject," he said before she could come up with something. "You said I needed endorphins."

"I'm not a doctor," she said, feeling herself start to smile, tiredness once again evaporating under the mystical powers of Oliver Shields. Maybe she was the one hooked on endorphins. The ones he provided.

"No, but you might be just what he ordered," Oliver said. "How about it, Amelia? Want to make me feel good?"

"Yes, I do," she said cheerfully and climbed into his lap.

On Friday, Oliver had another appointment to see his surgeon. Hopefully to get the stitches removed. They were itching like fury, which was annoying as hell, particularly when there was no way he was going to scratch and risk screwing something up.

His ankle was almost better. He was hardly limping. It was still sore, but he could walk and fit his foot back into a shoe. He used the stick when he went out of the apartment but got around inside without it. And he'd already defied doctor's orders to do almost thirty minutes on the exercise bike yesterday. It had made his ankle ache, even at the snail's pace that was all that he was allowed, but the movement had felt good and ice had taken care of the ache.

Maybe Amelia was right. Maybe he was an endorphin addict.

Well, there were worse things to be hooked on.

He was sitting in the waiting room, scrolling through his phone with his left hand, which still felt weird, when Lucas and Alex walked into the reception area.

His gut tightened. Why were they here? Had Dr. Banks called them here to be with him? Was he going to get bad news?

He'd had a second session of hand therapy the day before and had received the same noncommittal response when he'd asked about his prospects. But that was what the hand therapist had said to him. Who knows what she'd said to George Banks.

"Isn't two of you overkill for just getting some stitches out?" he said as Alex and Lucas joined him on the two chairs next to his.

"I'm just here to make sure it all goes smoothly," Lucas said.

That much he could expect. He wasn't actually that surprised to see Lucas, who'd been gate-crashing his appointments all along. But Alex? He turned to Winters, trying to decipher if there was any tension in the man's eyes. "What's your excuse?"

"Just protecting my investment."

"Dude, I'm not a stock portfolio."

"No, but you're damned expensive," Alex said. "So I wanted to hear what your doctors have to say.

"So you can figure out if you need a new first baseman?"

Alex shook his head. "You're still our first baseman."

"If I can play." He said the words that were left unspoken at the end of Alex's sentence.

"No reason to think you can't." Alex leaned back in the chair, crossed his legs. As usual he wore dark jeans and a sports jacket over a white shirt. A contrast with Lucas in his hand-tailored navy suit. But the two of them were a team. Friends for years. So he didn't think he'd get any help from Lucas in convincing Alex that he didn't need to be here. "Mal isn't going to suddenly appear, is he?" he asked grumpily.

"Mal isn't much on medical stuff," Lucas said. "I think he saw too much of it in the army. So, no. You're safe."

That, at least, was something. Though the look on George Banks's face when the three of them trooped into the consulting room was almost comical.

"Am I being graded?" Banks asked drily, directing his comment at Lucas.

"No. I'm just interested," Lucas said. "And Alex is paying the bills."

For a moment Oliver had a spark of hope that Banks was going to kick Alex out, but the doctor just shrugged good-naturedly and turned his attention to Oliver.

"How's the hand?"

"Sore. The stitches itch like a son of a bitch."

"That's normal. How's the hand therapy?"

Oliver was sure Banks must know exactly what was happening in his therapy sessions. "So far, so good."

"Any pain after doing the exercises?"

"Some."

"One to ten?"

"Six."

Banks studied him a moment. Then nodded. "All right." He pulled a wheeled table out from the wall, rolled it over to Oliver, draped it with a green cloth, and pulled out scissors, tweezers, some sort of antiseptic wash, and gauze. "Let's get those stitches out."

Oliver took off his splint. It was still a little awkward using his left hand but he'd gotten the hang of it. George took the bandage off then made him put his hand on the table to peel back the waterproof dressing. Without the splint, his fingers curled up. He resisted the urge to straighten them. For one thing he didn't want to discover that he couldn't. And for another, he wasn't meant to be doing anything that flexed his palm too much.

When the dressing came off, the row of stitches was the same ugly black mess it had been the last time his dressing had been changed. The skin underneath was red and angry looking. The line of stitches snaked across his palm from the top of his thumb joint to the base of his little finger.

The cut—as far as anyone had been able to guess, he'd somehow sliced his hand on metal or glass as his car had flipped—had been deep. As Banks touched the flesh gently with his gloved hands, Oliver tried not to flinch. The skin was tender. He tried to imagine the smack of a baseball hitting it right now, or the impact of a bat swung against a pitch. Just the thought made him vaguely queasy.

He set his teeth. Six months. He had six months. Or four and a half or so until the start of spring training. A lot could happen in six months. His hand would be fine.

Lucas leaned in and peered at his hand, too. "Nice work," he said to Banks.

"That's what you paid me for," Banks said and then set to work clipping and tugging the stitches free. It didn't take too long. After they were all out and Oliver's hand had been washed, the yellow of the antiseptic matched the bruising on his palm nicely, Banks made him do some of the tests the hand therapist had already been doing. He could flex his fingers a bit and wriggle them up and down but couldn't get anywhere close to straightening them fully.

Banks made notes and then poked and prodded some more. Some of it hurt but some of it Oliver couldn't feel. There seemed to be an area around the base of his thumb that had lost sensation. Banks made another note but didn't say anything more. Then he taped up the wound.

"No point letting you pull the scar open. You can wear the splint for another month unless you're doing your therapy. After that we'll see. Probably at night, for a bit longer than that. The risk is you overextending the tendons while they're healing and snapping or tearing one again." He looked sternly at Oliver. "You are not to attempt to pick up a baseball. Or a bat. Understood?"

Oliver nodded. He wasn't going to risk fucking up his hand any more than it already was. "Am I going to get the range of motion back?"

"I'm sorry, it's still too early to say. The motion you have now is a good sign. But full healing will take six months. Like I said before, we'll have a better idea a few months down the track. Do your therapy. That's the key. Whatever they tell you to do, no matter how strange it seems, just do it. I'll send them my notes from today. Come back in a week to get the taping redone—one of the nurses can do that so Mr. Winters here doesn't have to worry about my bill—and then see me a week after that and I'll assess how the scar is healing again."

"Maybe I'll start telling people I fought off a ninja," Oliver said, staring down at the fresh dressing on his hand.

Alex laughed beside him. "Yup. That sounds good. You'll have the girls swooning to look after your battle scars. That should keep you occupied."

Oliver didn't respond to that. He didn't want girls swooning. Or rather, he only wanted one girl. Amelia.

He looked forward to her arrival every night after she finished working with an eagerness that was almost disturbing in his intensity. She made him relax. Made him laugh. But also called him on his bullshit when he was cranky.

He just wished she would call Castro on his. Apparently the guy still hadn't spoken to her since the incident in the locker room. As much as she insisted that she was fine, he could see that Finn freezing her out was gnawing at her. See that she wasn't 100 percent happy no matter how brilliant her smile or how eager she was in bed.

Fucking Castro. Someone needed to show the guy how to be a man. Amelia was a good person. A fucking great one. She didn't deserve to be taken for granted by people she thought of as family. But she wouldn't appreciate him getting in Finn's face. So he didn't know how to fix the situation for her. Which pissed him off.

"Are you coming to the party tomorrow night?" Alex asked as they left the office.

Oliver nodded. Maggie had called him two days ago to announce she was throwing an end-of-season party on Saturday night. He was going. And Amelia was coming with him. No more sneaking around. They were together and he wanted people to know. He'd managed to convince her of that after a day or so of talking about it. It would be easier if everyone knew. Then they could all just deal with the situation. It had been a hard sell, but when Finn hadn't offered any sort of apology or contact after the first few days, she seemed to have swapped upset for "screw it." Which was fine by him. After all, Amelia could date whoever the hell she wanted, and he was damned lucky that he was the guy she wanted. He wanted everyone else to know that, too. Fuck Castro.

Chapter Fourteen

Amelia tried to look excited rather than nervous as she slipped earrings into her ears and then studied herself in the mirror. She twitched the skirt of the dress she'd bought the day before when she'd agreed to go to the party with Ollie.

A decision to go public deserved a new dress.

Battle armor of a kind. She smoothed the dark-teal-and-black lace over her waist.

It was a gorgeous dress. Sexy. It sleeked over her body like a glove, the green shade making her skin look even paler than normal. The neckline was high but scooped low in back so she'd put her hair up. Left her throat bare but she slipped on glittering green earrings. She looked good. She didn't know why she was so nervous. Other than Finn, she doubted that any of the Saints were going to have an issue with her dating Oliver. Unless him dating another player's friend or sister was against some arcane baseball bro code? Oh God.

She hadn't thought of that before. Had Oliver? Did such a thing exist? Men were weird about that stuff. But he hadn't brought that up as a possible complication when he'd been talking her into coming to the party, so he must not be worried about it. And it wasn't as though she was actually related to Finn.

No. The only one to worry about was Finn.

Trouble was, there was a lot to worry about when it came to him.

She'd texted him to wish him good luck with his photo shoot on Wednesday but he hadn't responded. Only the fact that he wasn't plastered over the news for being drunk and disorderly or starting a fight gave her comfort that he was okay.

Em had called earlier asking if Amelia had seen him. She'd said no. And that unless Finn called her, she wasn't going to run after him. Which meant Em was now cranky, too.

She sighed. Castros.

Impossible to imagine what her life might have been if not for them. They'd given her a safe place. Finn had given her more time with her mom. She loved them all. But maybe Oliver was right. She couldn't repay them. She could only love them. And that didn't have to mean putting herself last. Oliver was part of her life now, too. She hoped. She felt a twinge of guilt thinking about Monday and whether there would be a project announcement. Whether she might be offered a transfer.

What would happen then?

But no. No point borrowing extra trouble. Tonight might have enough of that as it was. She leaned forward, slicked on red lipstick. There. Battle armor complete.

So now to go and find her fellow warrior for the night and let him take her to a party.

She didn't know a lot about Staten Island real estate but it was clear, even though they were driving in darkness, that the area they were in was a wealthy one. The houses were large. Obviously expensive. They only got larger and more exclusive as Oliver's driver made his way up into the hills. So she was expecting something impressive when they got to Alex and Maggie's house.

She just hadn't expected quite so big. It was practically a mansion. There was even a valet at the entrance of the drive ready to park cars. In their case, he just pointed the driver in the direction he was to go and stepped back to talk to the driver of the low black sports car who'd pulled up behind them. The cars already parked were a mix of town cars like theirs, various BMW and Mercedes sedans, and a good smattering of sports cars. Right.

Money.

The Saints might historically have been one of the lower-performing teams in the majors, but that didn't mean that they weren't still big business. Everybody involved was wealthy by any standard. And Alex Winters had been a billionaire before he'd bought the Saints.

"Ready?" Oliver asked, squeezing her hand.

She looked over at him. He was in black tonight. Suit. Shirt. Tie. It made him look more like a pirate than ever. Out to take no prisoners and do no good. Hopefully with her. Later.

Once they made it through the party.

He was gorgeous and he made her happy. Made her heart beat faster and made her feel beautiful. So yes. She was ready to share that with the world.

"Ready," she agreed and waited for him to slide out of the car and come around to open the door for her. Apparently pirates prided themselves on good manners these days.

She slid out, tucking her arm into his good one. He'd left the sling off tonight, and the black plastic splint almost seemed like an extension of his clothing. "Let's party."

Everything went well for the first hour or so. She'd relaxed a little when she'd discovered that Finn hadn't actually arrived yet and even though she wondered where he was, she'd been too distracted by the exciting squeeing that her arrival on Oliver's arm had provoked from Maggie and Raina and Sara. There'd been hugs and cheek kisses and demands to know the whole story before Oliver had extricated her and started to introduce her around.

She met Brett Tuckerson, the starting pitcher, who was about Oliver's age, and his wife, Hana. Hana was a tiny dark-haired woman who looked like she was about six months' pregnant. She said hello to Amelia and then told Oliver that it was about time he found a woman with a brain after he told her that Amelia was an economist. Maggie, who was not so discreetly trailing them around the room, had laughed.

"That's what I told him," Maggie said to Hana, and the two women exchanged a look of deep satisfaction and understanding that made Amelia think that they were very good friends. She would have liked to keep talking to Hana, but Oliver made excuses and the introductions continued until the list of names and faces started to blur. She'd met a few of the players' partners at the games but hadn't spoken to anyone at length. As far as the players themselves were concerned, apart from a couple Finn had introduced her to the night of the party at Raina's club, she hadn't met many at all.

Oliver seemed determined to rectify that situation. Completely. After the players, he started on the coaching staff. They were talking to Dan Ellis, the team manager, and Indy Jones, the team doctor, when Amelia saw Finn appear at the far side of the room.

And she saw the moment when he noticed her. He smiled at first, then his gaze slid to Oliver standing next to her. Oliver, who had his arm tucked around her waist. The smile fled Finn's face like a blackout plunging a city into darkness.

She stiffened and Oliver looked down at her. "Everything okay?" he asked.

She tried to keep the smile on her face. "Finn just arrived."

Oliver's brows drew together. "Okay." His hand squeezed her waist gently. "It's going to be okay. How do you want to do this?"

No idea. Was that a valid answer? Because she really had no idea. But as she lost sight of Finn in the crowded room, and wondered if he was headed in their direction, she had to think of something. "Let me go talk to him alone. That might be easier. At first."

His frown deepened. "Are you sure about that?"

No.

But she had to do it anyway. She pasted a smile back on her face. "I'll be fine." She made her excuses to Dan and Indy and left Oliver with them. As she worked her way across the room, she could feel Oliver watching her. She turned and gave him a reassuring nod before she started looking for Finn again.

She found him, predictably, standing near the bar that was set up in another room off the main living area where the party was being held.

His face went stony as she approached, and he took a slug of his drink. The clear liquid in the tall glass could have been water but she doubted it. Vodka. Finn liked vodka when he wanted to get drunk. She'd even bought the odd bottle for him when he'd been at college and had sweet-talked her into buying booze when she'd visited. She hadn't seen the harm then. In retrospect she should have started saying no to him then. But she couldn't change the past. She could only set the ground rules for how things were going to be between them now.

"Hi," she said, determined to be the sensible one in the conversation.

"What are you doing here?" he asked. She could smell liquor on him. Not vodka. That didn't really smell. He must have been drinking something else before he arrived. Whiskey maybe. Which meant he was probably drunk already. Her stomach sank.

"I was invited—" she started.

"By Shields?"

"Yes." She lifted her chin.

"So you're screwing him?" His tone was harsh, eyes cold.

Temper flared. She was trying to be sensible but frankly, Finn was being an asshole. Had been an asshole too often lately. So maybe it was time somebody told him. "Oliver and I are seeing each other," she said flatly. "News flash. That has nothing to do with you."

"I told you he was trouble," Finn said.

"Yes. You did. However, I make my own choices. And since you're the one standing in front of me half drunk at eight thirty and he's sober, I'm pretty sure he's not the one who qualifies as trouble right now."

"Yeah? Well, you know, Milly." He almost sneered her name. "If you don't want me commenting on who you screw, then you don't get to comment on how I choose to entertain myself."

"Really? This is entertaining to you? Because I don't see someone having fun, I see someone who is sulking for America and making an idiot of himself in the process."

"You know what? You're right. You're not entertaining me. You're boring me. So you can just go, Milly. Leave me alone."

"So you can complete the process and make a dick of yourself at your bosses' house? You think that's a good idea?"

"You're shagging Shields. So I'm not all that interested in what you think is a good idea."

"What exactly is your problem with Oliver?"

"He's the enemy," Finn said viciously. "My rival."

"He's your teammate," she said, feeling sicker with the second. "You're on the same side."

"He's too fucking old and he should fucking retire."

"So you can have his position? Is that all you care about? Yourself?"

"I played well in those games." Finn drained his glass, shoved it toward the bartender. Amelia tried to make eye contact with the guy slinging the booze but he didn't look at her, just poured vodka into Finn's glass and topped up the ice before pushing it back without comment.

"You played great," Amelia said. "You should be proud."

"I did," he agreed. "That position should be mine."

"I'm sure it will be, one day. But right now it's Oliver's. Don't you want people to know you have the position because you earned it, not because you were the alternate and the first pick was hurt?" The words came rushing out of her mouth before she knew what was happening. She knew as soon as she spoke that they were a mistake. Finn's face went red, eyes blazing.

"Fuck Shields. You all think he's so fucking great. Look at everyone, so worried about him and his ridiculous hand. Even you."

"We're worried about him because he's injured," Amelia said. She tried to keep her voice low, aware that several of the people nearest them were starting to look in their direction. "An injury he got helping you."

"So it's my fault? I didn't drive that fucking Hummer. And I didn't lose the fucking series."

"No one thinks you lost the series," she said. She was really worried now. He wasn't entirely making sense.

"Yes they do. And they all take his side. Even you."

"I'm not taking sides," she said. "I'm still here for you."

He shook his head. "No. You aren't. If you were on my side you wouldn't be with him."

She put a hand on his arm. "Finn, it's not a case of either or. I love you and your family. You know that. But that has nothing to do with me and Oliver."

"My family," he said. "My family. Dad couldn't even fucking look at me on Monday night."

"I'm sure he was just worried that you were upset," Amelia said. "He's so proud of you, Finn. I was with him while he watched that game. He couldn't take his eyes off you."

Finn's face twisted. "Until I fucked up."

"You didn't fuck up. The Red Sox just played better that night. There will be other seasons."

"You don't understand what it's like," he said. "You don't care about me, either. You just want to fuck Shields."

She tried not to wince at the vicious tone. "That's not true. Look, why don't you come with me? We'll find you some coffee. Some food. You're upset about losing. I get that. Let me help you."

"No," he said, shaking his head vehemently. He shook off her grip, using all the considerable strength in his hand to shove her away. She stumbled back, only keeping her balance with difficulty. "No. You know what, Milly? I don't need you to take care of me. I have a family. Even if they think I'm a screwup. And you've muscled in on my family for long enough. So go. Go to Shields if he's the one you want. Just don't come crying to me when he fucks off like your dad did. You can find another fucking family to use when that happens. Until then, stay the fuck out of my life. You're not my fucking sister. So just leave me the hell alone."

He pushed past her and she stumbled back. By the time she'd caught her balance, Finn was gone and she was left standing there, unable to breathe. Feeling as though he'd slapped her.

Not his sister. Not his family. God. He sounded like he hated her. She felt sick. She was going to throw up. She looked around the room. Couldn't see anyone she knew. Couldn't see Oliver. Which might be just as well. He'd start something with Finn if he knew what had just happened.

God. Her eyes were stinging and suddenly all she could think was that she had to get out of the room before she started to cry.

"Amelia."

It wasn't Oliver's voice. Or Finn's. Not that she imagined for a second that Finn might be coming after her to apologize. He'd made his feelings about her pretty clear.

No, it was Maggie's voice. Maggie's whose house she was currently blundering through, no idea where she was going, just wanting somewhere to hide until she could make the sick feeling of hurt in her stomach vanish. Maggie who had been nothing but kind to her. So she stopped, waited. Blinked hard to stop the stinging in her eyes.

Maggie caught up to her, concern clear in her brown eyes. "Everything okay?"

Amelia gulped. Tried to talk through the acid burn in her throat. "Yes."

"Is that a big fat lie?'"

"Yes." She blinked again.

"Thought so. Come with me." Maggie tucked her arm through Amelia's, steered her a little farther down the hallway, and then opened a door. "Losses are never easy."

They stepped into a room that looked like a cross between a tiny living room and an office. There was a small carved oak desk tucked into the corner. A sleek silver laptop and a basket half full of paper sat on its gleaming surface. As did several scattered paperbacks. There was another bookcase holding books and files next to the desk and then a matching cupboard whose doors hid its contents on the other side. The rest of the room was filled up with three fat overstuffed armchairs in shades of blue velvet that cozied around a small coffee table. A small flatscreen hung on the opposite wall.

"Sit," Maggie said, pushing Amelia gently toward the nearest of the chairs before going over to the cupboard. She came back with two glasses, a bottle of scotch, and the biggest bar of Godiva chocolate Amelia had ever seen. "Which do you want? Booze or sugar?"

Amelia laughed, caught off guard. But she definitely didn't want booze. She could still smell the waft of alcohol Finn had breathed on her when he'd said those things. "Will you think badly of me if I chose the candy?"

"Sweetie, as long as you don't make me drink tequila with you, I will not judge." Maggie shuddered theatrically. "I hate tequila." She handed Amelia the chocolate, sat, and then kicked off her shoes with a relieved sigh.

"Deal. And I won't mention that I make killer margaritas."

Maggie looked mournful. "Margaritas sound tasty. But my loathing of tequila is the result of self-inflicted idiocy in high school. So I wouldn't know. I won't hold it against you that you aren't as dumb as me." She frowned. "Matter of fact, that particular incident was Ollie's fault."

Dark-brown eyes met Amelia's. "Is it weird if I talk about Oliver? About when we were dating?"

Amelia shook her head. She'd spent too much time watching Maggie and Alex together over the last two weeks to have any doubts that the two of them were madly in love. "No."

"He and I were a long time ago."

"I know." Amelia tore open the chocolate. "It's really okay."

Maggie looked relieved. "Good. So do you want to tell me what upset you back there? I don't like it when people get upset at my parties. It's against the Maggie, Sara, and Raina rules of fun."

"There are rules?"

"Definitely. Raina has views about what constitutes a good time, and I was hosting Saints parties for my dad when I was sixteen. But we were talking about you."

Amelia took a breath, broke off a piece of chocolate. She wasn't sure she could eat it, any more than she could have stomached alcohol. Finn's anger had shocked her. But Maggie was as good a person as any to talk to about it. It wasn't as if Amelia was ever going to tell Em. That was a guaranteed lose–lose conversation. And Maggie understood baseball players. She might have some good advice.

"I—" She stopped. Put the chocolate down. "Don't take this the wrong way, but how to do you survive all this—the pressure and the parties and—"

"The circus?" Maggie said. "It's overwhelming sometimes. But I grew up with it. So I guess I don't really notice how daunting it is most of the time. Raina or Sara might be able to shed some light. Is that what this is? You're not sure about taking all this on if you take on Oliver for good?"

Amelia froze. "For good?"

"Yeah. Never a good poker player, our Ollie. He can't take his eyes off you. He's seriously smitten." The *Don't break my friend's heart* was unspoken but clear in Maggie's tone.

Smitten? Maggie thought Oliver was smitten? She was just going to let that one go through to the catcher for now. "I'm not upset with Oliver. I must admit all this is daunting but it's not that." No. Oliver was another problem.

"Then what? Finn? He's taking Monday pretty hard?"

Amelia nodded. "Yeah. Finn." She wasn't going to tell Maggie exactly what he'd said to her. But she knew the fact that he'd said it, that he'd been so vicious, wasn't a good sign. He obviously wasn't handling the loss well. "I'm just not sure all of this is good for him."

Maggie looked sympathetic. "I hate to tell you this, but the only one who can really make that call is Finn. I've seen a lot of players come and go over the years. Watched them learn to cope with it all. They're all different, of course, but there are a few . . . well, call them categories . . . that they tend to fall into."

"Which are?"

"Well, there are the ones who reach the majors and settle right in. Who seem to manage to keep it about the game and don't let their heads get turned by the crazy and the circus."

"I'm not sure that's Finn."

"No," Maggie agreed. "Maybe not. Then there are the guys who arrive and try to cope with the pressure by jumping into the circus with both feet. The ones who blow off steam with parties and girls and soaking up the fame."

"What happens to them?"

"Either they get tired of that or learn that it affects their game badly and get their heads straight and settle down to the job of it or—"

"Or?" Her stomach twisted again.

"Or they blow it. Sometimes not badly enough that they can't win themselves a second chance. But sometimes completely. And then some of them just quit. Decide that the love of the game isn't worth the crap that comes with professional baseball. Or that they can't handle the crap."

"Do you think Finn is going to blow it?"

Maggie frowned. "Honestly?"

Amelia nodded. "Yes."

"I don't know. He hasn't settled, that's for sure. Even after we bought him cheap because the Cubs had decided he was difficult. He should be focused on behaving himself. But he played very well until Monday. I don't think Dan or the guys are ready to give up on him yet."

Amelia didn't want to imagine what might happen if the Saints actually ditched Finn. "I—"

Maggie held up a hand. "I know you love him. That he's kind of family to you, but the other thing I've learned is that adjusting to this is something they have to do on their own. I've seen wives and girlfriends and families break their hearts trying to help. The only one who can get his head screwed on straight and decide if he really wants this is Finn. So, if you want my advice, give him space. Let him figure it out. He needs to stand or fall on his own. And he needs not to have easy targets to take his frustration out on while he does it."

"That's pretty blunt."

"You asked. You had a fight, right? Earlier? That's what upset you?" Maggie sighed. "I'd say try not to take it personally but that's crap. He's not a boy. He's a man. He needs to learn to act like one on his own. Like I said.

Stand or fall. And sometimes a fall is what it takes. So if I were you, I'd focus on the guy with his head on straight."

"Oliver?"

Maggie nodded.

"Not sure how straight his head is, either. I know this hand thing is killing him, but he won't talk about it."

"They don't like talking about injuries." Maggie grimaced. "About what might happen if they don't come back. That's the other side of the coin. The ones who get their heads on straight, well, sometimes they have trouble on the other end. With what happens when the circus finally leaves town one day."

That made her shiver. "I asked him about that. Asked him what he might do after baseball."

"What did he say?" Maggie leaned forward, curiosity lighting her eyes.

Amelia shrugged. "Not much."

That drew a sigh from Maggie. A big one. "It's always been baseball for Oliver. Dad drafted him straight out of high school. Sometimes I wonder if that was the right thing to do. He was so young. Maybe if he'd gone to college, he'd know what might come next."

"He didn't want to go?"

"Dad offered. Said the Saints would even pay, if he wanted to wait and do that first. But Ollie said no."

"And he settled right in."

Maggie grinned. "Pretty much. Don't get me wrong, I'm not saying he hasn't had his party moments. But he's always had his eyes on the prize. Which for him has been baseball. And for some reason, the Saints. He could have moved to a better team. He's good enough. But he stayed. That's Oliver. Goes after what he wants with one hundred percent effort. Which is why it makes me happy to see him focused on you. About time he set his sights on someone worthy."

"Worthy?"

"Someone interesting. Someone who doesn't just want to sleep with a baseball player or date a rich guy."

"I'm not that interesting."

"He seems pretty interested. And you don't strike me as the out-to-land-a-rich-guy-for-his-money type. Otherwise you probably could have married one of those Wall Street money guys already and be a lady of leisure."

Amelia screwed up her nose. "Sounds hideous."

Maggie laughed. "Good answer. I think you're good for him. Particularly right now."

"I asked him about that, too," Amelia admitted. "About whether or not I was just a distraction because he'd injured his hand."

"Well, he was pretty cranky the night of the party at Raina's after you went home," Maggie said. "I didn't know why at the time but now I'm making a guess that not catching you first try might have something to do with that. That was before the accident. So he was already smitten before he got hurt. So, tell you what. You focus on Oliver. I think he might just surprise you." She smiled and shook her head before stretching out her legs and wriggling her toes. "Okay. I am going to go back out there and find some people to deal with Finn. Do you want me to send Oliver here or do you want to come back with me?"

Amelia hesitated.

"It's okay. I'm going to send Finn home before he does anything else stupid. You don't have to deal with him."

"Is it all right if I sit here a bit longer?"

"Sure," Maggie said. She bent and picked up one of her shoes. It was a wicked-looking black stiletto with heels that had to be four inches high. "Someday I'm going to learn that pretty doesn't equal comfortable when it comes to shoes." She flashed Amelia a grin as she pulled on the shoe, then its mate. "But hey, sometimes pretty is worth a little trouble, right?"

"Right," Amelia agreed, thinking of Oliver. He was definitely pretty. And definitely worth it.

Chapter Fifteen

"Ollie," Maggie said, appearing at his elbow.

He broke off his conversation with Hector Moreno, the Saints catcher. "Maggie J," he said. "Something I can do for you?" He half expected to see Amelia at her side. She'd been gone a long time. He'd just been about to make his excuses to Hector and go see if she was okay, Finn or no Finn.

"Seen Amelia lately?" Maggie said.

Something in her voice told him it wasn't a casual question. His instinct went on alert, gut tightening. "No. Is something wrong?" He let her tug him away from Hector.

When they had a little bit of space, Maggie said, "She and Finn had an argument. She's a bit shaken up."

"Fucking Castro." The words escaped him before he realized what he was saying. He lifted his head, searched the room. Maggie's fingers dug into his arm.

"No. You are not going to find Finn and punch him. I've already got Mal dealing with him. He'll be taken home."

"Let's hope he doesn't kill anyone in the process," Oliver snarled.

"He won't. But you need to forget about Finn and go look after Amelia. She's in my office."

"Thanks." He pressed a kiss to her cheek. "You're good people, Maggie J."

She rolled her eyes at him. "Don't try to charm me. Go charm Amelia. She's good people, too. Don't screw this one up, Ollie."

"Doing my best not to," he said and left.

He found Amelia, as Maggie had said, curled up on one of the velvet chairs in Maggie's office. She was licking melted chocolate off her fingers. Which made heat curl through his gut, pushing aside some of the urge to find Finn and pound him until he apologized. But only some. He and Castro were going to have a come-to-Jesus moment about how Finn would be treating Amelia in the future.

"Hey," he said.

She looked up, the surprise in her eyes melting into pleasure when she realized who it was. He'd do a lot of things to make sure she always looked at him like that. He went to the chair. Went to his knees beside her. "You okay?" he asked. "Maggie told me Finn did a number on you."

The pleasure in her eyes faded. "Yeah. But I don't want to talk about it. Not yet." She put a hand on his cheek. Leaned in and kissed him softly.

Chocolate and the taste of Amelia filled his mouth. Filled all of his senses. He let himself ride the sweetness of the sensation for a minute, letting her take the lead with the kiss. Whatever she needed.

Whatever comfort he could offer. Whatever strength he could lend.

He wanted to give it.

Awareness tumbled through him like a shower of sparks. He couldn't remember the last time he'd felt like this about a woman. Or if he'd ever felt like this about anyone. Not even Maggie.

This sense of rightness. Of home.

Amelia pulled back. "Thanks," she said. "I needed that. Now can we go back to the party?"

"Are you sure you're okay?"

She nodded. Then leaned in and kissed him again. "All good now you're here."

He couldn't help the goofy grin that filled his face. "Whatever you want," he said and let her lead him back to the party.

There was no sign of Finn, and after Ollie found Maggie's face in the crowd and she shot him a discreet thumbs-up, he relaxed and tried to shake off his lingering anger. Finn was not going to be an issue for the rest of the night, so he was going to forget about him and have fun with Amelia.

Who apparently had suddenly decided that she was in a party mood.

She demanded a margarita, which he procured for her. She downed it in a few gulps, asked for another.

He shrugged and went back to the bar.

She didn't drink the second one so fast. Instead, she sipped it, arm slipped through his, leaning into him, as Sara came over to them and started chatting. The music, which had been fairly soft until now, suddenly kicked up a few volume notches, the beat changing to something fast and sexy.

He didn't have to look to know that Raina would be clearing a space to form an impromptu dance floor. Or probably not so impromptu. Raina and Maggie and Sara ran Saints parties with military-style planning. Apparently they'd decided that what the party needed right now were some serious dance moves.

Raina led Mal into the space she'd cleared as a female

voice started singing about needing to party. Mal was laughing down at Raina, shaking his head as usual before he gave in to her pleas and pulled her close to start a bump-and-grind rhythm that had everyone clapping. Watching Mal and Raina dance probably needed to come with a parental advisory. The heat between them was so clear, it was surprising their clothes didn't catch fire. Other people started dancing around them, and Oliver realized Amelia was tapping her foot beside him.

"You wanna dance?" he asked.

She looked up at him, startled. "What about your ankle?"

"It'll survive a dance or two," he said, hoping it was true. Amelia smiled at him, clearly delighted at the idea. She knocked back her drink and held out a hand, tugging him toward the mass of dancers when he took it.

Hampered by his ankle, he couldn't really dance terribly well, but she didn't seem to mind as he put his hand on the curve of her back and pulled her close so that they were chest-to-chest and groin-to-groin while they moved to the music.

The scent of her, that unique Amelia smell he would probably recognize if he was half dead, filled his nose with every breath he took, and the heat of her skin under his hand made his palm itch to be touching more than the lacy fabric of her dress.

He'd gone hard the instant she'd pressed her hips to his. He pulled her closer, wanting more of the sensation, felt her suck in a breath then look up at him, devilry dancing in her eyes. She changed her movements then. Just a little. Just enough that she was grinding a little more forcefully against him. Her pupils flared, nearly drowning out the blue in her eyes as she pulled his head down for a kiss. One that went wild before he knew what was happening, her tongue tangling with his. He pulled her tighter against him instinctively, forgetting where they were.

"Get a room, Shields," someone yelled good-naturedly, and Amelia giggled against his mouth before she pushed him away. Her cheeks were flushed pink, the color a stark contrast with the creamy shade of her skin. No hiding her emotions from the world for Amelia. Anyone who looked at her could probably tell she had naughty thoughts dancing in her head.

The thought woke something primal and possessive deep in his gut. No one was going to help Amelia with her naughty thoughts but him.

No one got to see what she looked like when she gave herself over completely to those thoughts. Only him.

God.

He desperately wanted to drag her off into one of Maggie and Alex's million spare rooms and pull up her dress and bury himself in her. But he didn't think she was likely to play along with that idea.

So he was going to have to come up with Plan B.

Which wasn't that hard. All he had to do was pretend to stumble and let a completely fake wince cross his face.

Amelia's eyes flashed with concern, and he let her drag him from the dance floor.

"Everything okay?" she asked.

"No," he said. Then he bent down so his mouth was next to her ear. Blew softly so that she shivered. "I want to fuck you, Amelia," he said. "Let me take you home."

Her breath rushed out in a whoosh. And the breath she took after that was shaky. But she nodded.

He straightened. "Is that a yes?"

"It's a hell, yes."

He'd never cursed the distance between Manhattan and Staten Island quite so thoroughly as he did on the long drive home. The town car was hardly a limo, where he might have been able to close the privacy screen and pull Amelia onto his lap to have his way with her. So they had to sit and behave all the way back to his apartment. He'd put his hand on her thigh and she'd let her legs fall apart a little so that he could curl his fingers into the bare flesh above the stockings she wore but he limited himself to just stroking her skin. Even though her breathing became increasingly labored with every mile.

He knew how she felt. He was so hard, he ached. His cock screamed to be inside her.

They were both half blind with lust by the time they stumbled through the door of his apartment. He pushed her up against the wall and started to kiss her, shoving his hand into her underwear. Into heat and sliding wetness.

"God," he groaned. He needed her. Under normal circumstances, he would have probably just picked her up and had her against the wall. But that wasn't a move to pull off with one hand.

Instead he removed his hand, which made her curse him, and kissed her again. Hard. Fast. Deploying every dirty move he knew to make her want. Make her writhe. Make her beg. Then he steered her into the living room till the back of her thighs hit the back of the sofa.

"Turn around, Amelia," he growled.

Her eyes went round with shock, then her pupils widened, turning her eyes midnight dark. He'd thought she'd looked turned on before. Now she looked like pure sex. Like every fantasy he ever had.

She turned around, bent over for him, moved her legs wide. With a groan and a curse, he flipped up her skirt, pulled her underwear down. The sight of her, wet and waiting for him, sent him into near madness.

He was barely aware of what he was doing or where they were when he jerked down his zipper, pulled out his cock, and thrust into her with one sure motion.

Amelia moaned, head falling forward. "God, yes," she said.

It was all the encouragement he needed. He let go then, gave in to the need to be as close to her as possible. Each thrust into her, each slide of her flesh against his got wilder. Harder. Faster. And she urged him on. Met him with as much eagerness as his.

Until he felt her clench around him and start to come, her voice hoarse and dazed as she called his name. He couldn't have stopped the answered orgasm that roared through him like a tornado if someone had offered him all his wildest dreams to hold it back.

It felt so good, he thought he might just black out. And when his senses returned, he was bent over her, arms holding her close to his chest, their gasping breaths moving in sync. He backed off carefully, helping her straighten.

She moved slowly and he wondered if he'd gone too far. If he'd hurt her. But then he saw the smile on her face as she turned to face him.

God. That look. It undid him.

He wanted to see it every day.

She put her hands on his cheeks. Lurched up on tiptoe to kiss him.

"Thank you," she said. "I needed that."

Then she burst into tears.

It felt like she'd punched him. "Fuck. Amelia. What? Did I hurt you?"

She shook her head but kept sobbing.

He pulled her close to him. "What is it?"

She shook her head, sobbed harder.

Damn it. The sound of her crying was like being stabbed. He wanted her to stop. But what he wanted didn't matter. What mattered was what she needed. Heedless of his hand, he scooped her up, carried her through to his bedroom. Undressed her while she cried. Then coaxed her into bed before stripping down and climbing in with her. He pulled her close and just held her, whispering stupid meaningless words into her hair as she cried and cried.

Just him and her in the darkness. That was all that mattered. That he could make her feel okay. Make her feel safe. Make her feel loved.

Eventually her sobs quieted, slowed. Then stopped. He reached for the box of Kleenex on his nightstand. She wiped her eyes. Blew her nose. Hiccuped. Her makeup was smudged and her eyes were red.

She looked beautiful.

"Do you want to talk about it?" he asked.

Another head shake.

"Do you want to go to sleep?" he asked.

"No."

"Do you want me to stop asking questions and you can just tell me what you need?"

Her mouth curled up at that. "You," she said simply. "I just need you." She hooked a leg over his hip, moved closer, pressed her mouth to his. She tasted of salt and sex and herself.

This time, when they moved together, it was gentle. Slow. There was all the time in the world as he eased into her, as he worshipped her skin with his mouth, as he tried to take all her hurt away with his kisses. And this time, when she gasped and shuddered around him, he followed her down, letting the tide of pleasure pull him under and break him apart. Somewhere, far away, he thought he heard her say, "I love you, Ollie," before everything vanished into sensation.

On Monday, Amelia made a point of getting to work early. She and Oliver had spent Sunday playing hooky from the world, spending most of the day curled up in his big bed, napping, watching silly movies, making love, talking, and generally pretending the world outside his apartment didn't exist. After the stormy then sexy end to their Saturday, she had needed a day to regroup.

Oliver hadn't said anything about what had slipped out of her mouth when he'd made love to her after her ridiculous storm of tears. Right now she was grateful that he hadn't. In fact, she was hoping he hadn't heard it at all.

She hadn't meant to say it. Not yet. Not so soon. No one said *I love you* after two weeks. Yet it had spilled out. She loved him. She wasn't sure what that meant. She knew she cared about him. Wanted to be with him. Lit up when she saw him. But it was too soon for love, wasn't it?

So. Easier to pretend she hadn't said it. Wait and see what happened.

Sunday night they'd moved to her apartment so that she could get clothes for work on Monday. Oliver had stayed the night; nestled against him, his arm curving around her like a shield, she'd slept well. The day had eased the immediate sting of her fight with Finn but hadn't offered any sensible solutions as to how to fix things between them.

Finn was obviously struggling. She wanted to help. But maybe, as much as she hated to think about it, Maggie was right. Maybe the only one who could help Finn was Finn.

Right now, maybe she should just focus on helping herself.

She'd already checked her email on the way to work. Hong Kong was twelve hours ahead of New York. If there had been a project announcement, it should have already happened while she was sleeping. But no. Nothing in her email.

There was still nothing when she fired up her computer in her office. All right. Tomorrow then. The knot in her stomach that had ridden all the way from her apartment to Wall Street loosened a little. No point freaking out until she knew there was something to freak out about.

She took care of her emails and then turned to the latest project status report on the model. When she got to the end, she blinked. Then checked again. But no, all the issues on the status report were marked cleared. Which meant that they could start loading the sucker with test data and see what it spat out.

The urge to pump her fist in the air in victory surged through her but she restricted herself to a more discreet happy dance in her chair.

Sure, the testing would invariably throw up more problems to be fixed, but having the build of the actual model stable was a major milestone. Plus they were a week ahead of schedule.

Just the sort of thing Daniel loved to hear.

Especially if he was in the process of considering whether or not to recommend her for a transfer.

The knot in her stomach returned. A transfer.

Leaving New York would mean leaving Oliver behind. Maybe not for good, but for at least six months. More if she chose to finally use all that leave she'd been saving and travel at the end of her time in Hong Kong.

Nine months maybe. Nearly a year. She couldn't expect him to wait a year. Not when they were barely beginning.

She sucked in a breath against the pain that curled through her at the thought of losing Oliver. Tried to tell herself that she was borrowing trouble again. She didn't even know if she was going to be offered a transfer. And what then? What if she didn't get an offer? She'd always promised herself that she'd work in New York for six years. Time enough to sort out her finances and make sure her mom was okay.

Six years had been her goal, then she'd been determined to make a move. Apply for jobs overseas. Six years at a Wall Street bank, if she did well, would look good on a résumé. Of course it was a pretty cutthroat industry and there was always competition, but she had the credentials. She could find herself a job in London or Hong Kong or even Australia if she wanted to now that she'd put her time in.

See the world.

Have her dream.

Do something purely selfish.

Purely what she wanted.

And yet . . . was it the only thing she wanted now?

She didn't know.

So, she could sit here and drive herself crazy or she could get back to work. Dot the *i*'s and cross the *t*'s on her project update so she could take it to Daniel ASAP.

Do her job.

But in the end, Daniel beat her to the punch. He called asking her to come see him just after lunch.

The request made her pulse race. Stupid. He could want anything. So she had to be prepared. Deep breaths while she gathered the project report and her notebook so she could answer questions on the other projects she was working on calmed her slightly; she didn't feel quite so panicked when she walked down the hallway to Daniel's office.

It was about five times the size of hers, the windows looking out toward the Hudson and offering a glittering view of the city in the sunshine. Manhattan laid out like this always took her breath away. So much in one small space. So many lives. So many people. So many hopes and dreams.

She'd miss it when she left. Maybe she'd come back. She'd always thought she'd go home to Chicago eventually, but maybe not. Her mom was taken care of. She didn't have to go home, as much as she'd like to be close to Em and the Castros again

Always muscling in on my family.

Finn's voice rang in her head and she shook her head.

No. She hadn't muscled in. They'd taken her in. Offered help. They'd looked after her. Wanted her. Loved her like she loved them.

She told the Finn in her head to fuck off and sat when Daniel directed her to the small-glass–topped table that sat in one corner of his office.

Maybe it was just a project catch-up then. Whenever Daniel wanted to talk to her about performance reviews, he generally sat behind his desk. The power position.

But for other things, he used the table. She imagined he thought it was being casual. But nothing about Daniel Carling was really casual. He was cool and business-like all the way through. Or else he did a damned good impression of being cool. Not her cup of tea at all. Nope, she liked guys with passion. Warmth.

"Did you have a pleasant weekend?" Daniel asked.

She nodded. "Yes, thank you. And you?"

"Hamptons," he said.

She nodded. He wouldn't tell her more. That short exchange was pretty much the Daniel Carling version of cozy small talk. At least when it came to her. She wondered what he actually did in the Hamptons each weekend. It was hard to imagine him lying on a beach.

But she wasn't here to speculate about Daniel. She'd leave that to Em. She was here to get the job.

"You're probably wondering what I wanted to talk to you about?"

She nodded again, mouth feeling drier than dirt.

"Tomorrow the Hong Kong office will be announcing their acquisition of Li Huang Star."

"Really?" She tried to sound surprised. "That's a good fit for us." Li Huang Star was another small investment bank. One based in Hong Kong with roots there, and on mainland China. Effectively a gateway to build more business in China, which could be a tough nut to crack.

"Yes," Daniel agreed. "But they're also operating on some fairly archaic infrastructure and processes. So they are putting together a team to work on the integration of the business. Multidisciplinary. They want an economist familiar with the Pullman systems. So I thought of you."

And there it was. The sentence she'd been waiting to hear her boss say for years. An overseas transfer.

So why wasn't her first emotion a squeal of joy? "Thank you," she managed, trying to process what was happening. "When you say you thought of me does that mean you're throwing my name in the ring or that I have the job?"

"The team will be vetted but I'm fairly sure Henry will sign off on my recommendation in your case. I've always been impressed by your work, Amelia. I know Charlie Bucknell felt the same. So the job is almost certainly yours. If you want it." He cocked his head at her. "I'll confess you seem less . . . excited than I thought you may have been. Do you want it? Or have your plans changed?"

There was a lot unspoken in that sentence. Daniel knew about Oliver. Did he think she was the kind of woman who made choices based solely around what the men in her life wanted? She'd never done it before. Partly because there hadn't been that many important men in her life. Eddie Castro, she supposed. And Finn. But not a lover who had meant enough for her to change course. Yet here she was hesitating. She could understand why women made that kind of choice. A good relationship was worth some sacrifice. But . . .

"I'm just a little surprised," she said. "I wasn't expecting something to come up so soon. Do you need an answer right now?"

He waved a hand. "No. Not this minute. But I will need one by the end of the week. They want the project team on the ground in Hong Kong in early November. That's not a lot of time to get things arranged."

End of the week. Four short days to choose what life she wanted. It didn't seem long enough. But it was going to have to be.

Chapter Sixteen

On Tuesday, Amelia got to work early again. She tried to slide out of Oliver's bed without waking him but he caught her as she started to move, pulled her back against him. She'd resisted his best attempts at seducing her into morning sex and made her escape, guilt tightening her stomach as she let herself out of the apartment.

She hadn't told him about the job offer. She would tell him. She had to tell him eventually.

Just not yet.

She needed to know what she wanted before she told him.

Right now she still hadn't untangled it all in her head.

She wanted a few quiet hours at work to clear her mind. Of course, she'd forgotten about the project announcement. Which meant the morning turned into an impromptu celebration at Pullman, complete with champagne, cake, and lots of speculation about opportunities that the acquisition might bring. None of her fellow economists seemed all that interested in going to Hong Kong for any extended period of time. But they could be playing it cool.

If any of them had been approached like she had, they were keeping it quiet. So she did, too.

By the time she made it back to her office at lunchtime, she was wondering how she was going to get the day's work done in half a day. The thought gave her a headache and made the cake she'd eaten sit uneasily in her stomach.

Might as well start at the beginning. Make a to-do list. Prioritize. Break it down. All those things that were supposed to make tackling massive piles of work less daunting.

But the first message in her email was one of the firm's automated "you have voice mail" messages. The number attached was Em's cell.

Hmmm. Em rarely called her work landline. Usually went straight for the cell. The cell that was currently sitting in Amelia's purse, because she hadn't bothered to grab it when the invitation to this morning's celebrations had arrived. She hadn't expected to be gone for several hours. When she pulled the phone free of all the miscellaneous crap in her bag, the home screen told her she had three missed calls. All from Em.

Crap.

That couldn't be anything good.

She swung her office door shut and dialed, not bothering to listen to the voice mail. Thankfully, Em picked up straight away.

"Where have you been?" Em demanded.

"Work function."

"On a Tuesday morning?"

"End-of-project celebration," Amelia said, not ready to tell Em about the acquisition. Hopefully she was still too caught up in her case to be paying any attention to the financial pages. "What's up?"

"Have you seen Finn?"

"Not since Saturday night." She hadn't told Em what had happened at the Saints party.

"Saturday? At the Saints party?"

"Yes," Amelia said. "But not since. Is something wrong?"

"I called him this morning. He sounded drunk."

Okay. So he was okay. Alive, at least. She'd half expected Em to be calling to say he'd gotten into trouble somehow. "Sweetie, he's pretty upset about the loss. I'm sure the guys all get together and party for a few days. Blow off some steam."

"It's been a week. I'm worried about him. Can you go see him?"

Amelia sighed. "I'm not sure that's such a good idea."

"Why not?" Em sounded confused.

She was going to have to tell Em eventually. So now was as good a time as any. "We kind of had a fight."

"When? About what?"

"Saturday night. At the party," Amelia said. Damn. She hadn't wanted to tell Em any of this. Well, other than the Oliver part. She'd been trying to figure out how to tell Em the Oliver part. She'd half expected that Finn had done so already. But apparently not. Which explained the lack of Em calling her, demanding an update on her love life.

"As for why he was mad, well, I'd say seventy percent of it was him being half drunk and pissed off at the world."

"And the other thirty?"

"He objected to my choice of company." Amelia said. When Em didn't immediately reply, she added. "I was there with Oliver Shields, not because Finn invited me. We're kind of, um, dating."

"You're dating Oliver Shields?" Em shrieked.

Amelia couldn't tell if it was excitement or irritation because it was mostly just loud. "Yes."

"Finn hates that guy."

"Yes. I'm aware. But I don't. Like I've already told Finn several times, this has nothing to do with him."

"Which is reasonable," Em said, and the knot in Amelia's stomach eased a little. Apparently Em wasn't taking Finn's side on this particular issue. "So you finally broke the no-jocks rule, huh? You must really like this guy."

Amelia sighed. Em, unlike her brother, was probably too tactful to bring Amelia's dad into the conversation. Amelia had never even told her that she worried about her taste for athletes being some sort of weird looking-for-a-guy-just-like-Daddy thing. But she had told her she'd decided guys like that weren't a good idea. Which was true. "Yes. I do. Oliver is . . . different."

"Different, how?"

"He's . . . Oliver."

"Dude, you are in trouble," Em said, sounding half amused, half worried.

"I know. It's stupid. But I really like him."

"Doesn't stop this being kind of a messy situation."

"Why, because Finn wants Oliver's spot on first base? Well, tough. He's going to have to earn it."

"That's a little harsh."

"After what he said to me on Saturday, I'm not inclined to cut Finn much slack at the moment. Your brother can be a prick sometimes." She held her breath, waited for Em to leap to Finn's defense.

"I know," Em sighed. "But that doesn't mean I'm not worried about him. Can't you go see him?"

She could. But she didn't want to. It was definitely time to resign from Team Finn. Or at least the part of it that refused to acknowledge that Finn wasn't the perfect human. "I don't think it would help. He made it pretty clear that he wants me to keep my nose out of his business. I think you're right to be worried if he's still drinking after a week, but if I go charging over there, he's just going to be even more pissed off at the world. I think you're going to have to handle this one on your own."

"What the hell did he say to you?" Em asked, sounding upset.

"I'm not going to tell you that," Amelia said. "I don't want to put you in the middle of this. But if you want someone to check on Finn right now, then you're going to need a second choice." She took a deep breath. Now that she'd broken one piece of her news, she might as well just keeping ripping off the Band-Aid. "In fact, you might need a second choice in the future, too."

"Why?"

"There's an opportunity with Pullman in Hong Kong. Daniel is putting my name forward. If I want him to."

Em sucked in a breath. Then went silent.

"Em?"

"Wow," Em said. "So you're going to say yes?"

"I haven't decided."

"It's what you've always wanted. Isn't it?"

"Yes."

"Then why don't you sound over the moon?"

Amelia hesitated. "It's complicated."

"Because of Oliver Shields?"

"Yes."

"But you can't have been dating him very long?"

"No."

"Then what? You're in love with him?" Em's voice was disbelieving.

"Maybe. A little. I don't know." She shivered, feeling suddenly cold. Scared. No. Terrified. Of staying. Of going. Of what the hell being so scared might actually mean.

"How long *have* you been dating?"

"Two weeks."

"Nobody falls in love in two weeks. Other than in Hollywood," Em said.

"I know," Amelia said. "But it feels like it could be something. I know it sounds crazy."

"What does Oliver say?"

"I haven't told him yet. Daniel only told me yesterday. I need time to think. To figure out what I want to do." She pressed her thumb into the spot between her eyebrows where a headache was beginning to build.

"How long's the transfer?"

"Six months. Maybe a little longer."

Em blew out a breath. "That's not that long. Maybe he'll wait."

"Maybe. But he's not just any guy, Em. He's kind of famous. He's got women throwing themselves at him. Why would he?" It's not like he could come with her. He wouldn't want to stay away from the game he loved. Not for someone he'd known two weeks. Would he?

"If he cares, he'll wait. If he won't, then he's not the guy you want."

Amelia choked back a laugh. "That is far too logical."

"Sometimes logic is hard to beat. When would you leave?"

"End of the month."

"So soon?" Em sounded stricken.

"Like you said, it's only for six months. Hey, we don't live in the same city anyway. We could still Skype and do all the things we do now."

"It's not the same."

"Now who's being illogical? You and your big lawyer salary can afford a trip to Hong Kong, and I'd be back for Christmas." She hoped. If the project team was being assembled so quickly, then there was obviously a lot of work to get done.

"Okay," Em muttered. "You'll tell me when you decide?"

"You'll be my first phone call. Well, maybe my second. I'll have to tell Mom first." She didn't know what her mother would say. If Em was freaking out about the idea, then what would her travel-averse mom think? She squelched down the guilt. If she did this, it had to be for her.

The phone jolted Amelia awake sometime past midnight. Beside her, Oliver stirred as she rolled away from him, fumbling for the phone.

She squinted at the number. Raina Easton. Maggie had texted Amelia the day after the party to see how she was. And followed that up by sending her Sara's and Raina's numbers as well, just in case she wanted to talk.

Which was nice but what the hell was Raina doing calling her so late at night? She felt her pulse going into overtime as she hit the answer button. "Hello? Raina?"

"Amelia, is that you?"

"Yes?"

"Thank God. I was worried I hadn't put the number Maggie gave me in right."

Maggie, it seemed, was efficient when she distributed contact details. "Raina, what's wrong?"

"It's Finn," Raina said. "He's had an accident."

Amelia went cold. Struggled to breathe for a moment. "Is he okay?"

"He hit his head pretty good. Lots of blood. The paramedics are on their way."

"What is it?" Oliver asked beside her and she shook her head at him, focusing on Raina.

"Paramedics?" she asked, feeling sick. Paramedics meant serious.

"No messing with head injuries," Raina said.

"What happened?" Her hand was gripping the phone so tightly, it was digging into her palm. She tried to make her fingers relax a little but couldn't.

"He and a couple of the guys—Sam and Leeroy and Paul—have been here all night. Commiserating, I guess. Some harder than others."

By which she meant Finn, Amelia assumed. "And?"

"Well, some idiots came in with Yankees shirts on and they recognized the guys and it got a bit heated."

Heated. Heated was one thing. Paramedics were another. Raina Easton was apparently a master of understatement.

"There was a fight?"

"Yeah. Finn somehow climbed on a table. Then he fell."

"Is anyone else hurt?"

"Let me worry about that," Raina said. "Look, the closest hospital to me is Brooklyn Med. That's where the paramedics have taken people who've gotten hurt here before."

"You get this a lot?"

"No," Raina said. "We try to keep things smooth here." There was an edge to her voice. She clearly wasn't impressed with trouble at her club.

"Brooklyn Med. Right. I'll come now."

"Good. I've already called Alex and Lucas. I'm sure Maggie will let Finn's family know, but I know they're not in town. So I figured you'd want to know, too."

"Thanks. I do. I'm coming now."

"Good," Raina said. "Make sure you go straight to the hospital. Don't come here."

"Why not?

"We've had paparazzi hanging around the last week or so. Hoping for shots of Saints guys getting into trouble, I guess. There's not really a back entrance that would fit an ambulance so they're going to have to pull up in front.

So the photographers are going to see the paramedics. Then they'll go into a feeding frenzy. If someone hasn't already tipped them off."

Damn. It was bad enough that Finn had been in a fight and hurt himself. But to have the story get into the press, too? She couldn't see Alex and Lucas and Mal being impressed with that. "Thanks for letting me know," she said to Raina and hung up. For a second, she sat, pressing her fingers into her temples where her head was starting to throb. Her gut was churning, too.

"What?" Oliver asked, sitting up in the bed.

She pulled a face as she climbed out from under the covers. "How do you feel about a trip to Brooklyn?"

Oliver followed Amelia into the emergency room feeling a nasty sense of déjà vu. He didn't really remember much about what had happened between the car accident and waking up after surgery, but the smell of hospital hit him like a slap to the face.

And it was Castro's fault again.

Amelia had been tense and locked down all the way on the drive over. Not talking except when Em had called. Even then she'd finished the call fast after telling Em she didn't know anything yet and that she'd call her back.

He didn't like seeing her like this.

Didn't like not being able to fix the situation.

They hadn't even reached the reception desk when Mal loomed up beside them.

"Where's Finn?" Amelia asked.

"Getting some tests," Mal said.

"What sort of tests?" Oliver asked. Mal sounded calm, which was a good sign; then again Mal had had many years of practice staying calm in a crisis.

"A head CT for a start," Mal said. "They're not happy

with him having a head injury so soon after that concussion. Lucas is on his way, I'm sure he can tell you more." He looked down at Amelia, his displeasure with the situation clear in every inch of his rangy frame despite the control in his voice. "How much did Raina tell you about what happened?"

"Just the basics," Oliver said, seeing Amelia looking overwhelmed. "That the guys got into it with some Yankees fans."

Mal nodded. "Yeah. Kind of. From what I gather Finn started things. One of the guys he objected to has a broken nose and Paul has a fractured knuckle. Sam apparently was sensible enough to try and break things up but he has a pretty banged-up set of ribs for his trouble. The cops are going to want to talk to Finn."

Oliver had never really understood the phrase *deathly pale* until he watched the color drain away from Amelia's face, leaving her a ghostly shade that didn't belong on any living face. "Hey." He caught her arm, steered her to the row of plastic chairs nearest them. "Breathe. I've got you. Everything's going to be okay." He looked up at Mal. "Right, Mal?"

Mal blew out a breath. "I'm not going to lie, Ollie. Alex is pretty steamed. He's not the only one. This is the second time in less than a month, that Finn has gotten into trouble and someone's ended up hurt. And this time the cops and the press are involved."

Amelia pressed a hand to her mouth. Oliver wrapped an arm around her. "Ease off, Mal, none of this is Amelia's fault." He felt her shudder as she took a deep breath. Then another.

"Are you going to fire him?" she asked, staring up at Mal.

"Too soon to tell, darlin'," Mal said, tone softening slightly. "Let's worry about the immediate problem for now. We'll get you in to see Finn as soon as the doctors are done."

"As soon as the doctors are done" stretched into ninety very long minutes. By the time a nurse came to tell them that Finn was back in the examination room, Amelia's nerves were shredded. Lucas and Sara Angelo had joined her and Oliver in the waiting room. About ten minutes after they had arrived, Alex and Maggie had turned up.

They were all nice to her. Too nice, she thought. Oliver was speaking to her as if she was fragile. She wasn't fragile. Just worried.

Em called again to tell her that she had gotten a flight to New York and would be there early morning.

Which left nothing much to do but hold Oliver's hand and wait. It was taking too long, wasn't it? Raina had said it was a head injury. Amelia had figured Finn had whacked it on something. Cut it. But a simple cut to the head shouldn't take this long to sort out, should it?

She'd been about to snap. To ask Lucas to go and find out what the hell was happening when a nurse appeared.

The woman was short with dirty-blond hair scraped back from her face into a ponytail. She looked tired. Amelia knew how she felt.

The nurse regarded the group of them and her eyebrows raised slightly as she took in the four men. Understandable. The four of them were very nice to look at. Even at three o'clock in the morning.

"Are you all here for Finn Castro?"

"I am," Amelia said, getting to her feet.

"We are," Alex said at the same time.

The nurse looked from Amelia to Alex. "Anyone family?"

Amelia shook her head. "I'm a friend."

"I'm his boss," Alex said. "And Lucas, there, is his doctor."

"O-kay," the nurse said, clearly starting to think they were a little weird. "He can only have a couple of people in the exam with him at a time for now. He's got a pretty nice concussion going on, so we need to keep him quiet. So, who's it going to be?"

"Me," Amelia said firmly. She narrowed her eyes at Alex, daring him to disagree. He smiled at her and stepped back.

"Fine by me," he said. "You and Lucas go. The rest of us will stay here and drink some more bad coffee."

"There's a cafeteria," the nurse said. "The coffee is slightly less terrible there."

The room they were shown into had lowered lighting. Out of deference for Finn's head, Amelia presumed. She squinted a moment, letting her eyes adjust as she looked at Finn, lying on the hospital bed, half draped in a pale-green cotton blanket. A doctor was bandaging Finn's head. She finished the job and Finn didn't move as she eased his head back down on the pillow before she turned around.

Finn's eyes stayed closed as the doctor stepped away from his side. Amelia wasn't sure he was even awake, so she focused on the doctor. The woman ran a hand through close-cropped dark curls and then lifted her eyebrows a little at the nurse.

"Friend," the nurse said, pointing at Amelia. "Personal doctor, apparently." Her finger moved to Lucas. "Do you need me here?"

"No," the doctor said. "He's good for now." She focused big brown eyes on Lucas. "Personal doctor?"

He smiled at her. Extended a hand. "Lucas Angelo," he said. "I'm an ortho—"

"I know who you are, Dr. Angelo," the doctor said. "I'm Kala Simpson. Trauma."

"Ah," Lucas said. "Then I know who you are, too. Nice to know Finn's in good hands. Though I hope you won't be offended if we move him somewhere else if it's warranted."

"Fine by me if you free up one of our beds," Dr. Simpson said. "I know you can afford it." She looked across at Amelia. "Are you Mr. Castro's girlfriend?"

"No. Family friend. We grew up together. His sister is in Chicago, so are his parents. Em—his sister—will be here in the morning. But I'd appreciate it if you'd let me know whatever the news is before then so I can tell them."

Dr. Simpson nodded. Came around to the end of the bed and picked up Finn's chart. "Let's talk in the hall. He needs quiet more than anything else right now."

She ushered them out efficiently and then motioned to a row of seats a little way down the hall. When they were seated she opened the chart. "I'm sorry this has taken so long. CT was backed up. We're having a crazy night."

Lucas nodded. "We understand. What did the scans show?"

"Well, he has a decent concussion," she said. "Plus a nice gash in his forehead. I've cleaned that out, have a call in for a plastics resident. The paramedics said he fell off a table?"

"I wasn't there," Amelia said, tasting bile in the back of her throat. Plastic surgeon? How bad was the cut? "But yes, that's what I was told."

"He's probably lucky he didn't hurt himself worse." She glanced down at the chart again. Pressed her lips together for a moment.

"Let me guess," Lucas said. "Decent blood alcohol as well?"

"Gold star for the ortho guy," Dr. Simpson said. She

paused again, looked at Amelia. "The tests showed traces of amphetamines as well."

What? Amelia shook her head. "That can't be right. Finn doesn't do drugs. He's never done them."

They both looked at her, clearly not believing her. She lifted her chin. "His high school had a positively rabid anti-drug stance. He'd have been kicked off the baseball team if he was ever caught with so much as pot."

"Lots of people don't get caught," Lucas said.

"Teenage boys aren't masterminds." She refrained from adding any commentary about Finn's IQ. Damn it. He was exactly smart enough to hide it if he'd wanted to. But she just couldn't believe that he had ever wanted to. "He wasn't an angel. He got caught drinking a few times. But I've known him a long time and I've never seen him with drugs."

"Well, he took something tonight."

Lucas frowned. "Either that or someone slipped something in his drink."

Dr. Simpson looked surprised.

"If you know who I am then you presumably know I own part of a baseball team. He's one of my players," Lucas said. "It's happened before. Somebody thinking it would be funny to dope the famous guy."

"I'm sure it's possible," Dr. Simpson said. "Though in my experience, the less complicated explanation is more likely to be the truth. Either way, he's probably feeling crappy now and will feel crappier when the booze wears off. He already threw up in the ambulance, so we didn't pump his stomach. We're hydrating him but there's not a high enough level of whatever it is he took in his system to warrant anything more extreme. I'm more concerned about the concussion. The paramedics said they were told he'd had a concussion a few weeks ago?" She looked at Lucas for confirmation.

"Mild," he said. "Very mild. A little over two weeks ago."

"Mild or not, two concussions in a short period of time isn't good. I know you probably want to move him but I'd rather keep him here overnight for observation. Moving will just jostle him. Which in his current condition will hurt like a son of a bitch."

"Can't argue with that," Lucas said. "All right. We'll talk again in the morning?"

Dr. Simpson nodded. Then she turned to Amelia. "You can go in and sit with him, if you'd like. I suspect he's just going to sleep but I want him on hourly observations tonight so the nurses will be coming in to wake him up every hour. If he wakes up in between, tell him he has a concussion and try to get him to stay still. I'll send the plastics resident down to stitch his head as soon as they're free."

"Who's your plastics attending?" Lucas asked.

She rolled her eyes. "Our residents are excellent."

"I'm sure they are but I want the best for my guy." Lucas patted Amelia's arm. "Will you be okay for a few minutes? Dr. Simpson and I are going to discuss this some more. I'll get Oliver to come down if you want."

Amelia smiled at him. "No. Thanks but I'm okay. I'll just go in and sit with Finn for a while."

Chapter Seventeen

Finn didn't stir when Amelia came back into his room and closed the door as quietly as she could. So she curled up in the chair beside his bed and just watched him. She couldn't believe he'd taken drugs willingly. It wasn't him, no matter what they thought. But only Finn would know the truth on that one. And whether he chose to tell it would be another matter altogether.

She gnawed her lip, eyes gritty from lack of sleep. Lucas had been cool and professional dealing with the doctor and he'd been kind to her, but she was under no illusions that Finn hadn't fucked up big-time tonight. Other players injured. Cops. Press.

Shit.

If he couldn't handle losing the divisional series without getting wasted for a week and then into this much trouble, what would happen if the Saints dropped him?

She didn't want to think about it.

So she just watched him. The room smelled like disinfectant and sweaty man. There was a distinct odor of booze in that sweat. God. What if Finn had an actual problem with alcohol? He'd always liked to party, but she'd never thought he was out of control.

But falling off tables and picking fights and getting in trouble with the police seemed pretty out of control to her.

She didn't think he'd take kindly to her telling him that but she'd do it anyway. It wasn't as though she could screw up their friendship any more than it already was. But not tonight. Not while he was hurt and sick and alone in a goddamned hospital. Tonight she would just sit and be here if he needed her.

The door creaked open behind her. She turned, expecting Lucas, but it was Oliver. Oliver bearing a can of soda, already opened.

He held it out to her. "I thought caffeine and sugar might be easier to stomach than that hospital coffee," he whispered. Then he bent and pressed a kiss to the top of her head. "Are you okay?"

She nodded and took the can. "I'm fine."

Beside them, Finn stirred. Amelia froze. Finn opened his eyes. "Milly? And Shields? What the hell is he doing here?" He started to sit up then started retching halfway through the motion.

"Finn!" Amelia shoved the soda can at Oliver and stood, but Finn retched again and then suddenly slumped back on the bed. "Finn!" She put a hand on his arm, and he didn't move. "I think he's passed out."

"Hit the call button," Oliver said.

Amelia did but didn't move from Finn's side until the nurse came through the door at a run and muscled her aside. "What happened?"

"He woke up, tried to sit up, but then started vomiting—no, trying to vomit. He didn't actually throw up. Then he passed out."

The nurse hit another button on the wall. "Okay. It's probably just the concussion. But there're going to be a few more people in here in a minute. You're going to have to go back to the waiting room."

"I want to stay," Amelia said.

"Sorry," said the nurse. "You need to leave."

Oliver shepherded Amelia back down to the waiting room, feeling her reluctance to leave Finn in the tension running through her body.

Lucas looked up from his phone when they came through the doors. "What happened?"

"Castro woke up, started vomiting, passed out. We called the nurse. The nurse kicked us out," Oliver said. They were alone in the waiting room. Or rather, there were no other Saints people in the waiting room. "Where'd everybody go?"

"Sent them home," Lucas said. "No need for everyone to get no sleep." He yawned, stood, stretched. "Okay. I'll go see what's happening." He came over to Amelia. "It's probably just the concussion. Nausea is common. And vomiting. And if he sat up too fast then he could have been dizzy, and that could make him faint. They'll take good care of him."

Amelia nodded but her gaze followed Lucas as he headed back the way they'd come.

"It's going to be okay," Oliver said. "Come sit down."

She did and he put his arm around her, ignoring the ache that was beginning to set into his left hand. His painkillers were sitting safely at home back in his apartment. He hadn't thought about grabbing them when they left. But fuck it. This was a hospital. Lucas would be able to get him something if they didn't have a dispensary in the building. Amelia was very still next to him. He

remembered the soda. Which was now sitting back in
Finn's room. She should have something in her stomach.

"I'll get you another soda," he said, but she shook
her head and tucked her arm through his, resting her
head on his shoulder, hands gripping him so he couldn't
move.

"I'm not thirsty. I just want to sit here for a few minutes. I'll get something when Lucas comes back."

"Whatever you need, sweetheart," he said and pulled
her closer. It took a few minutes but gradually he felt her
relax against him, heard her breathing even out. And then
felt the extra weight lean into him as she fell asleep. He
struggled against the yawn that rose in his chest at the
thought. The clock on the far wall of the waiting room
told him it was nearly four a.m. Well. Let her sleep.

Lucas would be back soon enough with news.

But Amelia didn't stir when Lucas came back into the
waiting room and he smiled when he saw her, holding a
finger up to his lips. "Don't wake her up," he said. "They've
taken Finn for some more scans and then their head
plastics guy is going to stitch his face up so you won't
be able to see him for a while anyway. No signs it's anything other than the concussion so far."

Part of Oliver couldn't help feeling grimly satisfied
that Finn was now feeling as crappy as he had when he'd
woken up in the hospital after his accident. But most of
him was more worried about Amelia. So he just nodded
at Lucas and stayed where he was, watching over his girl
while she slept.

Two hours later, Em walked into the waiting room, and
this time Amelia did wake when Em called her name.
Lucas had vanished again about twenty minutes before, in
search of Finn's doctors, but he hadn't yet reappeared.

Oliver's arm had gone numb under Amelia's weight.

As she straightened, blinking at Em, he felt the first surges of pins and needles.

"Em?" Amelia said, blinking. "What time is it?"

"Six. Where's Finn?"

Amelia looked at Oliver. "How long was I asleep?"

He shrugged, "A couple of hours." He looked at Em, while he tried to flex his arm, to get the circulation flowing. She looked exhausted, dark hair piled up, black jeans and a rumpled gray hoodie doing nothing for her olive skin. "Lucas just went to get an update. Come and sit down. I'll text Lucas so they know you're here."

Em came and sat on the edge of the seat on the other side of Amelia. Her foot tapped nervously. "Why aren't you with Finn?"

"He—"

"They had to stitch his head," Oliver said smoothly. "They're limiting how much time he can have with visitors." Okay, not entirely the truth, but he didn't want Em to have a meltdown in the waiting room. "He has another concussion."

Em frowned at him. "I know. Amelia texted me."

"Good. Then you know as much as we do." He rolled his shoulders, looked down at Amelia, who was looking at Em with a vaguely guilty expression. "Does anyone need coffee?"

Em shook her head. "No. I've had enough. Did Finn say what happened?"

"No," Amelia said. "But he'd been drinking. And . . ." She hesitated.

"And what?" Em demanded.

"There were drugs in his system," Amelia said.

There were? Lucas hadn't mentioned that part. Oliver straightened. Hell, if Finn was doing drugs then he was on a short road to being an ex-Saint. The club had always taken a tough stand on drugs, even out of season.

"Finn doesn't do drugs," Em snapped.

"I know," Amelia said. "That's what I told them. But—"

"What? What did you tell them, Milly?" Em said.

"I didn't tell them anything they don't already know. That he likes to party. That he's always liked to drink a bit."

"Are you saying my brother's a drunk?" Em's face was turning red, eyes turning a poisonous shade of green. He knew that look. He'd seen it on Finn's face a few times. The look of a Castro in a rage. But he held back. This wasn't his battle to fight. Not yet.

"No. I know you're worried and tired and not thinking clearly. But Em, he hasn't been happy this season. And he has been partying. I think he did that in Chicago, too. He must have. The Cubs wouldn't have sold him cheaply if he wasn't doing something they didn't like."

Em shook her head. "You don't know that." Her gaze flicked to Oliver. "You're just worried that Finn's going to take your boyfriend's spot on the team."

Amelia sucked in a breath.

"Hey," Oliver said, feeling his temper start to curl. "Amelia has been nothing but good to your brother. Far better than he's been to her, as far as I can see."

Em's head snapped up. "He—"

Oliver held up a hand. "If you're going to tell me he saved her mom, I know. Just like Amelia knows. Just like I'm sure you know that she's always going to be grateful for that. But frankly, your brother has been acting like a brat all year." He watched Em suck in a breath, obviously ready to argue. "I don't care if he's rude to me. I can fight my own battles at the Saints. If Finn wants my spot then he's going to have to earn it the old-fashioned way. By being the better player. The better man." He narrowed his eyes at Emma, who was practically spitting anger now. "And your brother is a long way from the better man in this situation. But I'm not going to let him deal with his shit by taking it out on Amelia."

"Is that so?" Emma said, viciously. "How sweet of you, defending Amelia." She shot a look at Amelia, who glared right back. "I hope you're not expecting the same loyalty from her. After all, she's not sticking around much longer."

"Em!" Amelia gasped at the same time as he said, "What?" feeling like he'd been punched in the gut.

"Oh? Didn't she tell you?" Em said, looking satisfied. "Milly here is about to move to Hong Kong."

He shoved to his feet, ears ringing. Leaving? She was leaving. Beside him, he heard Amelia hiss something at Em. Then felt her put a hand on his arm. He shook her off.

"Oliver," she said.

"Not here," he said. "I'm not having this discussion here." Then he headed for the exit.

Amelia shot a disgusted look at Em, who only tilted her chin defiantly, green eyes gleaming—though whether with tears or satisfaction, Amelia couldn't tell. Quite frankly she didn't care. What the fuck did Em think she was doing, telling Oliver like that? But she wasn't going to stay and have it out with Em. Not when Oliver was walking away.

She grabbed her purse and went after him. Her head was spinning as she followed him down the corridor toward the car park where they'd come into the hospital. He was moving with barely a limp. Moving at speed and his long legs had hers beat. She didn't catch up with him until he was nearly at the taxi rank.

"Oliver," she said again. Her throat burned. Fuck. How had Em done this to her? He turned and the expression of fury on his face almost made her turn back. But then he opened the door of the cab and said, "Get in."

She did. What alternative was there? If she let him get in that cab alone she had a pretty good idea that she wouldn't be seeing him again anytime soon. She wasn't so sure she would be seeing him again anytime soon regardless, judging by how he was looking at her as she climbed into the cab. Oliver got in the other side, gave the driver her address.

"Oliver," she started again as the taxi pulled out of the rank. He would understand when she explained. He just had to let her explain.

"Not here." He turned to face the window.

They didn't speak all the way back to Manhattan. The traffic was building already and it took far longer than the reverse journey had earlier. She'd emailed Daniel while they'd been waiting for Finn's results the first time, told him there was a family emergency and that she'd be late. He wasn't going to be happy about it but he was just going to have to deal.

The silence continued all the way into her apartment. He headed straight for the kitchen where he poured a glass of water, drank it. Put the glass down far too carefully. Then nailed her with a look that possibly should have obliterated her entirely.

"All right," he said, voice rumbling slightly. "Talk."

"What do you want to know?"

"Is it true? What Em said?"

For a moment she wanted to say no. That it wasn't. To make the hurt and anger in his eyes disappear. But if she did that then she wasn't sure who she would become. "Yes. I have an offer to transfer to Hong Kong. Not forever," she added hastily. "For six months or so. Maybe a little longer."

"Hong Kong," he said, sounding almost as though he'd

never heard of the place. "How long have you had this offer?"

"Since Monday."

"Two days? And you didn't tell me?" He straightened, shifting his bad hand restlessly. "Wait. International job offers don't just happen out of the blue, do they? Did you know this was a possibility?"

She wasn't going to lie to him. She could give him that much. "It's always been a possibility. It's why I chose Pullman. I've always wanted to travel. I told you that. But there wasn't any indication that it was going to happen anytime soon. Then, about a week ago I heard rumors of a new big project."

"A week? You said nothing."

"It was the divisional series. You had other things to worry about and it was just a rumor. There've been rumors before. Nothing ever came of them."

"Yet two days ago it wasn't a rumor and you still didn't say anything. I thought you were quiet because of Finn. But it was because of this?" He was pacing now. Moving. As if movement could ward off bad news or something.

"I—" Her voice caught on the last word. She swallowed hard. Her head was pounding, her mouth dry. It was almost too much, coming after the night at the hospital. But she wasn't going to cry. Not now. If she cried, she wouldn't be able to stop. Wouldn't be able to explain. She needed to explain. "I didn't say anything because I hadn't made up my mind."

He stilled. "And have you now?"

"I don't know." She stared at him. "This is my dream, Oliver. The thing I've always wanted. You understand going after a dream."

"What about us?"

She wished there wasn't a counter between them. It felt like a continent. She wanted to touch him. To see if that would help. Trouble was, if she touched him, she wouldn't be able to think. "We're so new," she said. "Oliver, don't you see that?"

"You said you loved me. The other night. I heard."

She lost her breath. He had heard. "You didn't say it back."

"You didn't mention it again."

"Because it's crazy," she said. "This thing between us. It's crazy. Tell me you don't think that?"

"It's been crazy," he agreed. "Maybe crazy is what we both need. Maybe crazy should tell us something."

"Does that mean you want me to stay?"

"Of course I want you to stay." He was practically shouting.

God. She hadn't expected hearing him say it to hurt so much. To tear at her. She braced herself on the counter, dipped her head. Tried to think through the throbbing headache and the anger at Em and the soul-sucking fear of losing Oliver. Think about what she wanted.

For once.

"I can't do this based on what you want," she said. Her voice sounded odd. Distant. She lifted her head. "I have to do this for me. Choose for me. I've done what other people have wanted my whole life. Be a good girl. Get good grades. Go to college. Stay between the lines. Because my mom was terrified I was going to screw up and end up like her. I think she encouraged me to get so close to the Castros at first because she felt guilty I didn't have a dad. And I've always been so grateful to them for everything that I've tried to pay them back. Been there for Em. Been there for Finn. Been there for everyone. That's exhausting, Oliver. If I'd done what I'd wanted, I'd be working overseas right now. But I wanted to make sure my mom was taken care of. That everyone is taken care of. And now I'm taking care of you, too. I want to be with you. But I can't stay for you." She stared at him. "Can't you see that? You've chased the thing you've always wanted your whole life. Would you have given up a slot at the Saints because of a relationship after not even three weeks?"

His expression went stony. "That sounds like you've made up your mind to me."

She knew it was true. Knew it as she'd been saying the words. "It's not forever," she said. "People do long distance."

"Do they? After three weeks? When one of them thinks of the other as just something to be taken care of?" He stepped back, shaking his head. "No. I think better to stop now. Before we really fuck each other up." He stared at her for a long moment, face twisting. "So I think I should go now. Let you get on with this dream of yours. You're right. I understand it. And I think you should go for it." He came to her then, bent down. Kissed her one last time like he was drowning. Then pulled away. Straightened. Moved back. "I hope it works out, Amelia. For you. But I want you to know something."

She was going to break into pieces. Shatter where she stood if she breathed the wrong way or moved the wrong way or spoke the wrong words. He was leaving. She was getting the thing she wanted. But she was losing Oliver.

"What?" she managed to say. Rasped the word over a throat turned acid.

Oliver's eyes were fathoms deep. Fathoms cold. Not a pirate anymore. Maybe a shipwreck. Broken and sinking. "I was starting to think you were the thing I'd always wanted," he said. And then he was gone.

Chapter Eighteen

Somehow she made it into work. Showered, changed, pasted on a nothing's-wrong face, and arrived before nine. Still late by Pullman standards, but there. She went to her office, turned on her computer, and then sat staring at the screen. Still hearing Oliver's words in her head. The thing he'd always wanted.

God.

She pressed her hands into her temples, trying to think. It was simple really. Stay and keep Oliver. Maybe. If she could convince him to give her another chance after this morning.

Or go. Keep her dream and leave him behind.

And as much as the thought of not having Oliver was killing her, she knew that if she didn't go, if she didn't do this now, then maybe she never would. If she stayed, maybe her world would shrink like her mom's had. She'd be stuck in the playing-it-safe zone. Everything focused on not making another mistake. On minimizing risk. On avoiding another loss and not upsetting anyone. Amelia had been playing along with that mind-set for too long. She couldn't do it anymore. It wasn't the way the world worked, was it? There would always be pain. So she could have the life she wanted, mess and pain and all, or stay small and get hurt anyway. No. She couldn't be that person.

If that was the person Oliver wanted then she couldn't have him, either. She didn't want to mold and shift herself to suit yet another person.

She was going. She'd stand on her own two feet and leave Em and Finn to stand on theirs. And let Oliver find someone content to follow a baseball player and stand on the sidelines.

She shoved her chair back. Stood. Headed to Daniel's office before she could change her mind.

Daniel was there, which helped. No chance of changing her mind. He looked up as she breezed past his PA and through his door.

"Amelia," he said, coming to his feet. "Something I can do for you?"

She couldn't speak. Couldn't say it, not just yet.

He frowned. "Is everything all right? Your message said you had an emergency? Is it something serious?"

She shook her head, straightened. Found the nerve hiding deep in her gut, under the pain and the loss. "No. Not serious. Taken care of. I just came to tell you that yes, I want to go to Hong Kong. I can leave whenever they need me to. I have a résumé if they need one. So just let me know when you have an answer."

Daniel smiled. He didn't do that often enough. When he smiled maybe, just maybe, she could see what Em saw in him. "I'm glad to hear that," he said. "It's a smart move for you." Pale gray eyes studied her a moment and she thought maybe he was about to ask if there were any obstacles to her going but then he just gave a small nod. "I'll put your name forward to the project team now. With my strong recommendation. I'll let you know when they give me an answer. I don't think it will take long. I know they've already appointed a few people to the integration team. You have a passport, I take it?"

"Yes." She'd gotten one years ago even though, except for Mexico, she'd never used it.

"All right," he said. "They're pulling strings to get visas and all those details organized. I understand the plan is for us to organize accommodations. So all you should have to do is pack. Do you think you can fit your life into two suitcases for six months?"

"Yes," she said. And just like that, it was done.

Two weeks later and Amelia was beginning to think that whoever came up with the idea of only two suitcases for extended trips was a sadist. But every time she started to panic, she reminded herself that there were stores in Hong Kong. And tailors. Everything she could possibly want.

Except for Oliver.

No. She wasn't thinking about him. She hadn't heard from him since that morning in her apartment. She'd sent him a text to let him know she was actually going to Hong Kong.

She hadn't had a reply.

So that was that. No matter how many times she had cried about it. Even now her excitement at going to Hong Kong was tempered by the loss of him.

She'd forget when she got there, she decided. There'd be no reminders of him. Even with the season over, New York was a hard town to forget about baseball in. In Hong Kong she'd have a new apartment. New furniture. Nothing she could picture Oliver lounging or lying on.

She just had to hold on until then and remember she was making the right decision.

Because she was.

She hadn't spoken to Finn yet, either. Em had called

her when he had been released from the hospital. He was getting better but was still resting and limited in what he was allowed to do. The doctors weren't taking any more chances with his concussion. That conversation had been awkward and stilted. Em had apologized for her outburst in the hospital but Amelia wasn't sure she forgave her yet. They would patch it up eventually. But it might never be the same friendship it had been before.

She'd seen the story about Finn and the fight in the news of course. Lots of speculation about what the Saints were going to do to the players involved. Breathed a sigh of relief when it seemed no charges were being pressed.

And then Maggie Winters had called to ask if she would come to Deacon Field to talk about Finn.

So tempting to say no. But Maggie and the others had been nothing but kind to her. So she could do this last thing for them and for Finn before she left.

Which was why she was climbing out of a cab on a Saturday morning to stare up at the ugly concrete walls of Deacon Field one last time.

She kept her eyes averted from the larger-than-life banners of Saints players currently decorating the walls. One of them was Oliver. She didn't want to see him. Not even in a picture.

Maggie met her at the entry gate they'd agreed on. Gave her a quick hug, which Amelia returned. To Amelia's relief, she didn't mention anything about Oliver and Amelia, just chatted about safe topics—which Amelia interpreted as yes, she knew that Amelia and Oliver were over, but no she wasn't going to mention it unless Amelia did—until they got inside the office tower and reached Alex's office.

Where Lucas and Alex and Mal were all waiting. Along with Dan Ellis.

"I'm staying here, too," Maggie said in a low voice.

Then she frowned at the men. "You should all sit and stop looming. You'll make Amelia think she's on trial or something."

They all rolled their eyes at Maggie but smiled and sat. Maggie asked Amelia if she wanted anything to drink but she refused, keeping her attention on the men. She might not be on trial in this room but it was pretty clear that Finn's future was.

"Amelia, we wanted to talk to someone close to Finn," Alex said when they were all seated. "Lucas said that in the hospital, you said you didn't think Finn would do drugs?"

She nodded. She'd told herself she would tell the truth here. That was the biggest favor she could do for Finn, regardless of how he might feel about her afterward. "Yes. That's right. I've never known him to take drugs."

"That's what he says, too," Alex said. "Do you think we should believe him?"

"Yes. About the drugs. I just can't see it." Maybe she was naive to think it, but she had to go with her gut.

"Do you think he's happy?" Lucas said suddenly.

"He was upset about losing," she said. She hesitated. Truth. "But I think that was just the culmination of a lot of things. He's been putting a lot of pressure on himself since he got to New York. So, no, I'm not sure *happy* is the word I'd use."

"Does he drink when he's not happy?" Lucas said.

"Are you asking me if I think he has a drinking problem?"

"Yes," Alex said bluntly.

She sighed. "He's never been one to turn down a party. But he's also never let it interfere with his game. He's not eighteen anymore. I don't see how he could drink enough for it to be a habit and still play well."

"You might be surprised," Lucas muttered.

Amelia nodded. "He drinks, yes. I don't know how much or how regularly. I don't think more than I've known him to in the past but it's not like we live in each other's pockets." She hesitated. "Are you going to release him?"

Lucas shrugged. "That's what we're trying to figure out. How best to solve this problem. Because there's obviously something going on with him."

"What about the other players who were in the fight?"

"None of them has gotten into this sort of trouble before," Mal said. "But that's not the case with Finn. We knew that when we took him on from the Cubs. Even there he hadn't screwed up this badly."

"If someone put something in his drink—" she started.

Alex held up a hand. "We're taking that into account. That possibility. But that doesn't change the fact that Finn doesn't appear to be handling major-league baseball well. So the question becomes whether he can change that or not. Whether he wants to."

"He's wanted to play baseball his whole life," she said. "He loves the game. It's like the thing he's meant to do. I know that much."

Alex nodded. "Yes. Well. Sometimes dreams have to change." He looked at her a moment. "Now I think we've taken up enough of your time." He stood. Smiled. Which was dazzling. When Alex Winters focused on you and smiled, it was easy to see why Maggie had snapped the man up. "I know quite a few people in Hong Kong. Yell if you ever need anything."

Well, that answered the question of whether they knew about her and Oliver breaking up. He'd obviously told them that she was leaving. "Thank you," she said. "Finn's a good guy," she added. "Underneath it all. He's always been a good guy. So if you think you can give him a chance, I don't think he'll let you down again."

Maggie showed her out and they started back toward the elevator. "So, Hong Kong," Maggie said. "Are you excited?"

"Yes," Amelia said. "Excited and terrified."

"I get that," Maggie said. Then she stopped walking. Bit her lip. "Okay, I'm just going to say this. Tell me to go soak my head if you want but Oliver is kind of my Finn, so I have to ask. Are you sure you're doing the right thing here? He's crazy about you. I know that. He's been like a bear with a sore head for the last two weeks."

"I'm sorry," Amelia said. "I'm sorry I hurt him. But I have to do this. It's what I've always wanted."

"No way for you guys to work it out?"

"I raised the possibility of long distance," Amelia said. "It seems dumb. We only dated a few weeks. But Oliver said no."

Maggie frowned. "Men are stupid sometimes. Give him another chance."

"He's made his feeling pretty clear," Amelia said, shaking her head. "And as much as I lo—I mean, care about him," she amended. God, how had she let that slip out? She didn't love him. Couldn't love him. "I can't give this up for him. It's kind of like, well, to use a baseball analogy, it's like my shot at the big leagues. So I can either step up to the plate or stay on the sidelines. And even if the sidelines means I get to keep Oliver, I think that in order to be able to live with myself, I need to step up to the plate. I'd rather have the regrets that come with a swing and a miss than the regrets from never getting into the game. Does that make sense?"

The brunette smiled at her, something sad in the

expression. "Yes. It does. And I understand. I just wish you could have both."

"Well, if you figure out how to have your cake and eat it, too, let me know," Amelia said. "Now I need a taxi. I have to finish packing. I'm leaving on Wednesday."

"So soon?"

"Yeah. Big rush."

"I've never been to Hong Kong," Maggie said. "Maybe I can convince Alex we need a trip now that it's the off-season. We can come look you up."

"I'd like that," Amelia said, meaning it. "I wanted to say thank you. You've been so nice to me."

"You're easy to be nice to," Maggie said. Behind her, the elevator dinged and her eyes went wide. "Crap." She grabbed Amelia's arm. "Okay, I'm sorry for what's about to happen. I thought I had the timing right."

"What?" Amelia said, confused. Then Oliver stepped out of the elevator and she froze.

He looked good. No stick. And no splint on his hand. Just a bandage. That had to be a good thing. He wore dark jeans and a dark-green shirt and she'd never wanted so badly to be able to touch someone in her life.

"You're early," Maggie said, breaking the silence. Oliver kept looking at Amelia. Her face started to heat. And her heart started to break all over again.

"I have to go," she said. "It was nice to see you," she blurted at him and then rushed past him and into the elevator, hitting the CLOSE button and letting it carry her down to safety before she lost it completely.

"You're early," Maggie repeated, sounding exasperated. Oliver shook himself. *Amelia*. Had been here. And he'd said nothing. Fuck. She'd been standing right there, gorgeous in jeans and boots and a sludgy green sweater, red blond hair falling around her face. And he'd said nothing.

He turned his attention to Maggie. "Early? You mean you didn't plan that?"

Maggie shook her head. "I'm not a sadist, Ollie. I think you're being a big fat idiot if you let that woman walk away, but I'm not a sadist."

"I'm not letting her walk away. She's choosing to walk away."

"You're choosing not to run after her."

"What's the point if she's leaving?"

"Good grief, she's not leaving forever. What the hell do you have going on right now that means you couldn't go with her if you wanted?"

Go with her? He blinked. Then held up his hand. "Well, there's this."

"Call me crazy, but I'm guessing there are hand therapists in Hong Kong."

"My surgeon is here."

"That's only an issue if you need more surgery. Plus, they have these things called planes. Granted it's a long flight to Hong Kong, but you can afford to fly up at the pointy end. It's not exactly a hardship."

"There's also the small matter of her not asking me."

"Maybe it never crossed her mind that you would go." Maggie said. "I don't know Amelia all that well, but I get the feeling she's very good at putting other people first. She was just in there trying to help Finn despite everything. So no, maybe she didn't think about it. Or dismissed the idea for all the same stupid reasons that you just did. God. People in love are stupid sometimes."

She might as well have hit him in the gut. Was he doing what everyone else did to her? Expecting her to shape her life around his? Then the last part of Maggie's sentence registered in his brain. "In love?" he said. "Who said anything about—Did Amelia say that?" He sounded appallingly eager.

Maggie laughed. "No, you don't care at all, obviously. So think about it, okay?"

"Dan Ellis asked me whether I wanted to help out during the off-season. Get a feel for whether the coaching side of things is something I might want to do."

Maggie arched an eyebrow. "You thinking about retiring?"

He lifted his hand. "This is still going slowly. I have to figure out what I want to do when I grow up eventually, even if my hand does come good."

She grinned. "Well, well, well. Oliver Shields being sensible and finally planning for his future. Tell me again how you're not in love?"

He scowled and she laughed. "Ollie, there will be other off-seasons. You know the Saints will help you do whatever you want to do when you retire. You're family here. But I think you have a chance at a different kind of family. A chance you're currently screwing up."

"We've only known each other a few weeks. It's crazy."

She patted his shoulder. "That's exactly what she said. And you know, if there's one thing Alex has taught me it's that sometimes, when it feels like that, you just have to let the hell go and trust the crazy. Now come on, the guys are waiting for you."

He followed her down to Alex's office, mind whirling. Go to Hong Kong with Amelia. It did sound crazy. His life had been the Saints and Staten Island forever. The thought of leaving was hard to grasp. Even if he would be coming back.

"Oliver," Lucas said as they came into the room. "How's the hand?"

"Given I'm sure George is sending you copies of all

my reports, I'm sure you know the answer to that," Oliver said. He said hello to Alex and Mal and Dan. Truth was, as he'd said to Maggie, regaining his hand function was painfully slow. Every freaking fraction of an inch of movement was hard-won. "But you didn't ask me here to talk about my hand. So let's talk about Finn instead."

"Okay," Alex said. "What do you think of Castro?"

"I think he's a cocky little prick who's currently got his head up his ass," Oliver said. Then he held up his hand before they could start arguing with him. Amelia cared about Finn. So he would be honest. For her. "But I also think that if he can get his head out of his ass, then he's got a chance to be a pretty damned good first base man. He played brilliantly in a couple of those games. Reminded me of me when I was younger."

"Yes, he did," Dan agreed.

"Doesn't change the fact Ollie's right," Mal said. "The kid hasn't got his head on straight right now."

"Well, he's out of the hospital," Lucas said. "And his last checkup cleared him for light activity. The doctor said nothing strenuous for a few more weeks. So if we wanted to try and stick him in rehab or some sort of counseling place for a few weeks, this might be a good time."

"You think he needs rehab?" Alex asked Lucas.

Lucas shrugged. "I don't know. There's nothing in his blood work that suggests really heavy drinking. But I can't help thinking some time out might help him. If he wants to be helped."

"That's what it boils down to, isn't it?" Mal said. "The only one who can help him is him in the end."

"Yes, but we can support him. Regardless of whether we keep him or not," Maggie said. "We can still help. Amelia says he's a good guy."

"Even good guys can fuck things up," Lucas said, eyes fixed on Oliver.

"We're talking about Finn," Oliver growled. Fuck. Were they all going to read him the riot act about Amelia? And if all of them thought that way, did that mean he really was fucking up royally if he let her go?

"Who says I wasn't?" Lucas said with a grin.

"For me, I think some sort of rehab or counseling program is a given," Alex said. "If he won't do that, then I'm done with him. He's just going to keep fucking up. He's already put himself in the hospital, and Oliver. Not to mention Paul's hand and Sam's ribs. He's lucky those Yankees fans didn't press charges and land him in a lot worse trouble."

"Agreed," Mal said. "But if he agrees, then what do we do when he's out?"

"Send him to the Preachers," Oliver said. "Less pressure in AAA. Give him a chance to figure out if he really wants this enough to win his way back to the Saints. See how he does. You can always bring him back partway through the season if he turns things around and gets his act together. Some breathing room and a change of scenery might just be what the doctor ordered." Suddenly he didn't think he was just talking about Finn anymore. But before he could figure out his own life, if he was going to go after Amelia, he needed to make sure Finn understood a few things. Which meant he needed to get out of here.

"The Preachers? You think that's a good idea?" Dan said.

Oliver shrugged. "That's for all of you to decide. So I'm just going to leave you to it."

"What the hell are you doing here?" Finn said gruffly.

Oliver smiled a smile that felt more like baring his teeth at the guy. "Castro. Good to see you, too. Let me in." He put his hand on the door and, to his surprise, Finn fell back. Maybe the guy was still feeling like crap. Whatever. He walked into the apartment, shut the door behind him.

Finn stood in the small entry hall, hands shoved in the pockets of his jeans, scowling. Which made the pink scar that sliced across his forehead on an angle that just cut the tip of his right eyebrow wrinkle. "Okay. You're in. What do you want? If Dan Ellis sent you to give me another little pep talk, I'm not interested."

Oliver shook his head. "Kid, I'm not interested in saving your career. You've dug your own hole and you're going to have to pull yourself out of it. But you and I are going to have a little chat."

"About what?"

"About Amelia. And the way you're going to behave around her in the future."

Finn's scowl vanished, morphing for an instant into something Oliver would have called guilt on another guy's face, before the expression turned unreadable. "What do you care about Amelia? Em said you broke up."

Oliver just shrugged. "Whether I am or am not involved with Amelia isn't your problem. The fact that I'll take it badly if you ever talk to her again like you did at the party is."

Finn looked down at his shoes. "I'm going to apologize."

"You should have already apologized," Oliver said. "You should have groveled. You made her feel like crap. She's spent her whole life trying to please people and I'm guessing she's done nothing but support you over the years, even when you no doubt deserved a kick up the ass. And you tell her she's not part of your family because you're having a crappy week. Low blow. Don't you know how she feels about you all?"

Finn's head shot up, scowl firmly in place again. "I don't need you telling me I screwed up."

"Don't you? Because screwed up is hardly what I'd call it. More like comprehensively fucked things up. You do get that, right?"

"Yes," Finn gritted out.

"Good. Maybe there's hope for you yet," Oliver said. If the kid could accept that he'd been a dick and wanted to try a different approach, then maybe there was a chance he could make things right. "But regardless, you will treat Amelia the way she deserves to be treated or I will make you sorry. Understand me?"

Finn nodded. "Understood. Is that all you came to say?"

Oliver shrugged. "Yes." He turned, reached for the door. Then had a sudden image of Amelia frowning at him. If he was going to stay in her life that meant he had to be able to get along with Finn. "Look, Castro, I know you don't like me. I know you want my job. Fine. I'm not joining your fan club, either. Frankly, I'm not sure what Amelia sees in you. But she told me what you did for her mom and that tells me that once upon a time you were a good guy. A guy who thought saving a life was more important than anything else. Who put love for a girl who was part of his family over everything else. Maybe you've buried that guy under whatever mountain of bullshit it is that's fueling that chip on your shoulder. Maybe you've lost him for good. But if I were you, and I wanted to get my life back on track and save my career and my relationship with my sister, then I would try to find that guy again. That guy sounds like someone I could be friends with."

Amelia handed her passport and ticket over to the woman behind the airline checkout and tried to remember to breathe. She was leaving. Today. Going to Hong Kong. Leaving New York. Along with everything in it. She'd spent half an hour on the phone with Em earlier and somehow that had made the fact that she was leaving the country seem real for the first time. Em had managed not to cry, though she'd sounded weird. Amelia had also managed not to cry until she'd had a call from Finn. It had been short and awkward but he had at least apologized. She wasn't sure how she felt about it yet. Something to worry about once she was in Hong Kong. But the call had somehow made leaving feel overwhelming and she'd found herself in tears before the driver of the car she'd booked called up and she'd had to pull herself together.

"Ms. Graham, I have you as an upgrade," the woman said, with a flash of very white teeth.

"Um, I'm already in business class," Amelia said. She'd been surprised when she'd gotten her ticket. But apparently Pullman wanted her ready to work on the other end of her flight.

"Yes, but I have you in first." Brightly painted fingernails sped over the keyboard. She pressed a button and the computer spat out a boarding pass. "Once you get through customs, there's an elevator up to the first-class lounge. Just show your boarding pass and they'll take care of you from there."

"Okay, thanks." Amelia took the boarding pass, still confused. Maybe she had just lucked out. Airlines upgraded people sometimes, didn't they? She'd only ever flown coach, so she didn't really know how this all worked. But hell, first class sounded damned good to her, so she wasn't going to argue. She headed to security and made it through customs without too much hassle. Then she followed the instructions and went up to the first-class lounge, half expecting to be told it was some horrible mistake when she got there. But the man at the reception desk welcomed her with a smile. So she was none the wiser about why she'd gotten lucky until she walked through to the lounge itself and saw Oliver sitting in a low chair near the entry.

She stopped dead, which almost made the man walking behind her run into her. He stepped around her with a muttered, "Watch where you're going." She barely noticed. Because Oliver was there.

Oliver stood. Headed in her direction.

Her head was spinning. What was he doing here? She tried not to give into the frantic happiness spilling through her.

"You're blocking the path," he said when he reached her.

"You're here," she said. Brilliant reply. Not *Why are you here?*

He gestured back to where he'd been sitting. "Come and talk to me."

Talk about an invitation she couldn't refuse. She followed him to the chairs. Put her purse down and tucked her carry-on against the table. But she didn't sit. Neither did Oliver.

"Why are you here?" she asked.

"I had a thought," Oliver said.

"A thought?"

"About long distance," he said. "I don't think it's a good idea."

"I see," she said, not seeing at all.

"But then I had another thought," he said. "Which was that we don't have to do long distance. Because I don't actually have anything to do for the next few months, and the thought of sitting in New York doing nothing without you was making me crazy. So I bought a ticket to Hong Kong."

He reached into the pocket of his jacket. Pulled out a boarding pass. Which was for the seat next to hers in first class. Mystery solved. "Question is, do you want me to use it?"

"Yes," she said fiercely. "You idiot. Yes." Then she stood on tiptoe and pulled his head down to hers. Kissed him. Kissed him the way she'd been wanting to for two weeks. Only stopped when she realized there was a smattering of applause echoing around the beautifully styled sleek space of the lounge. Then she pulled back. Tried to catch her breath. Watched him trying to catch his. "But what about your hand? The Saints?"

"My doctors have hooked me up with a therapist and a surgeon to check on things over there. I might have to fly back here if the New York guys get concerned by what they hear from the Hong Kong docs or want to see me in person but hey, what's a plane flight or two? If I'm eased into spring training, I won't need to be in Florida until the end of February. Maybe even March. We'll figure that part out when we get there. If my hand is ready. It won't be for so long then if I have to come back. This is just for six months, right?"

She nodded, grinning. "Yes. Though I still want to travel."

"I'll take you wherever you want to go. I promise. If I can still play, then you give me the seasons and I'll do whatever the hell you want or need the rest of the year. And if I can't play—well, heck, maybe I'll just follow my globe-trotting executive gal around the world for a few years till we decide we're ready to settle down somewhere."

"Settle down?" she said faintly.

"Someday," he said. "When we get there. For now, I just want to be crazy with you, Amelia Graham. What do you say?"

"I say, I'd love to be crazy with you, Oliver Shields," she said. "So kiss me."

Read on for an excerpt from the next novel by
Melanie Scott

Playing Fast

Coming soon from St. Martin's Paperbacks!

Chapter One

Eva Harlowe had been many things at work. Happy, bored, sad, stressed, excited. Occasionally pissed off. She'd never before been one-hundred-percent mortified.

She looked down at the security pass she'd just run through the laminator and resisted the urge to flee the building.

Finn Castro.

That was whose face stared back at her from the otherwise innocent piece of plastic.

Finn Castro. Baseball player. Tall, dark, and trouble. Not to mention six years younger than her. On whom Eva had had an unreasonable, melting-underwear-level, unrelenting crush for, oh, at least a year.

There was nothing wrong with having a crush. Countless women swooned over actors and singers and, yes, athletes every day. Having a crush was harmless. Particularly a celebrity crush. Perfectly safe. Never going to be able to do anything about it except maybe one day pose for an awkward photograph if you ever ran across the person in real life and could summon the courage to ask. They could live in your head and cheer up your day and maybe, occasionally, when you were having one of those days, cheer up your nighttime fantasies, too.

One hundred percent A-OK.

Until of course, you found out that the object of your crush was coming to work where you worked.

Then it was mortifying. Totally, excruciatingly, horrifyingly, mortifying.

So mortified she was because, exactly six weeks ago, just after New Year's Day, the New York Saints had announced that they were sending Finn Castro to play a season at their AAA team, the Preachers.

Where Eva was the administration manager. Which was a glorified title for "does anything that really needs to be done and keeps things from falling apart at an inconvenient moment." Including getting new players set up with all the administrative things they needed to be set up with and, usually, giving them a quick tour of the place before they were handed over to the coaching team.

Which meant that any minute now, Finn Castro was going to come waltzing through her office door and she was going to have to act like a normal adult woman around him.

Seriously, life sucked.

She stared down at the picture and his way-too-handsome face merely smiled back at her. A smug smile. Like he knew her secret.

Thankfully, no one at the Preachers did. She'd worked there for a long time. Close enough to thirteen years. She wasn't dumb enough to admit a crush on a ballplayer to anybody on the premises, let alone a player from their parent team. She never would have heard the end of it. Nope, she'd kept her secret to herself and instead pretended to share her best friend Jenna's infatuation with Tom Hiddleston.

And she'd tried to get over the "Finn thing," as she had dubbed it.

Really tried. Ever since Don Mannings, the Preachers' manager had made the announcement that Finn was coming to Saratoga Springs at a management meeting back in January.

She had deleted every photo off her home computer. She'd unsubscribed from the Hotties of Baseball blog she'd been guiltily following. Stopped scanning the sports pages for mentions of him. Then she'd gone on a mad hunt for a guy who might distract her brain. She'd watched every TV show and movie she could think of. She'd scrolled through Pinterest boards for hours. And yes, there'd been a few guys who'd caught her attention. Men with beautiful faces and bodies sculpted to perfection. Men who made her girl parts happier just looking at them. She'd thought her plan had been working.

Until the photographs had leaked.

The ones from the sponsorship deal that Finn had lost when he'd gotten into a fight in a Brooklyn nightclub. A nightclub owned by Raina Easton who was married to Mal Coulter, who was one of the part owners of the Saints, what's more. Long Road Home, who made fancy fitness gadgets, had made polite public noises about wishing Finn well and then dropped him like a hot potato from being the face of their forthcoming ad campaign.

But somehow the pictures of Finn they'd taken for that campaign had leaked.

They were amazing. Finn being athletic and manly with a big black masculine Long Road Home fitness band clamped around his wrist, each shot showing off his well-honed body to perfection. Climbing rocks and sweat-drenched in gyms and riding a motorcycle. But it was the last shot that had gotten her. Finn standing thigh-deep in the ocean. Wearing a wet, white T-shirt and dark jeans, a storm brewing behind him.

Moody black and white and gray. Except the eyes.

Those they'd left enough color in to let you guess they were brilliant green. Predator eyes. Dangerous eyes to go with the dangerous body outlined in wet fabric. It was a magnificent photo. And she knew photos. It was brilliant. The perfect embodiment of the male animal, barely contained.

The picture had been everywhere. Impossible to avoid.

It had reignited her crush like a match put to gasoline.

The image was burned in her brain. Popped into her head at inconvenient moments. Made her pulse race and her body want.

Want things it could never have. Because she did not date baseball players. Particularly not bad-boy, only-in-town-because-it-was-a-pit-stop-to-the-Major-Leagues, never-going-to-stay baseball players. She'd seen enough of those in her time at the team to know one when she saw one. Finn Castro was definitely one. Sent to the Preachers in disgrace. Sent to redeem himself.

She didn't need a Taylor Swift song to know trouble was walking in her door.

So she would be rational and adult and treat him exactly the same way she treated all the other men here. Off-limits. Not an option. No crushes allowed.

It was the only sane thing to do. Even though she was planning on leaving the Preachers at the end of the season, there was no reason to go crazy.

Except, as the door to her small office opened and the man himself walked through, she realized that the picture had, it seemed, done little justice to the real thing.

And that a whole world of trouble had just landed in her lap.

Finn Castro looked down at the face of the woman behind the desk and got the feeling he'd done something to piss her off. Dark blue eyes studied him through narrow black-framed glasses, their expression distinctly cool. Not the first impression he'd been hoping to make. Or rather, needed to make. He'd been told to report to Eva Harlowe at the Preachers' headquarters today. The first day of his exile, as he'd been trying not to think of it.

What it really was was the grown-up version of a time-out. Because he'd done some dumb shit last year. Dumb enough to give himself a wake-up call.

Dumb enough to make Alex Winters, Lucas Angelo, and Malachi Coulter, the owners of the New York Saints, decide that he wouldn't be playing for the Saints this season. That he needed to prove himself all over again. The thought made his jaw tighten. He'd spent most of his life trying to prove himself when it came to baseball. And here he was starting from the fucking beginning again.

But he was the one who'd fucked up, so he was the one who had to suck it up. Keep his head down, work hard, get back to the Saints.

Be on his best behavior and make a good impression.

And here he was apparently screwing that up already. Or maybe he was just reading her wrong. He tried a smile. His smile usually worked on reluctant females. His looks were an asset. He knew that. So it would be dumb not to use them when he needed to. "Hi. I'm Finn Castro. Are you Eva?"

"Just like the sign on the door says," she replied, pushing back from her desk to stand. Her voice was slightly husky. But still cool.

Definitely unhappy about something. He studied her a moment. Dark brown hair pulled back into a bun, black sweater buttoned over a crisp white shirt. Dark liner highlighting the eyes that weren't impressed with him. But despite the demure attire, he got the feeling she wasn't all that demure. Because the lips that were painted a very neutral shade were full and the body beneath the clothes curved like a racetrack. Not that he let himself study it in any detail. She was already unimpressed. Staring at her chest wasn't going to improve the situation.

A trio of thin silver chains of varying lengths looped around her neck and thin small silver hoops hung from her ears. Except in her right ear, the loop wasn't alone. Next to the hoop was a small silver shape. At first he thought it was just a stud, but when she moved her head he realized it was actually a tiny skull.

Definitely not demure.

More like . . . intriguing.

But nope. He wasn't here to be intrigued. Let alone be intrigued by the woman who Maggie Winters—wife of Alex and currently Chief Operating Officer of the Saints—had told him was the heart of the Preachers' operations. The one who knew how things got done. The woman who had the respect and the ear of the coaching team. Not to be messed with.

And now they'd been staring at each other just that little bit too long.

Damn.

"Well, they told me to come find you when I got here," he said, to break the silence and the potential to grow more intrigued.

"Nice to see you can follow instructions, Mr. Castro," she said. She bent and scooped something up off her desk, held it out to him. "This is your security pass. It gets you into the building, the training complex, and the parking lot."

He took the pass. It was clipped onto a white lanyard with the Preachers' logo stamped in black along its length. Preachers. Not the Saints. His jaw tightened again and he relaxed it with an effort.

Suck it up.

"Now," Eva continued as she passed him a plastic

folder that had a matching logo on the front cover, "this folder has the map of the complex, your IT login, and your schedule for the week as well as the plans for the first week of spring training next week. Your schedule will be emailed to you once a week, and it and most other information is always available on our intranet. We have all your paperwork from the Saints, so unless you need to update any of the details you've given them in relation to your banking arrangements or uniform size, then that should be all set up."

Was he imagining things or had she just given him a quick once-over when she'd said "uniform"? He must have been imagining it. Her tone was definitely not enthusiastic.

"The only information we don't have is your address here in Saratoga," Eva continued. "Did you find an apartment or house yet? Or are you in a hotel for now?"

"I have an apartment." He'd rented a place not far from the Preachers' home field, Hennessee Park. His Manhattan apartment was sublet for six months. Alex Winters had told him he'd be in Saratoga Springs for a year, but he was determined to get back as soon as possible. So he didn't need anywhere flashy to live. Just somewhere close where he could crash. He wasn't here to party, after all.

Not that he was sure Saratoga Springs was much of a party town. The place seemed full of spas and, well, horse racing. He didn't know jack about horse racing and couldn't see himself getting interested anytime soon.

"Great," Eva said, not sounding at all like she meant it. "Once you log into your email, send me your details and you'll be all set. Now I'll show you around and then deliver you to Coach."

Finn kept his head down for the first couple of days. He went to his training sessions. To the gym. To team meetings. Took long runs around Hennessee Park and the area around his new apartment, trying to learn his way around. Spoke to his parents and his sister, Em, back in Chicago. Then he went home to his very boring apartment and slept. Focus, that was the key.

Head down, do the work, and be so damned good at his job that the Saints would have to call him back. No distractions. No thinking about the interesting Eva Harlowe.

Play it smart.

No trouble. Not so much as a hint. It was already clear that he had some ground to make up with most of his teammates. Who knew he'd been sent here in disgrace. Knew he'd blown it at the Saints. The guys hadn't exactly welcomed him with open arms. It was only the two real rookies, fresh out of college, who had spoken to him much at all. They were all enthusiasm, convinced they were going to conquer the world of baseball, eager to hear about his time in the majors. They reminded him of his idiot younger self. Which was kind of painful. But it was a start. The rest of the guys he'd have to prove himself to.

Work for it.

So head down and definitely no flirting with Eva, who was clearly a central part of the Preachers' organization. One that the players regarded as part of the family. He knew a little about how guys reacted when other guys tried to date their sisters, having a sister himself. Eva was off-limits. He would just have to ignore the fact that she kept popping into his mind and that the few times he'd seen her during the week, his attention had zeroed in on her like she was a lifeline and he was drowning.

It was an excellent plan until he tried to log into his email on Thursday morning, and the computer declared he didn't exist. Or rather his password didn't. Which meant he was going to have to go see the very interesting Eva after all.

No flirting, he reminded himself as he headed toward Eva's office thirty minutes later. Nice. Friendly. Cooperative, that was the key. She'd been all business when she'd given him a tour of the complex on Monday. Nothing but the facts. No shift in her demeanor despite his attempts to get her to relax. He hadn't figured out if it was him or if she'd been having a bad day. Hopefully the latter. Though she probably knew exactly how he'd washed up on her shores, so to speak. Knew all about his fall from grace at the Saints. She must have come across plenty of other players who'd been demoted. Maybe she gave them all the cold shoulder.

Smart woman.

He deserved the cold shoulder. It would remind him that he was walking the line, to steal a phrase from Johnny Cash.

He hadn't ended up in prison last year, but he'd been lucky to escape charges after a dumb bar fight. Luckier still that the Saints hadn't just sacked him and had instead sent him to a six-week program that wasn't exactly rehab. The consensus being that he wasn't an alcoholic but had definitely been in "Dude, you need to get a handle on things" territory. No booze, more health food than he ever wanted to see again, and daily sessions with a sports psychologist and the regular kind.

It had given him some clarity. Shown him what needed to change if he was going to be successful in MLB.

Now he just had to prove that he could do it.

So Eva Harlowe might just be a good test subject.

He knocked politely on her half-open door, waited for her to say "come in." When she did, he pushed the door open carefully.

Eva stood at one of the file cabinets behind her desk, rummaging through a drawer. Her dark hair was piled up and she'd stuck a pen through it at some point. She was smiling absently as she flicked through folders, as if remembering something happy. The deep blue sweater she wore over a black skirt highlighted some very nice curves. He pulled his eyes back to her face as she turned her head.

The cool look that quickly replaced her smile when she saw it was him clarified something else. She hadn't been in a bad mood on Monday. It was him she had a problem with.

He couldn't really blame her. She had to know his history. How badly he'd screwed things up to end up here. In her place, he'd have a problem with him, too. Which meant that he was just going to have to work a bit harder to prove that her low expectations were wrong.

"Mr. Castro," she said as she pulled a file from the drawer. "What can I do for you this morning?"

"It seems that your IT system has decided I don't exist. I couldn't get into my emails this morning."

"Did you try resetting your password?"

"Yes. But I got an error message. Plus, even if it worked, I can't log in to get the reset link."

She looked at him over the top of her glasses, expression suspicious. "No one else has mentioned having an issue."

He held up his hands. "I swear I didn't do anything to it. I logged in fine yesterday."

"I'll get the IT guys to reset the account. Was there anything in particular you wanted?"

"I wanted to check the schedule again. Coach said last night that there had been changes to the travel arrangements for Wednesday." Their first away game of spring training. He rolled his shoulders, suddenly nervous. He'd done fine in the training sessions this week. No reason for that to be any different when he got onto the field next week.

"Well, you're in luck. I just printed out a few copies to post in the locker room." She walked to her desk, lifted a big expensive-looking camera that was sitting on a pile of printouts, and picked up a piece of paper. "Here."

He took the paper. "Nice camera." He had no idea whether it was nice or not. Or whether it was hers. The Saints had an on-staff photographer who traveled with the team. He had no idea whether the Preachers' budget ran to that sort of thing.

She hitched a shoulder. "It does the job."

He nodded at the camera. "Do you like photography?" He knew he should really just take the schedule and leave, but he couldn't bring himself to quite make that first move toward the door.

"I dabble. I take shots around here to post to our social media."

"I'll have to check them out."

"You didn't list any social media accounts on the profile information you gave us."

"I closed them all last year when . . ." Exactly how much did she know about what had happened to him last season? Probably all of it.

"When you got in that bar fight?" she said coolly.

Yep. She knew. "Yes." No point trying to bullshit his way and put any spin on it. "Haven't really missed them much. But if you want me to set something up again, I can."

She shook her head. "It's not team policy that you have to have them, it's up to you."

He shrugged. "Trying to keep things simple. Keep my head clear."

Her brows lifted, just a fraction. "Well, as I said, it's not team policy."

He smiled and just for a moment he thought she was going to smile back. But then she looked away, reaching out to adjust a bright red photo frame on her desk. He knew he should leave, shouldn't get in her way. Not give her any reason to dislike him any more than she apparently already did.

The photo was Eva and three younger women. All dark-haired except the youngest who was sporting cropped platinum blond hair. All with the same deep blue eyes as her.

"Sisters?" he asked.

For once she actually smiled as her gaze dropped to the photo. "Yes. Kate, Lizzie, and Audrey."

"Eva, Kate, Lizzie, and Audrey?" he asked. His mom was an old Hollywood movie fan. "Tell me, is Kate short for Katharine?"

"Yes," she said. She shrugged. "My mom loved old movies."

"Katharine Hepburn, Audrey Hepburn. Elizabeth Taylor." He ticked the names off. "But wait, I assume you're Ava Gardner? Didn't she spell her name with an A?"

"My dad wasn't such a movie fan. He filled out the birth certificate and spelled it with an E. My mom almost strangled him when she saw it but the deed, so to speak, was done."

"So that's why you're Ay-va not Ee-va?" He looked from her to the photo again. Her mom had obviously been psychic. All four of her daughters were gorgeous. Though Eva had that something . . . more than mere prettiness.

"Yup. There you go, the great mystery of my name solved." She stroked a finger over the photo and then turned it slightly again so he couldn't see it clearly. "Now, is there something else I can do for you, Mr. Shields?"

3-1-16